THE JAKE HELMAN FILES
HUMAN MONSTERS

GREGORY LAMBERSON

THE JAKE HELMAN FILES
HUMAN MONSTERS

GREGORY LAMBERSON

MEDALLION
P R E S S
Medallion Press, Inc.
Printed in USA

DEDICATION

Dedicated to my wife, Tamar,
for allowing me to put Jake through his paces

Published 2015 by Medallion Press, Inc.

The MEDALLION PRESS LOGO
is a registered trademark of Medallion Press, Inc.

Typeset in Adobe Garamond Pro

Printed in the United States of America

ISBN# 9781605427300

10 9 8 7 6 5 4 3 2 1

First Edition

"He shall deliver thee in six troubles; yea, in seven there shall no evil touch thee."

—Job 5:19

"He who lives by fighting with an enemy has an interest in the preservation of the enemy's life."

—Friedrich Nietzsche

ONE

A gasping sound in the dark basement snapped Jake Helman awake. Propping himself up on his elbow, he slid his right hand—his only hand—along the sofa bed and located the warm impression Maria Vasquez's supple body had left in the mattress. He sensed her beside him, her breathing labored. He traced the sweaty ridges of her spine, which he followed to her shoulders, her soft hair spilling over his wrist.

"Are you okay?" he said.

"Yes." Maria lay down, pressing her buttocks against him, and he wrapped his arm around her sternum. She pulled his hand between her breasts, holding it over her heart.

This was not the first nightmare she had suffered since their return from Pavot Island and their survival of the supernatural hurricane that had almost destroyed New York City. Jake was no stranger to nightmares, and he regretted that his world had seeped into Maria's subconscious mind. He checked the alarm clock—3:11 a.m.

glowed red in the dark. He kissed her shoulder. "Go back to sleep."

"I can't." She drew back the sheet and slid off the bed.

He heard the rustling of fabric against her soft skin. "You don't have to go right now."

"Yes, I do." She crossed the basement, flipped on the stairway light, and climbed the stairs, a shiny pale blue robe tied at her waist. When she reached the top, the light went off again. At least she didn't close the door.

Jake draped one arm over his eye. Twelve days had passed since Lilith's storm had displaced him from the back room in his Manhattan office where he had lived for almost two years. The Jackson Heights house belonged to Joyce Wood, who had moved down south with Jake's friend and ex-partner Edgar Hopkins, and their son, Martin. Maria had become their tenant, and Jake had moved in with her while waiting for his office to become accessible. Despite their deepening relationship, the temporary move had been dictated by necessity, not romance.

Due to the state of emergency in Manhattan caused by the storm, they had seen little of each other except at night. The city needed every member of NYPD to work overtime to deal with the flood's aftermath, and Maria served as a detective in the Special Homicide Task Force, Jake's old unit. He admired her for the life she was attempting to build and wondered, not for the first time, if he could ever have a normal life again.

2

Jake awoke with early morning sunlight in his eye. His sleep had been sound, undisturbed by monsters with tentacles or sawdust for blood. He got out of bed and stretched. His body felt strong, not battered. His joints did not snap when he stretched, and he felt younger than he had in years. Twelve days earlier, when Lilith had almost destroyed his body, Laurel Doniger had used her psychic healing powers to save him, sacrificing herself in the process. He felt renewed.

Jake pulled on a pair of shorts and an old NYPD T-shirt and took his glass eye from the cup full of cleaning solution on the bedside table. He pressed the eye into his socket, then sat at the computer in the corner and checked his e-mail.

Every day he searched for Carrie Scott, his former assistant, who had stolen his laptop, files, and cash from his office safe during the hurricane. The laptop had been dedicated to Afterlife, a compendium of supernatural knowledge funded by the late billionaire Nicholas Tower. Even though Carrie's betrayal angered him, he had no desire to punish her. He just wanted Afterlife returned so he could destroy it and prevent the possibility of it falling into the wrong hands.

The apartment Carrie had shared with her boyfriend, Ripper, had been abandoned, and she had closed her mobile phone, social networking, and e-mail accounts.

Her credit cards and bank account showed no activity. As far as Jake could tell, she had not left Manhattan by train, plane, bus, or boat, and she had neither rented nor purchased a car. She could have hitchhiked or bought a junk vehicle with cash, but his instincts told him she was hiding in one of the city's five boroughs. How hard could it be to find a goth dwarf covered with piercings and tattoos?

Jake went upstairs to the kitchen. Maria, dressed for work in black slacks and a purple blouse, stood with her back to him at the stove. The television on the counter was on, and she didn't seem to hear his footsteps. Jake slid his hands over her hips and she flinched. He kissed her cheek.

"You of all people should know better than to sneak up on someone like that," Maria said.

She was right: he had startled Sheryl, his late wife, the same way once. "You don't have to cook for me. I just need coffee."

"Shana doesn't drink coffee," Maria said.

Maria fostered Shana Robbins, the seven-year-old daughter of Papa Joe Morton, a drug kingpin. Shana was orphaned when Joe and her mother were killed last year. Maria had rescued Shana during Hurricane Daria after the girl's custodial aunt, also in the family business, was murdered. With the death toll still rising and many Manhattan residents rendered homeless by the storm, he imagined Child Services had been eager to place Shana with Maria, resulting in Jake's relocation from the main bedroom to the basement.

Jake poured himself a cup of steaming java. "What's new at work?"

Maria turned to him. "No one knows who the Romance Killer is, if that's what you're asking."

Lilith, an ancient being posing as Lilian Kane, the head of romance publisher Eternity Books, had sent three employees and members of her coven to kill Jake. One of them had killed Ripper, and Jake had killed all three women. Because they had worked at Eternity, the media had dubbed their slayer the Romance Killer.

"Do I have anything to worry about?" Jake said.

She held his gaze. "I don't think so. There was no security footage during the blackout."

"What about before that?" Jake had gone to the Flat-iron Building to negotiate Laurel's freedom with Lilith. Lilith had subjected him to Black Magic, a powerful supernatural narcotic, and Maria and Ripper had shown up and taken him home.

"There's no security footage of any of us in that building," Maria said in a flat tone.

"Meaning you destroyed it?"

"Not me. Lilith must have been covering her own tracks since she planned to kill us."

"I'm sorry you're in this position."

"I'm supposed to solve three homicides and one suspicious death resulting from your raid on that building. By pretending I have no knowledge of what happened, I'm an accessory. So is Bernie. I pray you and Edgar covered your tracks."

Bernie Reinhardt served as Maria's partner. Jake knew the funny little man disapproved of him and probably carried a torch for Maria. "We did but you just never know . . ."

"I don't like it but I made my choice. If we're caught, no one will ever believe the truth, even with everything else that went on."

"How's Bernie holding up?"

She hesitated. "He likes it even less than I do, but he's loyal, and he's in the dark enough to maintain plausible deniability. If you get caught and I go down with you, we keep him and Edgar out of it."

"Agreed."

"Four more cases under my name that will go unsolved in addition to sixty zonbie corpses. I wonder how long it will be before I get transferred. Maybe that'll be for the best. I'd like to have a normal life again someday."

Jake and Maria desired a real relationship, but his life would always be threatened by the supernatural forces he had crossed. He could not hide from them.

He sat at the table and looked at the TV. He recognized the thin and pale man, with wispy dirty blond hair and the blonde woman beside him. Pierce Freemont and his wife, Beth, headed the Anti-Cloning Creationist League (ACCL).

Old Nick and Kira Thorn had said the Freemonts were also associated with a domestic terrorist organization called RAGE: the Righteous Against Genetic Engineering. They had lied. RAGE did not exist. It had been fabricated by Tower to justify his elaborate security needs and to cast doubt on the Freemonts—scientific extremism pitted against religious fanaticism.

"Hurricane Daria was sent to Manhattan because of the sins perpetrated here," Pierce said.

"That's right," Beth said, with a permanent smile on her perfect face. "With all the cheating, stealing, lying, fornicating, and perversion in this city, it's a wonder God didn't wipe it clean off the map."

The interviewer had dark hair and wore a gray suit. "Isn't forgiveness divine?"

"The Lord demonstrated forgiveness when he stopped that hurricane," Pierce said. "The storm circled the island like a watchdog for hours. Every scientist agrees this was impossible. When science can't explain an occurrence, look to heaven above."

"Look what happened to Sodom and Gomorrah," Beth said. "And the great flood. And Job."

"Those are all Old Testament references," the interviewer said with a wry smile.

"There's nothing wrong with that," Beth said as if

speaking to a child.

Pierce leaned forward. "We're not here to argue theology. It's obvious to everyone that Hurricane Daria was an unnatural catastrophe. We're here to raise money for the victims of this disaster. Twelve thousand people—over five thousand in Manhattan and the entire population of Roosevelt Island—have been left homeless. Hundreds of thousands of people are now out of work, and hundreds of thousands more are without power. With the economy spiraling downward, it's only going to get worse. The food shortage is devastating. FEMA is doing what it can, but we the people need to help. That's why Beth and I returned to New York."

Maria lowered the volume and set the table. "They came back because Pierce is going to run for the senate. Do you plan to go out today?"

"Just to my appointment."

"You've got to stop being self-conscious about your hand."

He raised his stump. "What hand?"

"Very funny. You're not afraid to be home alone with Shana, are you?"

Jake sipped his coffee. "Wouldn't she be better off in day care?"

"I haven't had time to find one. School will start soon. God, I have to register her out here."

"The prospect of meeting your mother scares me

more than babysitting."

"She isn't any scarier than the witch doctors on Pavot Island."

"Great."

"Once Mom's here, you won't have to worry about Shana. You can go out if you want."

He saw right through her. "That isn't on my dance card."

"You haven't been to the city since you moved out here."

"Queens is a city."

"It isn't *the* city."

"It's where I grew up. I like it here. There's electricity and running water, and I can see the sidewalks."

"The water's off the streets in Manhattan, and you know it."

"Leaving mud, debris, and garbage. I do watch the news."

"The trains aren't running but the buses are."

"There's no point in me going back until I can at least get into my office."

The stretch of East Twenty-third Street where his office building stood had been declared the new Ground Zero One after an immense waterspout had toppled two skyscrapers, which in turn had crushed four smaller buildings on Madison Avenue.

Maria sat opposite him. "I think you should forget about Carrie and move on."

"I can't."

"You mean you won't."

Jake stood. "Let's not discuss it."

Standing as well, she draped her arms around his neck. "Meaning you're going to spend all your free time looking for her."

"More or less."

She scratched his beard and frowned. "Go shower."

He set his coffee mug on the table, walked into the living room, and climbed the stairs. In the upstairs hallway, he stopped in his tracks: Shana stood outside the bedroom that had belonged to Martin, staring at him. He had not been alone with her yet, and he knew she had been traumatized by everything she had been through. "Are you okay?"

She nodded.

"Do you need to use the bathroom?"

She shook her head.

"Breakfast is almost ready. Why don't you go downstairs?"

Shana gave him an uncertain look, her eyes shiny. He stepped away, making room for her, and she passed him and hurried down the stairs.

Wondering how he was going to entertain her until Maria's mother arrived, Jake went into the bathroom and locked the door. He stood before the sink, gazing at his reflection in the mirror. He needed a haircut, and the beard hid almost half his face. Sliding the medicine cabinet mirror open, he located a pair of scissors. He closed the mirror and clipped his whiskers, which collected in the sink.

Within minutes the lower half of his face and the four long scars from his left cheek to his jawline, which the beard had masked, had returned. Staring at his visage, he wished he had left the beard.

When Jake returned to the kitchen, wet hair clinging to the back of his neck, a computer-generated cartoon, not one of the hand-drawn classics he had grown up watching, played on TV. Maria and Shana sat at the table, eating pancakes and scrambled eggs. Shana's gaze did not leave the cartoon.

Maria smiled at the sight of Jake's shaved face. "I don't believe it. Who is this stranger?"

Jake took his seat and Shana turned to him. He kept his stump below the table on his thigh, so as not to disturb the child.

"It was itching me in this heat," he said.

Maria caressed his face, smooth other than the scars. "It's a definite improvement."

Jake looked at Shana. "What do you think?"

"You look okay, I guess."

"This may surprise you, but people used to find me handsome."

"I still find you handsome," Maria said.

Jake served himself a stack of pancakes. "Beauty and the beast."

Shana smiled.

"Oh, you like that, huh? How do you know I'm the beast?"

Her smile broadened.

"I might be Prince Charming." Jake nodded at Maria. "And *she* might be the beast."

Shana laughed.

"I think you two will get along just fine. If not, there's always TV." Maria stood and gathered the dirty plates.

"We're going to see Long Island," Jake said to Shana.

Maria rinsed the plates. "Drive carefully."

"I'm the best driver in the city. Everyone else is nuts."

"Don't forget the booster seat."

"I don't need one anymore," Jake said.

Shana giggled.

"I have to go." Maria hugged Shana and kissed the top of her head. "Have fun today. Don't let Jake get into any trouble. My mother will be here after lunch. I'll try to be home for dinner."

"I'll walk you out," Jake said. He followed Maria into the living room.

Maria opened the door and stepped outside.

"Catch some bad guys today," he said. "Just not this one."

"No fast food for Shana for lunch."

He kissed her cheek, and she walked down the steps

and got into her Toyota, parked in the driveway, and drove off.

The sky was clear, and the sun shone on the neighborhood. Men and women of all ethnicities walked in the direction of the subway station while others got into their cars. In another hour, children would be playing in the heat. Everything here was different than in Manhattan.

TWO

Maria entered the Detective Bureau Manhattan on East Twenty-first Street. Power had still not been restored to the neighborhood, and generators droned. The homeless citizens who had crowded the building's stairway and corridors had been relocated to emergency shelters.

She climbed the rubber-coated stairs, nodding to patrolmen and detectives, and walked into the Special Homicide Task Force squad room. The windows were open, and fans blew air around the space, flipping the corners of loose paperwork. Bernie sat reading a newspaper at his desk, a cup of coffee before him.

She draped her jacket over the back of her chair. "Good morning."

"Hey, kid," Bernie said.

Maria sat at the desk previously occupied by Jake. It faced Bernie's desk, which had been Edgar's. "Shana's settled in."

Bernie sipped his coffee. "That's great. Who's watching her now?"

Maria booted up her computer. "As if you didn't know."

"He's some role model."

"You're repeating yourself."

He folded his newspaper. "You're setting up house with a guy who's making our job increasingly difficult."

Seeing Bernie planned to press the issue, she lowered her voice. "I'm not setting up house with him. He's just staying with me until he can get into his building. Show some compassion."

Bernie lowered his voice to match hers. "I thought I showed compassion when I took you and that Korean hood to get him from the Flatiron Building. Now Ripper and three women who worked in that building are dead, with I don't know what on the roof, and guess who's supposed to catch their killer? You and me."

Maria gave him a pleading look. "I understand you're upset. I'm not happy, either. I don't want this assignment, but we're stuck with it. Do you want another partner? Because I'll understand if you do."

"I didn't say that. You know I don't. But you have personal reasons for wanting the Romance Killer unidentified. I don't share those reasons."

Maria rolled her chair over to Bernie and whispered, "If Jake is implicated in those killings, I could go down with him."

"It's the only reason I'm keeping my mouth shut."

"I appreciate it."

"You're not just risking your career; you're risking

mine, too. I hope he's worth it, but I don't see it that way. He looked strung out when you brought him out of the building."

Jake had been strung out on Black Magic when Maria had collected him from Lilith, but that wasn't his fault.

"Things are a lot more complicated than you think, and I'm not talking about my relationship with him. He's saved people's lives. He may have saved this whole city."

"He resigned from the department—from your desk—to avoid taking a drug test."

"It isn't what you think."

"Convince me."

"Not here."

Bernie frowned. "L.T. said he wanted to see us when you got in."

Maria followed her partner into Lieutenant Mauceri's office.

The short, silver-haired man looked up from his monitor. "My dream team. Let's get this powwow started."

Maria and Bernie sat in chairs facing Mauceri's desk in the cramped office.

"I've got the ME's report on your female DOA from the roof of the Flatiron Building." Mauceri handed a folder to Maria. "Dental records confirm Lilian Kane, the Queen of Romance, is no longer missing."

"That's good for Missing Persons," Bernie said. "What about us?"

"There are two hundred six bones in the human

body, and every one of them in Kane's was broken, which explains why her corpse practically had to be scooped off the roof."

"How is that possible?" Maria knew what had happened to Kane's body, but she felt like she had to say something.

"The ME refuses to classify her death as a homicide."

"Thank heaven for small favors," Bernie said.

"Funny you should say that. He's classifying it as a 'suspicious death, attributable to an act of God.' I don't know if he's been born again due to recent events, but he's blaming Daria."

One less problem to deal with, Maria thought.

"Don't look so happy," Mauceri said. "If Kane was killed by the storm because she was trying to escape from whoever killed her three employees, her death still falls under your investigation. Where are you on the Romance Murders?"

"Somewhere between nowhere and *Lost in Space*," Bernie said.

"Do you think Kim's our guy?"

Samuel Kim went by the street name Ripper.

"I don't," Maria said.

"He was an ex-con."

"Harla Sota was stabbed. Chloe Sanderstein was stabbed and shot with a machine gun. Jada Brighton was shot with the same machine gun. Kim wasn't packing a knife or a machine gun."

"They could have been blown away by the storm. Or maybe Kim belonged to a crew that covered his tracks. You want a scenario? This crew took advantage of the hurricane to burglarize Eternity Books. Or maybe they wanted to kidnap Kane and hold her for ransom. That broad had a lot of money. Something went wrong; that's when Kane bolted. Kim ran onto the roof after her, and the storm flattened her and chucked him off the roof. Then the rest of the crew killed the other three women because they were witnesses."

"I think Kim's death is completely unrelated," Maria said. "Daria snatched him from the flood and dropped him on that signpost."

"Anything's possible these days," Mauceri said. "But if Kim didn't kill those women, the perps are still out there. I don't believe the Romance Killer is one guy who killed Sanderstein in a stranger's car, threw Brighton out of a broken window, and stabbed Soto on the sixteenth floor. That's some Michael Myers shit."

Maria wondered if Mauceri was suggesting they pin the murders on Ripper to make their lives easier. "There's no evidence left. The storm blew or washed away whatever might have been there."

"Well, in that case, maybe we should forget about these DOAs and write them off to inclement weather. I suggest you treat Kim as a person of interest and look up all his associates. That's the only lead I see." He smiled.

"Let's put this one down."

Maria took Mauceri's comment as a dig at her. "I think we'd better revisit the crime scene."

"That sounds like a good idea," Mauceri said. "Do you concur, Reinhardt?"

"She took the words right out of my mouth."

Maria and Bernie exited Mauceri's office.

"Why are we going back there?" Bernie said.

"To talk in private," Maria said.

Maria and Bernie entered the lobby of the Flatiron Building carrying coffee, their shoes covered with mud. The building lacked air-conditioning, and the doors were propped open. Furniture ruined in the flood had been removed, and mats covered the floor where tiles had buckled. A sign on a stand read, Please Excuse Our Appearance. At the far end of the lobby, contractors installed new tiles.

Maria showed her shield to the security guard behind the warped counter. "We need to go back onto the roof."

"I'll call Mr. Davis," the guard said.

A minute later Willard Davis, the building manager, emerged from his office. "Good morning, Detectives. You need to go back upstairs?"

"To the roof," Maria said. "We can get up there ourselves."

"I'd hoped our role in this mess was over."

"Five dead people in and around your building means five cases. All of them are still open."

"I understand. It's just the publicity . . ."

"We can't help that."

"Have there been any new developments?"

"Nothing we can discuss."

Maria and Bernie boarded an elevator.

"You're a real chatterbox," Maria said.

"I'm not sure what I'm allowed to say about anything anymore."

"Passive-aggressive doesn't suit you. I prefer sarcasm."

"I'm beginning to feel like the woman in this marriage."

"That's better."

They got off on the top floor, where yellow crime scene tape covered the dark entrance to Eternity Books. Maria doubted she would ever read a romance novel again. Bernie opened the stairwell door for her, and they climbed the stairs.

Sunshine beat down on them, and Maria crossed to the edge of the narrow, triangular roof. She faced the Tower across the street. Then she gazed at the ruins of the skyscrapers Lilith's storm had toppled across the street from the four-story building where Jake kept his office. Several smaller buildings on Madison Avenue had been crushed by the Metropolitan Life North Building when it fell. Now that the water had been pumped from street level, caravans of dump trucks carted away debris, hundreds of workers busied themselves, and helicopters crossed the sky.

Bernie joined her. "Memories."

She turned to him. "Sixty DOAs packed with sawdust."

"You mean the ones with no fingertips, toes, or teeth? I remember."

They had worked the Machete Massacres together as part of the Black Magic Task Force. "It's been almost a year. What theories have you formed about them?"

"I try not to think about them."

"How do you manage that? We're responsible for solving their murders. It's on us. There have been frigging documentaries about them on TV."

"I said I try not to think about them. I didn't say I succeed. It's impossible to control your thoughts when you dream."

"I have dreams, too," she said.

"I bet you do."

"I've kept things from you."

"No kidding."

"But only because I wanted to protect you. I still do."

"That might have worked before but not now. I'm stuck in the middle of this."

"I didn't mean for that to happen." Maria drew in her breath. "What do you think about the hurricane?"

"The scientists call it an impossible phenomenon. The

religious nuts say it was God. I think they're both right."

"It wasn't God."

"You know this?"

She nodded, afraid to say more.

"What's on your mind?"

"I want to tell you. I *need* to tell you. You deserve to hear the truth. But I'm worried you won't believe me."

"I'm your partner; you can tell me anything. Would it help if I told you I believe those DOAs were walking dead people who had their plugs pulled?"

She sipped her coffee. "Okay, then, here it goes. I met Jake after Marc Gorman, the Cipher, killed his wife. I was the primary on Sheryl Helman's murder. When Gorman was killed by an anonymous vigilante, I wanted to interview Jake again as a possible suspect."

"You had good instincts back then, especially in light of recent events. Jake was the obvious suspect."

"Sheryl was the Cipher's thirteenth victim. There were a lot of suspects."

"But none of the Cipher's other victims had ex-homicide cops as relatives. Helman knew how to track him down."

She nodded at the Tower. "At the time Jake was working there as the director of security for Old Nick. His supervisor, Kira Thorn, provided him with an alibi. Then she disappeared."

"I remember. A lot of people in Helman's life do that."

"After Old Nick died, Jake set up shop as a PI." She gestured at Twenty-third Street. "There."

"We seem to be standing at Ground Zero One for Mister Rogers' neighborhood."

"Edgar and I were working Black Magic and the Machete Massacres when the city became scarecrow central. That's when Edgar disappeared. Then Dawn Du Pre was murdered in a construction site."

"Du Pre was Edgar's girlfriend. He was a suspect for a short time. I'm guessing he didn't do it."

"Du Pre was in bed with Prince Malachai."

"Also found dead—very dead—at the construction site. I was there, remember?"

"Du Pre and Malachai were behind the Black Magic, which turned junkies into a zonbie work force."

"Zombies."

"Jake and Edgar killed those zonbies at the plant in the Bronx."

Bernie grew animated. "Son of a bitch, I knew he was involved . . ."

"Du Pre was also behind Edgar's disappearance."

"How did she manage that?"

"She turned him into a raven."

Bernie blinked. "A raven."

"She was a voodoo witch. Jake stopped her and Malachai—"

"You mean he killed them."

"He stopped the Black Magic."

"Let's go back to the raven."

"I saw him—first in Jake's office, then in Miami."

"Helman kept Hopkins in his office."

"Miriam Santiago was Du Pre's aunt."

"The new president of Pavot Island?"

"Pavot is where Black Magic was created. Miriam told Jake and me she would return Edgar to human form if we went to Pavot and freed her husband, Andre Santiago, from El Miedo prison. Things didn't exactly go as planned."

"Imagine that. Jesus, you two started that revolution!"

"It was Jake's idea." She paused. "There was an army of zonbies on Pavot. I killed a lot of them. Jake figured out a way to use them to our advantage. That's how we got out of there alive."

"You're as crazy as he is."

"Miriam kept her word, even though her husband was killed on Pavot. She turned Edgar human again and we brought him home."

"Does Hopkins know he was a raven?"

"Yes."

"I'm having trouble with that one." He pointed at the roof at their feet. "What gets us here?"

"Lilian Kane. Her real name was Lilith."

"Lilith, as in Adam's first wife?"

"You've heard of her?"

"She's part of my religion. That doesn't mean I

believe she was the Queen of Romance."

"Erika Long wasn't just a member of Lilian's stable of romance writers; she was also a member of Lilith's coven. She disappeared with one hundred million of Kane's dollars and set up shop in Jake's building as Laurel Doniger, a psychic healer."

"Oy vey."

"Jake came here to negotiate with Lilith on Laurel's behalf. Lilith messed with his brain. That's where you came in."

"And the song remains anything but the same."

"I looked that bitch in the eye, and I can tell you she wasn't human. She was a storm demon, and she created the hurricane to trap Jake and force him to turn Laurel over to her. She was willing to destroy the entire city to get to them."

"How did our DOAs score their initials?"

"They were members of Lilith's coven. Jake and Ripper came here during the worst of the storm to stop her. According to Jake, she turned Soto, Sanderstein, and Brighton into monsters and sent them after them. He killed them but not before one of them killed Ripper."

"Monsters?" Bernie frowned. "They looked human enough to me."

"They turned back to their original forms when they died."

"So Jake is the Romance Killer. What happened to Kane?"

26

"He killed her, too." She elected not to mention Edgar's involvement.

"I'll say. He broke every bone in her body. Some hero."

"There's more to all of this than I've said. If I told you everything, we'd be up here for a week. Jake saved this entire city. I saw things on Pavot Island, impossible things. There's more to this world than we know."

"I'm not saying I believe you, but if everything you've said is true, even more trouble follows Helman than I thought. Is this why Hopkins left town?"

"Yes."

"So what the hell are you doing with Helman?"

She sighed. "He saved my life, and I saved his more times than either one of us can count. If he takes the fall, no one will believe the truth. And Ripper died a hero. He doesn't deserve to have this pinned on him."

Bernie gestured at the cityscape. "Is this over?"

"Lilith is over. There will always be something else. Jake's told me so himself. He's got a big fat target on his back."

"He's not exactly my idea of the world's most eligible bachelor."

"I'm stuck with him, Bernie."

"Oh, kid, I'm sorry. Does anyone else know about this? Anyone who could tie him to everything you say has gone down?"

Maria thought about it. "No."

"You're not a very good liar."

"His assistant, Carrie Scott. She was in his office

27

during everything that happened with Lilith. She was also Ripper's girlfriend. She took off with Jake's files, and he can't track her down."

"What kind of files?"

"The detailed kind."

"I call that a very big problem."

THREE

Dressed in jeans and a short-sleeved button-down shirt, Jake left the house with Shana in tow. The sun had already made the surface of the Plymouth Edgar had entrusted with him hot to the touch. Jake's Nissan Maxima remained underwater in a Manhattan parking garage near his office. Edgar's car had occupied Joyce's garage during his absence, and Jake had been unable to secure a rental in the wake of the hurricane.

He opened the driver's side door, positioned the booster seat, and watched Shana climb in. "Do you need help?"

"No," she said in a quiet voice.

Shana had withdrawn into her shell after Maria had left, making conversation difficult. Not that he had much to say to a seven-year-old.

She sat on the booster seat, buckled herself in, and took out a handheld video game.

Jake slid in behind the steering wheel, started the engine, and pulled into the street. He turned on the radio.

A commercial jingle played on his jazz station, so he switched to news.

"The body of a woman discovered on the roof of the Flatiron Building has been identified as Lilian Kane, the so-called Queen of Romance," a man with a deep voice said. "According to police, Kane's death was caused by Hurricane Daria. The murders of three of her Eternity Books employees at or near the same location are still under investigation. Police believe the Romance Killer is still at large."

With the sound of the video game beeping behind him, Jake drove onto the Long Island Expressway and headed toward Amityville.

"Why do you sleep in the basement?" Shana said in a soft voice.

Jake glanced in the rearview mirror at the girl's inquisitive eyes. "That isn't my house. I live somewhere else."

"Where?"

The kid was being nosy, but he didn't want to discourage her from speaking to him. "I sleep on a cot in my office, which is across the street from those buildings that fell during the storm. I'm only staying at Maria's until I can get back in there."

"She's your girlfriend, isn't she?"

"We're friends, yes."

"So why don't you sleep in the same room? My aunt slept in the same bedroom with her boyfriend."

Jake increased the air-conditioning. "Who's the private investigator, you or me?"

"Do you catch bad guys?"

"Maria's the police detective; she catches bad guys."

"Then what do you do?"

I help the bad guys meet well-deserved ends. "I follow people and take photos of them without them knowing it."

"So you're a spy."

"In a way."

"What happened to your hand? And your face?"

Jeez, learn to pull your punches. "Life is never as easy as you expect it to be."

In Amityville, Jake parked in the lot of a three-story medical building and took Shana inside. She played her video game in the waiting room while he watched the news on TV.

"President Baldwin is back in Washington after his visit to New York City to tour areas hardest hit by Hurricane Daria and to ring the bell at the reopening of the stock exchange," a blonde female news anchor said. "He took questions from reporters in the White House briefing room this morning."

President Baldwin appeared behind a podium embossed with the presidential seal. "People are struggling in Manhattan, but they're coping with this national disaster. We've deployed FEMA trailers throughout the city, and people are getting the assistance they need. New Yorkers are resolute in their determination to rebuild, and so am I."

The news anchor reappeared. "When asked about the spiritual questions that seem to be on everyone's mind these days, the president had this to say."

A closer shot of the president. "There has never been a storm like the one that struck New York City. We've all seen the radar maps. Hurricane Daria formed, struck, and maintained a pattern that defies scientific explanation or even scientific rationalization. I'm a man of faith, and I accept that Daria was created by a power greater than we can comprehend."

Jake grunted. He had encountered angels and had battled demons, but it was the work of Lilith, an ages-old being who came from neither the Realm of Light nor the Dark Realm who had reawakened in the world a belief in higher powers. He looked around the room: everyone watched the TV with rapt attention.

"Mr. Helman?" A woman in dark blue scrubs stood in the doorway next to the admissions desk.

"Right here." Standing, he took Shana's hand and led her inside.

The woman escorted them into another room where a man with graying hair and a beard waited.

"Hello," Raymond Arbogast said to Shana.

"Hi." She stared at the items set out on a table: a metal hook attached to a harness and a prosthetic hand.

"Can she have a sucker?" Raymond said to Jake.

"Sure, why not?"

"I'll get it," the woman said, closing the door behind her.

Raymond gestured to the prosthetic devices. "They've been custom fitted to the impressions we took of your stump."

Jake picked up the harness. "Do I put it over my shirt?"

"You can, but it will be less obvious if you wear it under your shirt and over a T-shirt. For now, wear it over the shirt you have on." Raymond handed him a gym sock. "First put this on."

Jake took the sock and pulled it over his stump, stretching it past his elbow.

"Now pull the prosthetic over your arm."

Jake slid his stump inside the prosthetic, which fit him like a glove.

"The sock will make it more comfortable, and it will absorb perspiration. You're going to sweat in there a lot."

Jake swung the harness around his back and slid his arm through it as he would a shoulder holster. A strap circled each shoulder, forming an *X* where they joined between his shoulder blades. The metal cable ran from a lever on the prosthetic to below his left shoulder, and rubber bands held the hook.

"The rig is body powered. When you apply tension

to the lever, it opens the hook; when you draw your arm closer to your body, it closes the hook. Give it a try."

Jake raised his elbow, then moved the prosthetic away from his chest. He felt the cable tighten, and the halves of the hook opened. He brought the prosthetic close to his chest, and the hook closed. "It feels weird."

"It's not part of your body, but it's functioning like it is. You'll get used to it. You'll also figure out different ways to move your arm to open and close the hook. In a few days, you'll be able to do any number of small tasks without thinking about it. You're lucky you're right-handed."

Someone knocked on the door, and Larry Metivier, Jake's regular doctor, entered. Larry had an office in the same building, where he serviced wounded cops and criminals alike, no questions asked, for cash. He held a large envelope in one hand and an orange sucker in the other. "Sorry I'm late. I was told to bring this." He held the sucker out for Jake. "For you?"

"No, for me," Shana said.

"Oh, for you." He handed the sucker to Shana and smiled. "I'm Larry."

"Like in *The Three Stooges*," Jake said.

"That's right. Only I'm a doctor." Larry turned to Jake. "You look like a Transformer. How do you like it?"

Jake opened and closed his new claw. "It will be a while before I can juggle again."

Raymond picked up the prosthetic hand, which had a hollow forearm. "This one is purely cosmetic. It's made of silicone, with an armature inside to keep the fingers from wiggling. You can adjust the positions of the fingers, so they'll look reasonably natural when you go running. Just pay attention to when it loosens, or you'll surprise bystanders far more than if you wore the hook. The racing glove is on the house."

Jake held the artificial hand with his right hand. "I appreciate you rushing these."

"Any friend of Larry's is a suspicious patient of mine. You'll pay for the rush."

"I'm sure."

"Speaking of which, I'll go make sure your paperwork is ready. You can keep that case. Some patients feel uncomfortable walking out of here with a new prosthetic."

"Thanks."

Raymond exited and Larry raised the envelope. "I have your X-rays. I can see why you came all the way out here to have them done. Let's step out in the hall for a minute."

"Shana, wait here," Jake said.

Jake and Larry stepped into the hall, and Jake closed the door behind them.

"Cute kid," Larry said.

"Yeah, I'm growing on her."

"Is she yours?"

"No. I still haven't sired anyone to follow in my footsteps."

"Good."

"We can't all be doctors."

"I was so surprised by the X-rays that I spent an entire afternoon studying them," Larry said. "Can you guess what I found?"

"Healed broken bones?" Jake said.

"That's the understatement of the century. Two hundred six healed broken bones—every damned one in your body. And every internal injury that could be associated with them—punctured lungs, ruptured blood vessels, torn arteries, fissured brain tissue—all healed, just like your bones. You have more scars *inside* your body than outside it. There's no record of these injuries in your medical file, so I looked at that MRI we did a year and a half ago. Surprise, surprise, you had none of these injuries then. They're all recent. If I cut you open in the name of science, I bet I'd find you suffered these breaks at the same time.

"By all rights, you shouldn't possibly be standing here. You shouldn't be standing anywhere. You should be lying six feet underground or tits up on a slab in Area 51. What the hell happened to you, and how the hell are you still alive?"

Jake took the envelope from Larry. "You don't want to know."

Larry glared at him. "You're right; I don't. You know, I was raised Catholic."

"I bet you go to church every Sunday."

"Don't be so surprised. I've been reevaluating my life

since this holy hurricane scrubbed the city."

"There's a lot of that going around."

"I've decided to live my life differently."

"No more hookers behind your wife's back?"

Larry's lips tightened. "No more anything that could be deemed unscrupulous."

"Congratulations."

"What I'm saying is, I can't be your doctor anymore."

"Am I the only patient you're dropping?"

"No, but you're at the top of my list."

"I scored higher than mafia goons, drug dealers, and crooked cops?"

"Don't take it personally. Just forget my number. Forget my name. We never did any business together."

"It's not like you give receipts."

"You've got your new hand. Please don't come back here. Stay off Long Island altogether if you can."

Jake raised the envelope containing the X-rays. "What do I owe you for these?"

"Nothing. That's on the house. I'll pay the tech out of my own pocket. I just want to forget I ever met you."

"I can't begrudge you for that. Will you also forget all the cash I've paid you for your services?"

"That feels like a lifetime ago. The world was a different place then." Larry turned and walked away.

Yes, it was, Jake thought.

On the trip back, Jake closed his hook on the Plymouth's steering wheel. He had grown accustomed to driving with one hand, but this felt steadier. He released the wheel with his right hand, and the car veered to the left. He seized the wheel again and righted the vehicle's course. This was going to take time.

"Do you believe in monsters?" Shana said.

Jake glanced in the mirror. The girl stared at him with eyes that had witnessed too much. "Why do you ask?"

"I believe in them. Zombies killed my father."

Jake had not been prepared for such a brutal statement.

"The doctor at social services said I was wrong, and my aunt told me never to talk about it. Even Maria says I shouldn't think about it."

Jake didn't want to contradict Maria, but he didn't intend to lie to a girl who had experienced horrors no child should even know existed. "Yes, I believe in monsters."

"Do you think I'm crazy?"

"No."

"Have you ever seen any?"

Avademe flashed through his mind: fifty feet tall, with two brains, four eyes, and eight massive tentacles. "Yes."

Shana grew quiet, and Jake felt he owed her an explanation. "There are different kinds of monsters, honey. There are make-believe monsters, the kind you read about in books or see in movies."

"Like in *ParaNorman* and *The Nightmare Before Christmas*."

Jake had never heard of *ParaNorman*. "Right. Those monsters are just for fun. They can't hurt you. Then there are supernatural monsters, like the ones you and I saw. We both know they can hurt us, don't we?"

She nodded.

"They don't belong in our world. That's why most people don't believe in them. Sometimes they slip through and that causes trouble. Only people like you and me know the truth, and we have to be on our guard for the sake of everyone else."

"But I'm just a kid."

"I know. It isn't fair. But you have to keep watch, even though others won't believe you. It will be easier for you if you don't tell people the truth."

"What do I do if I see them again?"

"You won't. The zombies are gone. But if you do, tell me and I'll take care of them."

"Do you promise?"

"Yes. And if I'm not around, tell Maria. There's nothing she won't do for you."

"Are there other real monsters besides zombies?"

He debated how much to say. "There are monsters who look just like me, who do terrible things to people, even kids. They'll try to trick you so they can hurt you. They'll come to you with a piece of candy, they'll invite you to see a puppy or a video game at their house, or they'll say they're going to take you to Maria or me. They're the worst monsters of all, and you have to worry about them more than zombies or anything else. Never trust any grown-up you don't know."

"Do I come to you if any of them ever try to trick me?"

"Anytime, anyplace—you tell me, and I'll take care of it."

.·*·.·.

Back home, Jake opened McDonald's bags and set the packaged items around on the kitchen table.

Seated, Shana tore the cellophane from the toy in her Happy Meal.

"What do you want to watch?" Jake said.

The girl shrugged.

He turned on the TV and left it on the educational kids' programming station Maria had selected. He sat next to Shana and attempted to unwrap his Big Mac with his hook but succeeded only in disfiguring the burger, which elicited laughter from Shana.

"You think that's funny?" he said.

She nodded.

Opening the claw, he managed to move the burger around the table, which resulted in more laughter. Frowning, he used his hand to peel back the layers of wrapping, then raised the burger to his mouth.

The doorbell rang before he could take a bite.

"Damn. Wait here." Jake walked into the living room, then peered through the peephole, which revealed the top of a head of orange hair. He unlocked and opened the door for a five-foot-tall Hispanic woman holding a bag of groceries.

"Mrs. Vasquez?"

The woman smiled. "Paola," she said in a heavy accent.

Jake held out his hand. "It's nice to meet you."

Still smiling, Paola searched his face.

He pointed at his left eye. "It's this one."

"How you get those scars?" she said in broken English.

"They're from a work-related injury." He stepped back from the door. "Please come in."

Paola entered the house and looked around. "Where's the little girl?"

"She's eating," Jake said, pointing to the kitchen.

Paola went into the kitchen and he followed.

"Hello, I'm Paola, Maria's mommy," she said.

Shana offered a nervous wave.

"My daughter left McDonald's for her?" Paola said.

"Uh, no, we picked that up on the way home from a doctor's appointment," Jake said, gesturing to his hook.

Paola gave him a stern look. "How you do that?"

"It's a long story."

Shaking her head, Paola set the groceries on the counter, then opened cupboards and inspected the contents of the refrigerator.

"Would you like something to drink?" Jake said.

Paola removed milk, rice, and chicken from her bag. "No, but this little girl needs some real food."

Jake suspected Paola was going to report his catering infraction to Maria. "Do you need some help?"

"Where's the broom and the mop?"

Jake's smartphone rang. "Just a minute." He took out the phone and checked it. No name appeared, but the numbers 206 followed area code 212.

A public pay phone, he thought. When was the last time he had received a call from one of those? "Hello?"

"Jake, it's me."

Every muscle in his body tightened. He recognized the speaker.

Carrie Scott.

FOUR

"Just a minute," Jake said to Carrie. He turned to his guest and pointed at the phone. "Excuse me. I have to take this."

Paola waved at him, and he went into the living room.

"Where the hell are you?" he said. *Manhattan*, he knew that much.

"Did you get the letter I sent you?"

"How could I get any letter? No one's been allowed near the destruction zone, including mailmen."

"I explained everything in that letter."

Jake kept his voice low. "I don't have time for games. You don't know what's in that laptop. I want it back. And my files."

"I want to give them back. I need your help."

"I'd laugh if I wasn't so pissed off at you. Do you have any idea how much time and effort I've spent trying to find you? Your parents couldn't be prouder, by the way."

"They're going to kill me."

"I don't blame them."

"Not my parents, though I've always been a disappointment to them."

His brain switched gears. "Who wants to kill you?"

"I don't have time to explain it now. I have to keep moving or they'll catch me."

"Who?" he said through clenched teeth.

"I'll only tell you if you agree to meet me."

Carrie held all the cards. He couldn't throttle her over the phone. "Where?"

"Someplace public, where they'll think twice about trying anything."

"How about the destruction zone? We'll be close to the Detective Bureau Manhattan, and there will be plenty of security around. No one will hurt you—not even me."

"That's the last place I'll go."

"Where, then?"

"Meet me at the fountain across the street from the plaza at two o'clock."

"That's a little tight for me. Make it three."

"I'll see you then."

"Carrie?" His voice conveyed enough urgency to keep her from hanging up.

"Yes?"

"Do you even care that Ripper got killed?"

"Later, Jake." Carrie hung up.

Jake saved the pay phone's number, then returned to the kitchen, where Paola had started cooking. "You're staying until Maria comes home, right?"

"*Sí.*"

"I just got an emergency phone call. Do you mind watching Shana for two or three hours?"

"Go ahead."

Shana shot him a worried look.

"Remember what we discussed in the car about my job?"

She nodded.

"I have to do that now."

Jake went to the basement and sat at the computer. He searched for a list of the pay phones in Manhattan, then scanned the results until he located the one Carrie had called from: Union Square. He selected a nylon Windbreaker from a coatrack. It would be hot for early August, but he wanted to hide the harness and his shoulder holster, which he put on next. So many straps crisscrossed his back that he felt like a fly trapped in a spiderweb.

He unlocked the top drawer of the metal desk, then took out his Smith & Wesson Model 325 Thunder Ranch revolver with a black matte finish. He didn't have to check the cylinder. The weapon had become his favorite since his return from Pavot Island, and he always kept it loaded.

Jake pushed the revolver into his shoulder holster, then slung a black canvas bag over one shoulder. The bag contained two speed loaders holding six rounds each, an HD camera and spare batteries, a can of pepper spray, and other assorted goodies. The only other item he needed already hung around his neck: the Anting-Anting amulet, a bronze medallion with a carved image of a warrior wielding a sword against a demon. It had saved his life before, and he never knew when a demon would rear its ugly head.

In the kitchen, Shana blinked at the TV, which now showed a telenovela. Jake stood before her, but she did not look at him.

"Leaving now?" Paola said.

"Yes," Jake said. "I'll try not to be long."

"Don't worry. We'll stay busy. I brought my dominoes."

Jake rapped his knuckles on the tabletop, and Shana raised her eyes.

"Don't look so glum. Maria will be home for dinner, and I'll try to get back before then." He managed a sympathetic smile. "You can watch TV in the living room when you're done eating."

"That's right," Paola said, drawing out her words.

"I have to go." He faced Paola. "Thanks again."

Jake exited the house and locked the door behind him. Then he climbed into the Plymouth, started its engine, and headed toward Manhattan. At the Queensboro Bridge traffic slowed to a crawl. Once on the bridge, traffic stopped altogether.

"Come on, damn it."

Jake wanted to reach the Grand Army Plaza an hour early to check out the area. He didn't put it past Carrie to set him up, and he planned to take every precaution possible in the time he had. The drive should have taken twenty minutes, but with the subways in Manhattan closed due to flooding, people were driving into the city. He could only imagine what the commute had been like during rush hour.

Traffic crept forward, and halfway over the bridge Manhattan skyscrapers became visible. A feeling of intense dread made Jake nauseous. Lilith had wreaked destruction on the city because Jake had rattled her cage by rescuing Laurel. He could never turn his back on a friend, and Laurel had helped him more than once. But had he known the level of damage his actions would result in and the number of lives lost, would he have done the same thing? He did not know the answer.

Taking the Second Avenue ramp, he made his way into the city. Battered cars still lined the streets, some upside down and some blocking the sidewalks. Windows had been blown out of buildings. Mud and garbage clung to outside walls. At every street corner men and women clutched signs asking for food or money. People camped out in abandoned vehicles. Police officers on horseback and on foot patrol watched for crime. A pregnant woman fanned herself in the blazing heat while the Plymouth's air-conditioning kept Jake cool. He had never seen anything like it in his life.

He stopped at a red light, and dirty children seemed to appear out of nowhere. They surrounded his car and pressed their faces against the windows.

"Help," a boy with grimy features said.

"We're hungry," a girl with tangled hair said.

Jake grabbed a handful of change he kept handy for tolls, then lowered his window with his hook and tossed the coins at the children, hoping to distract them.

High-pitched voices called out, and young bodies fell to their knees, fighting over the money. More children surged at the car, reaching inside to claw at Jake.

He raised the window, and when the light turned green he moved forward, scattering the children before the car.

One boy, who looked only a year or two older than Shana, climbed on top of the hood and lunged at the windshield. He rolled off the car as Jake increased speed.

He turned on Central Park South and searched for a parking space. A fleet of tow trucks removed damaged vehicles, and he pulled into an evacuated space. Climbing out of the car, he locked the doors and slung his bag over one shoulder. The doors of businesses were boarded over, and workers wearing orange vests jackhammered the jagged sidewalk.

Jake walked in traffic until he emerged from the

cool shadows of the buildings in Grand Army Plaza, crowded with hundreds of people, and faced the Pulitzer Fountain where he had agreed to meet Carrie. The statue of the Roman goddess Pomona had been toppled, and Jake wondered if Lilith had harbored a grudge against it. Behind it on the far side of the plaza, dozens of National Guards protected a twenty-story building of high-end condominiums. The wealthy rated armed protection from the rabble.

To his left, workers dismantled the marquee of a movie theatre that had collapsed on the sidewalk, and the fifty-story tower beside it stood like a hollow monument, its glass facade destroyed, revealing desecrated offices. Streetlights lay twisted on the sidewalk, and emergency lights had been set up in their place.

Jake moved through a crowd surrounding the pedestal where the bronze equestrian statue of William T. Sherman had once stood. Cigarette and marijuana smoke lingered in the air. Portable toilets had been set up in clusters. A filthy street musician strummed his acoustic guitar, and two evangelists with loudspeakers competed for attention.

"God has punished us," a black preacher said. "But he's punished us for our wicked ways because he loves us. Do not turn your backs on him. Embrace his love, and see his punishment as a gift from heaven above. Be grateful that he made an example of us for the entire world to see. Get down on your knees and beg for his forgiveness and pray for his love. This is not the end but the beginning!"

Jake gazed at Central Park. Not one tree remained standing. Some had snapped, leaving split trunks and stumps, and others had been uprooted. White FEMA trailers, surrounded by growing mountains of mulched trees, gleamed in the sunlight as far as the eye could see. Large tents had been erected, and campers with the Red Cross symbol lined the park. People of all ages wandered around the giant refugee camp, looking weary and hopeless. Police and National Guards stood at thirty-foot intervals while orange-vested men and women wearing safety helmets took chain saws to the fallen trees. Children played in the mud. Jake wanted to vomit.

A dark-skinned woman spoke to a camera near another toppled statue. The cameraman panned across the crowd, shooting B-roll footage.

Jake shifted his weight from one foot to the other. He didn't like being photographed.

A young woman with long brown hair approached him, her dark eyes shiny with religious fervor. He had seen that look before. "Excuse me. Do you have the time?"

Jake checked his watch. "It's 3:35."

"Are you waiting for food?"

"Nope."

She held out a flyer. "Can I give you one of these?"

"I have one at home."

"You don't even know what it is."

Oh, those crazy eyes. "It's an invitation to join Sky Cloud Dreams and become a Dreamer."

Her voice and the look in her eyes hardened. "Are you making fun of me?"

"Not at all. I think your whole movement is sad."

She gestured at the evangelists. "Don't listen to these men, brother. Watch the stars and rejoice! Imago is returning to earth."

Jake wanted to slap some sense into her. "There is no Imago, sister."

The Dreamers worshipped Imago, an alien being from outer space. Their religion had been created by Benjamin Bradley, based on his father's science fiction. Bradley had built Sky Cloud Dreams corporation into a profitable cult with all the protections afforded any religion. He had belonged to the Order of Avademe, a cabal of wealthy industrialists who served the giant mutant octopus god Avademe. Unlike Imago, Avademe had been real until Jake helped destroy the creature. Bradley and the other members of the order were killed in a ferocious battle, but the cult survived.

"You're wrong," the young woman said. "Imago is alive and he is love."

"Take a walk," Jake said.

The young woman smiled. "I'll see you on the other side in a silver spaceship." She sashayed away.

Before Jake could return to his task the reporter and cameraman took her place. The reporter held her microphone in his face. "Sir, we're with Manhattan Minute News. Can we interview you?"

"No," Jake said in a quiet voice.

"Can you spell your name for the camera?"

Jake smiled. "I don't want to be interviewed."

"Did you lose your hand in the hurricane?" the reporter said.

"No."

"We're looking for human interest stories. Real interviews with real survivors . . ."

"I'm sure you can find someone else to give you a sound bite."

She moved on, cameraman in tow.

Jake turned his attention to the fountain. A pair of troop transport trucks covered in green canvas rumbled into the plaza, and the crowd cheered. The trucks circled the fountain and stopped. A dozen armed guards jumped out of the first truck and surrounded the second, their machine guns held at the ready. Jake hoped the weapons held rubber bullets. What was good enough for crowd control on Pavot Island was good enough for the USA.

A guard set up a table, and a woman in camouflage spoke into a megaphone. "Listen carefully. We are about to disperse food rations of bread, cheese, fruit, and water. Each person will have his hand stamped with today's date. When we run out of rations, we will leave. Please remain in line; another truck will be here soon."

"I've heard that before," a sunburned man with long hair and no shirt said.

Since he could not stand at the fountain, Jake scanned the crowd for Carrie. He thought he had chosen a pretty conspicuous spot and hoped she would see him, but at about four and a half feet tall, she had certain disadvantages in a crowd this size. He watched the National Guards distribute food and water until they ran out of inventory and left. The crowd grumbled but behaved and no shots were fired.

At 4:30 p.m., he sat on a bench.

At 4:45, he clenched his jaw.

At 5:00, he gave up. Carrie wasn't coming.

Lost in thought, Jake returned to his car. So much dust covered the vehicle that he almost failed to recognize it. Standing at the driver's side door, he removed a tissue from his pocket and wiped the window. It took a moment for him to discern the reflection of a man standing behind him. Then cold, hard steel pressed against the back of his neck.

FIVE

"Give me your keys," the man standing behind Jake said.

Jake raised his hand and hook in the air. "I just got this car."

"Put your arms down and give me the keys."

Jake lowered his arms and turned so the revolver in the man's hand pointed at his chin. "Don't you have anything better to do than rob a cripple?"

"I didn't tell you to turn around."

"I'm a busy man. I don't have time for this. You're making a mistake. Walk away now."

The man dimpled Jake's chin with the tip of the gun's barrel. "Big man, huh? Or *what*?"

Jake drove his hook between them, ensnaring the man's wrist. He jerked the gun hand away and gave the hook a sharp twist. The man's wrist snapped, and he screamed as his gun clattered on the sidewalk. Jake punched the man's jaw, popping it and reducing his scream to a strangled whimper. The man crashed to the sidewalk. Jake picked up the gun and held it away from the man, who rolled from side to side on the sidewalk.

"I warned you," Jake said.

"You broke my wrist, motherfucker!"

"You'll live." Jake stepped into the street and tossed the revolver down a storm drain. Returning to his door he debated whether or not to help the man stand.

"Police!"

He turned as a policewoman galloped toward them on horseback. The carjacker got to his feet as she slowed the horse to a stop at the car. Jake and the carjacker stood at attention while she dismounted.

"What's going on here?" the policewoman said.

"It was a misunderstanding," Jake said.

The policewoman's nametag identified her as Sanchez, and she looked at each of them. "What kind of misunderstanding?"

"This gentleman mistook my car for his, and I mistook him for a carjacker."

"So you laid him out?"

"Something like that."

"He broke my fucking wrist!"

"He tripped and fell," Jake said.

"Let's see some ID, gentlemen."

Jake took out his wallet and handed it to Sanchez, who looked through his credentials. "PI, huh?"

"Ex-cop," Jake said.

"Oh, hell, no," the carjacker said.

"Really? Where did you work?" Sanchez said.

"Special Homicide Task Force. What I do now is boring in comparison."

"Why did you quit?"

Jake leaned closer. "Bullshit with the bosses. You know how it is."

"I hear that," Sanchez said. "I only see a business address, and that's in Ground Zero One."

"I'm staying with a friend in Brooklyn. She's on the job. I guess you could say my car is my office right now. That's why I overreacted when I thought this gentleman was trying to take it."

Sanchez looked at the robber. "What about you?"

"I forgot my wallet at home."

"At least you didn't say the dog ate it. What's your name?"

"Roberts."

"Roberts the robber?"

"Calvin Roberts. I'm innocent."

"You got a job, Roberts?"

"Not anymore. The hurricane washed away the TV repair shop where I worked."

"Like I said, a misunderstanding," Jake said.

"Sounds to me like someone doesn't want to fill out paperwork," Sanchez said.

Jake winked at her. "I've got a full dance card."

"So you don't want to press charges?"

"No."

Sanchez gestured at Roberts. "How about you? You want to press charges?"

Optimism blossomed on Roberts's face.

"If you do, I'll have to press countercharges," Jake said.

The optimism darkened. "Nah, I don't want to press charges. It's like he said—it was all a misunderstanding."

"What about your busted wrist?" Sanchez said.

Roberts grasped his wrist and winced. "I think it's just sprained. My fault. My wife always says what a klutz I am."

"You'd better have it looked at."

"There are medical tents set up in the park," Jake said.

"Thanks," Roberts said in a dull voice.

"I guess my work here is done," Sanchez said

"Sorry we wasted your time, Officer," Jake said.

Sanchez mounted her horse and nodded to Roberts. "Be on your way. I want to make sure you don't trip again."

"No problem." Roberts looked at Jake. "No hard feelings."

"Same here."

Roberts headed east.

"I recognize your name," Sanchez said. "What happened to you was bullshit."

Jake smiled.

Sanchez reined her horse in the opposite direction, and Jake got into the car. Maybe his reputation with his former colleagues wasn't as bad as he had believed.

.𝕒ﭔ𝕒 ꞉ ꞉

The landline on Maria's desk rang. She glanced at it, then returned to the file on her monitor. In all the years she had read the romantic fiction of Lilian Kane and Erika Long, she never expected to investigate their murders or cover them up. The phone continued to ring.

"Are you going to get that?" Bernie said.

"Don't we have enough on our hands?" Maria said. "Let someone else get it. Our shift was supposed to end an hour ago."

Bernie looked around the squad room. "Everyone's out or busy."

"We're busy, too."

Bernie answered the phone. "Special Homicide Task Force, Detective Reinhardt speaking."

Maria bit her tongue. She wanted to go home and have dinner with Shana, her mother, and Jake—her family.

Bernie scribbled an address on his notepad. "Got it." He hung up and turned to Maria. "Sorry. I know you don't want the overtime tonight, but we're going to the Bowery."

"You're breaking my heart."

"You need to toughen up." Bernie tore the sheet

from the notepad and walked to Mauceri's office.

Bernie drove the unmarked Cavalier downtown. By the time they reached the Bowery, dirt caked the white vehicle. Dried mud covered the streets and sidewalks, and movement stirred up dust. A police cruiser vacated a spot in front of the Roseview Hotel, leaving only one other unit at the scene.

"Watch this." Bernie pulled beside the remaining police car and parallel parked.

"Nice," Maria said.

"I passed my driving test the first time."

"So did I."

"But I can parallel park."

They got out of the car.

Maria surveyed the grimy facade of the four-story hotel. "Drug deal gone wrong or a dead john?"

"Maybe both," Bernie said.

A policewoman stood in front of the hotel. Bernie and Maria showed her their shields.

"What's doing?" Maria said.

"Victim's on the third floor," the policewoman said.

They entered what served as a lobby: a couple of ratty chairs facing a console TV next to a counter surrounded by bulletproof glass. A skinny Indian man sat in the protected area.

Maria held her shield up. "What's going on?"

"A man came in here an hour ago to see one of our guests," the man said. "A few minutes later another guest called down complaining of fighting sounds and screaming, so I called the police. Before they arrived, the man left."

"I'm having a hard time hearing you in there. Come out of the cage."

The man exited through a side door and stood before them.

"Did you go upstairs with the police when they got here?" Maria said.

"Yes."

"What did you see?"

"The woman's dead. Beaten, too."

"Was she your guest?" Bernie said.

"Yes."

"What's her name?"

"Just a minute." The man went back inside his station and checked a computer screen. "Joan Smith."

Rolling her eyes, Maria picked up a clipboard on the counter. "What room was Smith staying in?"

"Three B."

Maria scanned the visitors' log. "*John* Smith signed in but he didn't sign out."

"Brother and sister," Bernie said.

"Did Mr. Smith show you any ID?"

The man shook his head. "We don't require that."

"How about Ms. Smith? Do you require guests to keep credit cards on file?"

"Ms. Smith paid for a full week in advance and left a five-hundred-dollar security deposit."

"The woman knew how to manage her business," Bernie said.

"What did Mr. Smith look like?" Maria said.

"He was a white man with light hair," the man said.

"Dead hooker," Bernie said under his breath.

Maria pointed at Bernie. "Like him?"

"Darker than that."

"Was he taller or shorter than my partner?"

"Taller. My height."

"Six feet?"

"Yes."

Maria looked around, then nodded at a corner inside the booth. "Has that camera been recording all day?"

"Yes," the man said.

"Hallelujah," Bernie said. "Let's go home."

"We need to see that footage when we come back downstairs," Maria said. "While we're up there, feel free to burn a copy of it on DVD or a USB drive."

The man nodded. "I'll do that."

"Thanks for your cooperation," Bernie said.

Maria smiled at Bernie and they walked upstairs. Wallpaper in the halls peeled, and so many stains covered the rug that they resembled a pattern.

"Lovely," Maria said.

On the third floor, a policeman holding a clipboard stood outside a door.

They showed their shields again.

"Maria Vasquez. Special Homicide Task Force."

The PO recorded her name.

"Bernie Reinhardt, same."

"Too bad Smith was taken," Maria said.

They pulled on latex gloves and shoe covers.

An emaciated black woman stood in the next doorway. "I called the manager."

"What did you hear?" Bernie said.

"Screaming. A lot of it."

"Male or female?"

"Female," the woman said. "I heard furniture turning over, too. That was a fight."

"How long did it go on?"

"Maybe only five minutes but it seemed longer."

"Did you see anything?" Maria said.

"I saw the manager come upstairs with the police."

"Did you know your neighbor?"

The woman shrugged. "We said hello a few times."

"Thanks for your time, Miss . . . ?"

"Wanda Dumont."

"We'll need to get a full statement from you before we leave."

"I'm not going anywhere."

Bernie opened the door and Maria followed him

inside. The hotel room was larger than she expected. A chair had been knocked over. Clothes lay scattered across the floor. The wastebasket overflowed with soda bottles and food cartons. The bed had not been made. Maria moved around the bed and saw a still figure on the floor. She narrowed her eyes and her blood turned cold.

"Please tell me that isn't a dwarf," Bernie said, joining her.

"That's her," Maria said.

Carrie Scott wore pink panties and a cutoff T-shirt. Bruises covered her arms and legs. Her right eye was swollen and both lips were split. Half a dozen stab wounds punctured her chest and sternum. Blood covered her flesh and the rug.

Staring at the corpse, Maria debated her next course of action.

"Don't even think about it," Bernie said.

She looked at him. "What?"

"You're not calling Jake."

"Who said I was going to?"

"It's written all over your face. From where I stand, he's a suspect. We're going to recuse ourselves from this investigation and tell L.T. why."

"Jake didn't do it," she said in a flat tone. "He's home with my mother and Shana."

"Then the investigation will bear that out."

"Let's just have a look at the security footage downstairs."

64

SIX

When Jake returned to the house, he found Shana and Paolo playing dominoes on the kitchen table. "Who's winning?"

"I am," Shana said.

"Why am I not surprised?"

"She's very good," Paolo said in an exaggerated tone.

"Do you want to play?" Shana said.

"Maybe later," Jake said. "I have some work to do first."

Jake went to the basement and fired up his laptop. He took off his hook and harness and peeled off the wet sock that covered his stump. Then he pulled on a fresh sock and tried on the prosthetic hand. It fit him like a glove. Sitting at the computer, he ran an updated check on Carrie, with no results.

The doorbell rang.

Rising, he went upstairs. Paola and Shana stood in the entrance to the kitchen.

"I've got it," he said.

Looking through the peephole, he saw a familiar domed head. He slid his prosthetic into his pocket, then unlocked the door and opened it for Detectives Storm and Verila. Both men worked under Teddy Geoghegan in the Major Crimes Unit at One Police Plaza.

"This is a little far out of Manhattan for you fellas, isn't it?" Jake said.

"Major Crimes covers all five boroughs," Storm said, his blond hair gleaming in the sunlight.

"Okay, I'll bite. What can I do for you? And how did you know where to find me?"

"We need you to come to One PP with us. You'll get answers there."

"You'll have to do better than that."

Storm glanced at Paolo and Shana inside. "You don't want to make it hard. Not this time. One way or another, you're going downtown."

Jake saw they meant business. What the hell was going on? Geoghegan had been a thorn in his side since Black Magic and the Machete Massacres. "I'll be right out."

He started to close the door, but Storm held it open.

"Just give me a minute."

"Make it fast," Storm said.

Turning from the door, Jake faced Paolo and Shana. "These men are police detectives. I have to go downtown with them. Are you okay with watching Shana until Maria gets home?"

"Of course."

"They don't have a warrant, so don't let them or anyone else inside for any reason." He winked at Shana. She had probably seen her share of cops come and go while she lived with her aunt. "Nothing to worry about."

He went into the kitchen, then hurried to the basement, where he shut down his computer. If they came back with a search warrant while he was downtown, he didn't have to make checking his files easy for them.

"Call Maria and tell her what's going on," Jake said to Paolo when he returned to the living room. "Tell her it's no big deal." He hoped.

Jake stepped outside and closed the door. "Okay, fellas, I'm all yours. But I have to be home by midnight or I turn back into a kitchen maid."

"We'll see how funny you are in about an hour," Verila said, his smooth head sparkling with sweat.

Jake wondered if new evidence had emerged linking him to the vigilante execution of the Cipher. If the time had come to pay the piper, so be it. He would plead temporary insanity and let the chips fall where they may.

Storm and Verila escorted him to an unmarked car across the street. He was surprised he hadn't made them when he had come home.

I'm slipping. Getting careless. Too many distractions. "Can I ride up front and play with the siren?"

Storm opened the rear door. "Just get in."

Jake faced the detective. "Hey, how did you guys know where to find me, anyway?"

Storm stared at him.

Jake got into the car, an uneasy feeling settling over him. Only a handful of people knew he was staying at Joyce's with Maria. Whatever had happened, he hoped Reinhardt had been the one who blew him in, but the knot in his stomach told him otherwise.

Storm and Verila got into the front seat, and Storm started the engine.

Jake listened to radio calls on the drive into Manhattan. "How about this weather, huh? We could use some rain."

"You think that's funny?" Verila said. "A lot of people died in that hurricane. A lot more are displaced. Not everyone gets to move into a nice house when they lose everything."

Jake stared out the window at kids playing in a stream of water gushing from a fire hydrant. "No, it's not funny at all. I'm just making conversation."

"Save it for Geoghegan. He's looking forward to talking to you."

"Sure, Teddy's always a lively conversationalist."

Storm crossed the Queensboro Bridge and drove into Lower Manhattan. One Police Plaza, the fortified Puzzle Palace, rose before them on Park Row, showing little wear and tear in the wake of Daria.

Storm parked in a lot a couple of blocks away, and they got out and walked toward the nerve center of NYPD operations. Jake had spent more time there as a private investigator than he had on the force. They passed protective barriers and entered the air-conditioned building. Storm and Verila flashed their shields and walked him around the metal detector, leaving Jake to wonder if his prosthetic hand would have triggered the alarm.

On the elevator ride, all three men watched the numbers change on the floor indicator. On the fifth floor, Jake surveyed the reception area. He didn't recognize the woman sitting at the desk.

"Tell the lieutenant we've got his fish," Storm said.

The woman reached for her phone as Storm guided Jake down a quiet corridor to an interview room. Jake had been in the room before.

The detective gestured at the table and chairs. "Have a seat."

"My choice?" Jake said.

Storm smiled. "Facing the mirror would be best."

"Of course." Jake sat in the metal chair facing the two-way mirror and wondered who stood behind it besides Teddy.

"What can I get you to drink? A cola? Coffee?"

"Why don't you give me a syringe full of Sodium Pentothal?"

Storm snapped his fingers. "I think we're all out."

"I guess I'm good, then."

Storm exited, and Jake sat with his right hand on the table and his prosthetic in his pocket. He looked around the drab room. Only the interview room at Internal Affairs Bureau, where he had resigned from the force after refusing to take a drug test, had looked any different from the rest. He resisted the urge to drum his fingers on the metal table.

The door opened, and Storm and Verila rolled in a wide-screen TV and a digital player on a metal cart.

"Are you guys in the AV club, too?" Jake said.

Ignoring him, they connected the player to the TV and plugged in the devices.

Teddy Geoghegan entered the room with a file folder in his hands. The fifty-year-old lieutenant wore a sports jacket, and his gray hair had turned white. "Jesus, Helman, what happened to your face?"

"I get that a lot. I got jumped by some punks a little while after our last talk."

Geoghegan dropped the file folder on the table. It made a small sound, just loud enough to remind Jake he was in hot water. "You lost your left eye when you were jumped by hoods, too, didn't you?"

"Is the interview starting already?"

Geoghegan sat opposite him. "I guess you're not the tough guy you pretend to be. You get messed up a lot."

"It's been a tough couple of years."

Verila left the room and closed the door, leaving Storm to stand near the TV with his arms crossed.

"This interview is being recorded," Geoghegan said.

"I'd expect nothing less."

"This is Lieutenant Theodore Geoghegan with Major Crimes Unit, NYPD. The subject is Helman, Jake." He stated the date and a case number. "Where do you live, Helman?"

"You already know because you sent your boys to pick me up."

"Tell the folks at home."

Jake gave the address of the Queens residence.

"How long have you lived there?"

"A week and a half, since Daria creamed my office."

"Who owns the house?"

"Joyce Wood."

"What's your relationship to Ms. Wood?"

"She's a friend."

"Elaborate."

"She's the mother of my ex-partner's son."

"Your ex-partner when you were in Special Homicide in this department?"

"Let me save us some time. Joyce is the mother of Martin Hopkins, Edgar Hopkins's teenage son. Edgar and I were partners in Special Homicide. I resigned from the unit when I refused to take a drug test. Edgar disappeared for almost a year, then resurfaced. He and Joyce were separated but got back together. They moved down to North Carolina, and my girlfriend, Maria Vasquez, is watching the house for them. Maria's in Special Homicide now. She and Edgar were partners, too. I'm staying with her."

Geoghegan's smile tightened. "How long have you and Vasquez been an item?"

"None of your business."

"Was she your girlfriend when she interviewed you as a possible suspect in the murder of Marc Gorman?"

"No, that's when we met."

"You must give a hell of a good interview."

"That never made you and me any closer, but I guess there's still time to be optimistic."

"Was Vasquez your girlfriend the first time I brought you in here?"

"You mean when those drug dealers caused me to flip my car outside? We'd just had our first date, but we didn't become involved until after Edgar disappeared. Why all the interest in my love life? I don't ask you about yours."

"Where was Hopkins all that time?"

"I don't know. Neither does he."

"Does Vasquez know?"

"No."

"I take it you saw Hopkins before he moved down south?"

72

"Sure, we're friends."

"What did he tell you?"

"Nothing he didn't tell you when you railroaded him out of the department."

"His case was still pending when he left town."

"I guess the handwriting was on the wall, and he'd had enough of your bullshit. But enough about Edgar. Why am I here, Teddy?"

"Where were you last month?"

"New Orleans. Then Miami. Then Pavot Island."

"Southern heat and tropical heat. Were you on a case?"

"No." Jake had not been around this bush with Geoghegan yet.

"So you were on vacation?"

"More like a sabbatical."

"You were finding yourself?"

"Something like that."

"With Vasquez?"

Jake began to suspect Maria was Geoghegan's target. "She came to New Orleans a little after I did."

"But you didn't stay in the same hotels."

Geoghegan had run checks on their credit cards. He knew every stop they had made when they hadn't used cash. "You don't know where we slept."

"So tell me."

It's none of your damn business. "We weren't holding hands yet. I went on to Miami, and she was supposed to come back to New York, so she joined me later."

"Why did she change her mind?"

"It must have been my blue eye. We went to Pavot Island as a couple since you're so hot to know."

"Just days before the revolution broke out. Those must have been some fireworks."

Jake said nothing.

"When did you come home?"

"I don't remember the date. You tell me."

"How does July 22 sound?"

"Sure."

"The day before Vasquez returned to work and Hopkins suddenly reappeared."

"If you say so."

"And the two of you had nothing to do with his return?"

"No."

"I don't believe you."

Jake shrugged. "The burden of proof is on you."

Geoghegan smiled. "You just keep dancing around one coincidence after another, don't you?"

"It's a crazy city. A crazy world."

"Are you working on a case now?"

"No."

"When was your last case?"

Jake hadn't expected this. His last client had been Marla Madigan, the wife of Mayor Myron Madigan.

Avademe had eaten her and Cain had killed Myron. "It's been a while."

"And yet you can afford to spend months on sabbatical, moving from one love nest to another."

"You've obviously seen my credit card statements. You know how I paid for everything. I'm not paying rent now."

"Aren't you lucky?"

"My wife was murdered by a serial killer. *Lucky* isn't the word I would use to describe myself." *Cursed is more like it.*

Geoghegan set his hand on the file folder. The look in his eyes told Jake he couldn't wait to spring its contents on him. He opened the folder and removed a color photograph. "Do you know this woman?"

Jake felt his confidence draining like dirty dishwater from a sink. "That's Carrie Scott."

"How do you know her?"

"She was my part-time bookkeeper, then my full-time office manager and assistant."

"Did she work for you while you were traveling?"

"Yes."

"You employed her for months even though you weren't working?"

"Let's just say I needed a change in direction, and I hadn't decided what to do with my business yet. My second quarter taxes still needed to be filed, and she took care of my bookkeeping while I thought about my next move."

"When was the last time you saw her?"

"During the hurricane. We were holed up in my office, waiting things out."

"Just the two of you?"

He chose his words carefully, even though he had rehearsed them. "No, her boyfriend, Sam Kim, was with us. He went out looking for food, and when he didn't come back, I went looking for him."

"Did you find him?"

"No. But later on the news, I learned he'd been killed by the storm. The waterspout must have thrown him onto a post that impaled him. When I returned to what was left of my office, Carrie was gone."

"Did she contact you after that?"

"No. She wouldn't have. She didn't leave empty-handed. She stole a laptop, some case files, and cash from my safe."

Geoghegan's expression didn't change, but Jake pictured the wheels turning in his head. "How did she get into your safe?"

"I must have left it unlocked. There was a lot going on right across the street, with those buildings collapsing."

"What was on the laptop?"

The secrets of the supernatural. "More case files."

"What the hell would she want with those?"

"I have no idea."

"How much cash did she take?"

"Five hundred bucks."

"Did you report the theft?"

"No. I preferred to handle it internally. Carrie was a friend. I trusted her. I just wanted my files back. I didn't even care about the cash."

"What did you do to find her?"

"I went to her apartment, which was abandoned. I contacted her parents. Former employers. Friends. Anyone who might know where she was. I got no leads. I tracked her credit cards but she stopped using them."

"So you would have let her go if she returned your files?"

Jake would not even admit the truth to himself. Carrie had sent Ripper with Jake to the Flatiron Building so she could get away. She had sent him to his death, and she deserved to pay for that. "Yes. I didn't want to punish her. She's young and more stupid than I thought. Everyone screws up."

"She's dead."

Jake had begun to suspect as much. "How?"

"She was beaten and stabbed to death in the Rose-view Hotel earlier today."

Jake knew about that dive. Carrie had been hiding, just like she said on the phone. But from whom? "Were my files at the scene?"

Geoghegan shook his head. "No files, no laptop, no five hundred bucks."

Damn it. "Do you have any leads?"

"As a matter of fact, we do." Geoghegan nodded to Storm, who powered on the TV and the player. The image of a gloomy interior filled the screen. "This is surveillance footage taken from inside the Roseview. The camera's mounted behind the counter, facing the entrance. The image is a little cloudy because of the bulletproof glass. We've edited what's here."

Jake stared at the time stamp in the lower right-hand corner of the screen.

"As you can see, this was at 3:30 p.m. today," Geoghegan said.

A figure entered the lobby and approached the counter. Jake's good eye twitched. The man wore jeans and a polo shirt, and scars covered the left side of his face.

"Look familiar?"

That's me, Jake thought.

SEVEN

"There's no audio," Geoghegan said. "According to the desk clerk, this man asked for the guest by the alias she was using, Ms. Joan Smith. The clerk called upstairs, and Miss Scott gave him the okay to send you up."

"That isn't me," Jake said. "I've never been inside that fleabag hotel in my life."

"Those scars are pretty distinctive. You used to be so pretty. Now here's the best part."

On the screen, Jake's double exited the lobby in a hurry, carrying a laptop and some file folders. Jake felt an invisible noose tightening around his neck.

This is where everything catches up to me. But he did not intend to pay for a murder he had not committed.

"That's ten minutes later. Sure looked like a laptop and file folders to me. Five minutes after you went upstairs, a woman in the next room complained about a racket in Scott's room, with a woman screaming. Some blues showed up one minute after you left."

Jake's temples throbbed. "That isn't me. I'm being set up."

"You just provided me with your motive, and HD doesn't lie. You want to stand in a lineup, or do you want to sign a confession now? If you make things easy for me, I'll do the same for you."

Jake grunted. "That isn't me."

"Okay, have it your way. Detective Storm, read Helman his rights."

"Storm, rewind that footage to the beginning," Jake said.

Storm gave Geoghegan a questioning look.

"Sure, rewind the footage," Geoghegan said. "It isn't going to change anything."

Once again, the footage showed Jake entering the lobby and approaching the counter.

"Freeze it right there," Jake said.

Storm froze the frame. On screen, Jake stood at the counter with both hands on its surface.

"See my hands?" Jake said.

Geoghegan crossed his arms. "Yeah, so?"

"Now fast-forward to the part where the guy exits."

Geoghegan nodded and Storm fast-forwarded the footage.

"Freeze it," Jake said.

Storm froze the image as Jake opened the front door.

"He's carrying the laptop and files in his right hand, and he's opening the door with his left."

"Again—so?"

"He grabbed the handle on the door with his left hand and pushed it open. See the way his hands are curled around the handle?"

"What a tricky son of a bitch you are. I never would have imagined doing such a thing. What else were you going to do, open it with your teeth?"

Jake took his time standing.

Storm moved closer to the table, but Geoghegan raised one hand to stop him.

Jake removed the prosthetic from his pocket and used his right hand to detach the prosthetic hand, which he tossed onto the table before Geoghegan like a gauntlet. The prosthetic hand slapped Carrie's photo inside the file folder. Geoghegan's eyes widened and Jake raised his stump. In his mind, he also raised a phantom middle finger.

"Jesus Christ," Storm said.

"I lost my left hand on Pavot Island," Jake said. "Someone went to a lot of trouble to find someone who looks like me, fake the scars with makeup, and send him to that hotel to kill Carrie and steal my files. They must not have known about my hand. Everything's in the details."

Geoghegan stared at the prosthetic, then at Jake. His features darkened. "Sit down."

Jake returned to his seat.

"Play the footage again."

Storm replayed the footage, and all three men

watched Jake 2.0 use his left hand to open the door.

"How the *fuck*?" Geoghegan said.

"You said the perp beat Carrie to death," Jake said. "What does the evidence show?"

Geoghegan spoke in a slow cadence. "Her body was covered with bruises and stab wounds. It looks like he finished her off by choking her."

"It would be difficult for a one-handed man to choke a woman to death. It would even be hard for a one-handed man to stab a woman to death, unless she was tied up or otherwise incapacitated."

"She was a small woman. You're a resourceful six-foot-tall man."

"The footage shows a man who looks like me—"

"*Just like you*, you're ugly as sin."

"—using his left hand to open the door. He clearly bends his fingers. I don't have a left hand."

Geoghegan stared at Jake. "What happened to it?"

"Bill Russel hacked it off with a machete."

"Who?"

"He was ex-CIA, working for Ernesto Malvado. They apprehended me, I guess because I'm an American."

"And he chopped your hand off just for the hell of it?"

"No, he did it to make me suffer."

"Is Mr. Russel dead now?"

"According to the news."

"Make me believe you."

"When Maria and I got off the airplane from Pavot Island in Miami, two guys from the State Department detained us and interviewed us separately. I gave Weissman the full story about my hand. He must have documented it."

Geoghegan's gaze returned to the prosthetic. "Where were you today between three thirty and four?"

"At three thirty, I was parking my car. I walked over to Fifth Avenue and Central Park South and stayed there until five."

"What were you doing there?"

"Today was my first day back in the city since I moved to Queens. I wanted to see the refugee camp FEMA set up in Central Park. While I was there, the National Guards distributed food. I've never seen anything like that before, so I stuck around."

"Were you alone?"

"Yes."

"Did anyone see you?"

Jake was about to answer in the negative, then snapped his fingers. "A reporter from Manhattan Minute News was conducting interviews. She asked me a couple of questions before I gave her the brush-off. I didn't give her permission to use the footage, but her cameraman definitely rolled on me."

"What time was this?"

"If I had to guess? Three forty. I couldn't have been

at the hotel and in that square at the same time. When I left at five, a guy tried to jack my car, and I roughed him up. A mounted policewoman came to investigate. Me and the perp played stupid. The cop was named Sanchez."

"But you didn't file a report?"

"That was the last thing I wanted to do. But how many mounted policewomen named Sanchez can there be?"

"Where were you before you came into the city?"

"I spent the morning with Shana Robbins, the little girl Maria's fostering."

"Papa Joe's daughter."

"We picked up that prosthetic on Long Island, then went back home. Maria's mother came over. I was with both of them until I drove into Manhattan, and I went straight home after I tossed the guy who tried to steal my car. Storm and Verila saw them at the house."

Geoghegan turned to Storm, who nodded. "Get Verila and get busy."

Storm left the interview room.

"Get that hand off my file."

Jake grabbed the prosthetic and reattached it.

Geoghegan glared at him.

"I'll take that coffee now," Jake said.

Sitting alone in the interview room, Jake took out his phone and called Maria. She answered midway through the second ring.

"Keep dinner warm for me," he said.

"You're coming home?"

"Did you have any doubt?"

"I saw the surveillance footage. So did Bernie. We turned it in to Mauceri."

He hesitated before answering. "What else could you do?"

"As soon as your name comes up in a case, it goes to Geoghegan. I wanted to warn you but I couldn't."

"Forget about it. You did what you had to do. I'm not angry."

"Did you get a lawyer?"

"I don't need one. I didn't do anything wrong. I was nowhere near that hotel."

Her brief silence made him uncomfortable. "What's happening now?"

"I'm sitting in a room waiting while Teddy's toadies check my alibis."

"Verila already called and spoke to my mother. You sure know how to make an impression." There was no mistaking the sadness behind her joke.

"Kiss the kid good night for me. I'll see you later." He hung up feeling none too convinced Maria believed him.

Two hours later, Geoghegan entered. He had removed

his sports jacket and had rolled up his sleeves. Jake took this as a sign the man didn't plan to announce his arrest anytime soon.

"Manhattan Minute News located the footage just like you said."

"Time stamped?"

"From 3:39 to 3:40."

Thank Christ. "You seem disappointed."

"Officer Sanchez confirmed she spoke to you as well."

"Just like the cavalry."

Geoghegan sat down. "We're still waiting for State to get back to us, but I've spoken to the ADA and you're free to go."

"Then I guess I'll be on my way."

"Who the hell would want to kill Carrie Scott? Besides you, I mean."

"I have no idea."

"Someone who wanted your files just as badly as you did. Someone who knew she worked for you. A former client? You must have had incriminating evidence on someone. Maybe he convinced her to steal those files in the first place."

Jake gave the lieutenant a passive look. "If I think of anyone I'll let you know."

Geoghegan slapped the table. "Goddamn it, stop jerking me around! You know who's behind this. Someone who not only wanted those files bad enough to kill for them but who wanted to set you up to boot. They made someone *look* like you. That's some crazy *Mission: Impossible* malarkey."

Jake had an idea or two. He just couldn't share them. "You've got your work cut out for you. I don't miss being a detective. But I'm glad to know you have my back."

"You never stop with the wisecracks, do you?"

"You mean you don't have my back?"

Geoghegan's jaw tightened.

Jake stood. "You've had a hard-on for me for over a year. Then you had one for Edgar. Now you have one for Maria. You keep coming after me and winding up empty-handed. You should have seen yourself sitting there across from me, salivating at the prospect of cuffing me."

Geoghegan stood, too. "It still might happen."

"You had surveillance video and it still wasn't enough. I've got alibis. Even if you dig deeper, you'll only find more to support my innocence. You're obsessed with me and it isn't pretty. If you ever make a run at me again, you'd better come to the table with incontrovertible proof, or I'll slap you with a harassment suit that will set your reputation back a decade. I can show the pattern. Same thing if you make a run at Maria."

Geoghegan snorted. "This is the part where I tell you I'll be in touch and warn you not to leave town."

"This is the part where I tell you you've wasted enough of my time. You've got my number. Now, you brought me down here, so how about a ride home?"

Jake rode in the back of a police cruiser, staring at Queens beyond the bridge. His phone rang and he took it out, expecting to see Maria's name. Instead he saw Edgar's. "Hello?"

"I'm glad to hear your voice," Edgar said.

"How are things down there?"

"Not as boring as I'd hoped. Did you forget to tell me you had an identical twin brother?"

Jake's stomach tightened. "No, why?"

"Because I just killed you ten minutes ago."

EIGHT

"Thanks," Jake said to the police officers who drove him.

He ran up the steps and unlocked the door. Maria and her mother sat on the sofa, watching television. Maria rose as he entered the room.

"Everything's cool but I'm in a hurry." Jake rushed to the basement, removed his prosthetic hand, set it on the desk, and peeled off the wet sock. Then he started packing.

Maria came downstairs. "What the hell is going on?"

"I've got to make a short trip."

"Where to?"

"I'd rather not say."

She crossed her arms. "I thought we were done keeping secrets from each other."

"No offense but you kept a big one today."

"You said you understood."

Jake moved close to her. "I do. You've got to cover your own ass, or you'll be out of a job. And I'm sure you get that it's better for you if I don't tell you where I'm going." He snapped his fingers. "Your mother can watch Shana tomorrow, right?"

"Yes. When will you be back?" she said in an arch tone.

"We'll have that family dinner tomorrow."

"What am I supposed to tell Geoghegan if he checks up on you?"

"See? Now you get it." He slung the bag over his shoulder.

Maria picked up the prosthetic hand.

"It looks different than what that guy pretending to be me had, doesn't it?"

Maria stared at the false hand.

"You didn't catch that, did you?"

She shook her head.

"Did you believe it was me?"

She raised her eyes to his. "In my heart, no. But the time my mother said you left the house jibed with the time stamp on the footage. And that guy looked just like you."

Jake took the hand from her and set it down. "It's okay. When I watched that footage, even I thought I was guilty for a minute."

"Who's doing this and why?"

"I've got my share of enemies. Prewitt from Sky Cloud Dreams, for one. I'm willing to bet every member of the Order of Avademe had a second in command who knew what was going on. That means White River

Security, Reichard Shipping, the Reichard Foundation, and three munitions contactors. All of them have the resources and the motivation to come after me and a reason to want Afterlife. One or all of them reached out to Carrie and turned her."

"That doesn't say much about her."

"I was gone for a long time. They had time to work on her."

"What are you doing on this trip?"

He wanted to tell her. "You're out of this one. I'm on my own. You've got Shana to worry about."

"Are we in danger?"

If Edgar had killed Jake's double, then that person couldn't strike out again. But who had controlled the marionette's puppet strings?

"Carrie's killer may no longer be a problem, but I don't know who sent him, and now that this address is in the NYPD data bank, my location isn't as secret as I'd like it to be."

Maria sighed. "I just went back to work after my leave of absence. I can't stay home."

"Tell Reinhardt to take a personal day and stay here."

"Even though it could mean risking his life?"

Jake touched her cheek. "If I thought you and Shana were in danger, I wouldn't be going."

She closed her hand over his. "Promise me you'll come back."

"This isn't a dangerous trip. It's more like a fact-finding

mission. I need to verify something with my own eye."

"That isn't what I meant."

He kissed her. "You know me better than that. I'm not going on the run. I'm putting a name to whoever ordered the hit on Carrie, so I can take the fight to him."

She hugged him and he held her.

Jake drove the Plymouth to LaGuardia Airport in Queens and parked it in a massive lot, then took a shuttle bus to his terminal. The security line was short this late at night, and he located his gate without trouble.

The incoming flight arrived twenty minutes late, causing a slight delay for his midnight flight. He boarded a narrow air taxi with a ceiling so low he had to bow his head while walking the aisle, which divided single seats from pairs. He sat overlooking one wing and watched the ground crew at work below while other passengers boarded and took their seats.

Shutting his window shade, he closed his eye. The flight to North Carolina was scheduled to last one hour and forty minutes, and he had a long morning ahead of him. Drifting asleep during the flight attendant's safety instructions, he awoke when the plane taxied out to the runway, then slept through takeoff and awakened again when the flight attendants, illuminated by soft lighting, served drinks. He closed his eye and didn't open it until the plane circled its destination: Raleigh–Durham International Airport.

Inside the airport, he passed open shops en route to the car rental agency, where he checked out a black Ford Escape from a pretty brunette who lowered her gaze from his scarred face to his stump, which he had set on the counter without realizing it.

Heat rose from the concrete bottom of the enormous garage as he searched for his vehicle, and his polo shirt damped. He programmed the address Edgar had given him into the GPS and left the garage. The luminous dashboard clock showed the time was 2:20 a.m.

He drove west toward Jordan Lake. Edgar, Joyce, and Martin were staying with Edgar's relatives, just outside Pittsboro, a little farther west. The city gave way to the country, and the darkness grew denser. The GPS directed him to get off at an exit, and five minutes later a gas station with an attached convenience store came into view. He pulled over to the side of the store, away from the pumps, and parked beside a large pickup. The truck appeared to be black, but when he got out he saw it was dark green. A tarp covered the truck's bed.

Edgar leaned out the driver's side window. He wore a short-sleeved shirt. "You're late, just like I expected."

"If that's what you expected, I wasn't really late." Jake gestured at the truck. "Is this monster yours?"

"It belongs to my cousin. You look a lot better than

the last time I saw you, and I don't mean in Queens." Edgar started the truck's engine. "Follow me. It's about a twenty-minute drive."

Jake had expected a warmer welcome. He got back into the Escape and followed Edgar out of the parking lot. They drove through the darkness, then turned onto a dirt road that cut through woods, the headlights of the two vehicles causing the trees around them to glow. Edgar slowed down and Jake did the same, the Escape bouncing and rocking from bumps in the little used road.

They reached a clearing where the road ended, and Edgar stopped and switched off his engine. Jake followed suit. The dome light in the truck came on as Edgar climbed out of the cab: he wore jeans and hiking boots. When he closed the truck door, darkness greeted Jake, who got out and joined his friend at the truck's hatch. Crickets chirped around them, and sweat formed on Jake's flesh.

"How are Joyce and Martin?" Jake said.

"They're both good. This place takes getting used to. It's a lot different from the city. Everything's slower here . . . much slower. Martin's already made some friends, and Joyce is going to start job hunting next week."

"How about you?"

"We'll see. There's only one thing I know how to do." Edgar lowered the hatch and set a lantern on it, which he fired up. The glow of the lantern illuminated fishing rods and tackle boxes.

"Are you fishing these days?" Jake said.

"That's just my cover story. I had to tell Joyce something. Martin wanted to come along, so I told them I wanted to be alone. I didn't like lying." He unsnapped the tarp and drew it back, revealing a man-size shape wrapped in canvas.

Jake shuddered. "What happened?"

"I'll tell you on the way. We don't have any time to waste." Edgar grabbed the body by what Jake assumed were its heels and pulled the cadaver out. "Don't just stand there. Put that hand to use."

Jake wrapped his right arm around the ankles and squeezed them to his chest.

Edgar slid the handle of the lantern over Jake's stump, positioned it in the crook of Jake's arm, and raised the stump. "Put that thing to use, too."

Edgar wrapped his arm around what should have been the torso and used his free hand to hold it from beneath, and they lifted the body out of the truck.

"We're only going a quarter of a mile, but it won't be easy."

Mosquitoes and gnats swarmed over the lantern. They carried the body, Edgar leading the way. A flap of canvas fell loose and rubbed against Jake's jeans. Twigs snapped beneath their weight and an owl hooted. The moon could have been full, and its light still wouldn't have penetrated the dense tree branches.

"How do you know about this place?" Jake said.

"I scoped it out after we spoke on the phone. There was no way I was burying this thing on my cousin's land."

"Tell me what happened."

Edgar heaved the body higher for a better grip. "My cousin lives in a big house on what used to be a farm. He owns close to eighty acres but doesn't do anything with it. A couple of hundred yards behind the barn, there's a field filled with tall grass, and beyond the field there are woods, all owned by him. There's a bunch of paths crisscrossing the field and the woods, and I've taken to walking them alone."

"Bird-watching?" Jake said.

"Something like that. I'm definitely drawn to nature in a way I never was before."

Jake tightened his grip around the ankles.

"I was coming back from a long walk when I saw a man standing behind the barn. As I got closer, he waved to me, and I could have sworn it was you. What the hell, right? Then he turned and walked around the side of the barn, and I lost sight of him. I walked faster, wondering what the hell you were doing in Pittsboro.

"When I reached the front of the barn, I saw no sign of him . . . you. I opened the barn doors. My cousin keeps a little motorboat on a trailer and a riding lawn mower and God knows what else in there. There's no electricity, but sunlight shone through the slats in the walls. You think it's humid now? The barn was like an oven and reeked of rotting wood. And of course I heard bees buzzing. I just love bees, and they're nice and fat out here, like cotton balls.

"I stood in the doorway, adjusting my eyes to the darkness, but there are plenty of hiding places. I began to think I'd imagined seeing you, which made more sense than you hopping a plane to North Carolina to play hide-and-seek. I called your name in a low voice. You didn't respond. So I walked inside, moving along the near side of the boat. As I reached the end of it, I saw gardening tools next to a workbench covered in dust. I was looking at those tools when the doors started closing. I turned around, just in time to see you before the doors shut.

"I asked what the hell you were doing here. You didn't answer and I heard you running. A silhouette passed along one wall, blotting out the slats of light. The hair on the back of my neck stood on end—you know what I mean?"

"Yeah," Jake said, grunting from the weight he carried.

"I didn't get the feeling you were there to play touch football in the dark. I only brought a .38 here, and I keep it locked up, so I was unarmed. I dropped to all fours and ducked beneath the boat. I had to lie flat to get beneath the trailer, and I wasn't exactly quiet about it.

When I stood, clumps of dirt stuck to my skin. I ran for the tools, but before I reached them a weight slammed into me like a linebacker, knocking me to the dirt floor. I got to my feet, but so did you—I heard you breathing and sensed where you were. I raised my fists but held my ground. The only way I could see you was if I held still, so I could look for gaps in the light."

"Stop saying 'you,'" Jake said. "It wasn't me."

"I took a punch in the chin, which snapped my head back. I raised my fists close to my face, and my right arm blocked a second punch, but the son of a bitch punched me in the stomach. I swung out blindly and missed and took a kick inside my left thigh that must have been meant for my balls. I staggered and fell to one knee, then I heard running footsteps again.

"Before I could figure out what was happening, two feet plowed into my chest, driving me to the floor. I gasped for air but couldn't breathe and couldn't get up. Before I knew it, he climbed on top of me and started pummeling me. I kept my fists in front of my face and fended off most of the punches. Slats of light revealed glimpses of his face. It was you; I was sure of it. But your features were angry, hateful. And as I fought off the punches, I knew you—he—wanted to kill me with his bare hands. Then it occurred to me: you don't *have* two hands. Whoever it was, it wasn't you.

"Whatever reluctance I'd felt to fight back with

everything I had evaporated. My chest ached, but I managed to regain my ability to breathe. I couldn't reach his face, so I went straight for his solar plexus, which made him lean forward. I went to town on his face as much as I could from that position, one punch from each hand, and that was enough to knock him off me."

"Then you really knew it wasn't me," Jake said.

"I got to my feet and staggered over to the workbench. He got up behind me, and I heard his feet stomping the dirt. I patted the workbench, searching for anything I could use to coldcock the guy. He threw his arm around my throat and squeezed. I couldn't breathe again. So I planted one foot against the top of the workbench and kicked out, driving us both back and off our feet.

"He landed on the floor, with me on top of him, and grunted, and I figured this time I'd knocked the wind out of him. I got up, ran to the bench, and grabbed the long wooden handle of a gardening tool. He came after me. I whipped around and swung the tool so its metal end bit into his side. He cried out and I jerked the tool free, then swung it behind me and overhead and brought its end down so hard the handle snapped in two. I expected him to scream but he didn't; he just fell to his knees and then pitched forward.

"I stood there, gasping for breath, sweat pouring down my face, and waited for him to get up again, but he didn't. I opened the barn doors, filling the interior with sunlight. When I walked back to the guy, I knew he was dead. Dropping to one knee, I rolled him over. The tool had been a steel rake. I brained him and blood covered his face. But it was your damned ugly face, scars and all. I grabbed his wrists and raised his arms, inspecting his bruised hands. They were flesh and bone. I searched the barn for some place to hide the body until I had a plan and ended up stuffing him in the boat.

"Then I called you. I didn't know what to expect. After I hung up, I went into the side yard, where there's a manual water pump. I washed myself clean and told everyone I'd just been hot from my walk. I asked my cousin if I could borrow his truck, so he took Joyce's car to go play cards with his buddies. As soon as everyone went to sleep, I drove to the barn, loaded the body into the truck, and drove off."

Jake stumbled and regained his balance. "How much farther?"

"We're almost there," Edgar said. "Do you mind telling me what in the hell is going on? Just the parts that affect the safety of me and my family."

Jake told Edgar about Carrie's murder, his interrogation by Geoghegan, and the surveillance footage of his look-alike arriving and departing the Roseview Hotel.

They reached the crest of a deep slope.

"Down there," Edgar said.

They set the body down, and Jake held the lantern high.

The darkness swallowed its light. "I can't see anything."

"That's the point," Edgar said. "There's nothing down there but fallen trees and poison ivy. We'll leave the body here and go back for the shovels."

"I need to see it first."

Edgar held the lantern over the wrapped figure. "Go ahead."

Kneeling, Jake rolled the figure toward him, then unwrapped the canvas. The figure wore the same clothes he had worn at the Roseview. Jake peeled back the top flap and stilled his breathing. Even caked in blood, he recognized his own features. He traced the scars with his fingers. They were real, not makeup applications. He poked the corpse's left eye: it was hard, not soft. He parted the eyelids.

Edgar leaned closer. "I already checked that."

The eye was made of glass.

"This is *me*," Jake said.

NINE

"What do you think I've been telling you?" Edgar said.

Jake just gaped at his double.

"It's like one of those pod people from *Invasion of the Body Snatchers*."

Jake's expression hardened. "Did you check its pockets?"

"Empty."

"Then he didn't fly out here via conventional aircraft."

"Or he hid his ID before he came to kill me."

"I don't suppose you have a fingerprinting kit in that truck?"

"I improvised." Edgar took a sealed envelope out of his pocket. "This isn't my first homicide investigation, just the first one where I did the deed."

"Thanks." Jake slid the envelope into his own pocket.

"Let's go back to the truck and get the shovels."

"No way," Jake said. "I came out here to bury this thing. If I go to the truck with you, it'll be gone when we get back."

"It's dead," Edgar said. "It isn't going anywhere."

"I'm not taking any chances."

"Fine, but I'm using the lantern." Edgar walked away.

Jake took out his phone and set its luminosity on bright, then brought the phone close to his doppelganger's face. He parted its lips and forced its stiff jaw open. Shining the phone inside the mouth, he saw silver fillings reflecting light. He didn't know how many fillings he had, but that sure looked like the inside of his mouth.

Darkness pressed around him. A mosquito droned in his ear, and he flattened it with his palm, smearing blood across his cheek. Crickets chirped. Somewhere in the darkness, a bullfrog croaked.

The duplicate had killed Carrie, then hopped a plane to North Carolina to kill Edgar. But what name had it traveled under? And how had it reached the property where Edgar was staying?

Fifteen minutes later, Edgar returned with two shovels. "I suppose you expect me to dig the grave on top of everything else."

"I can help," Jake said.

"Do you have any idea who's behind this?"

Jake wrapped the body. "Maybe."

"Why does whoever it is want me dead?"

"Because you're my friend. They want to make sure I have no one to turn to for help."

"That's reassuring. Why this way? They could have picked me off with a sniper rifle before I even reached the barn."

"I don't know but I'm going to find out. Did you search the area around your cousin's for any vehicles at the side of the road?"

"Affirmative. Nothing stood out. There's a whole lot of land and not a whole lot of houses. How do I know they won't come after me again? That I won't open the front door and someone who looks just like Maria won't shoot me in the face?"

"I won't let that happen."

"I don't need to know the whole story. Just let me know when it's over."

"Roger that."

They picked up the body, swung it three times, then threw it into space. A long moment passed before the body struck the ground and rolled, snapping branches on the way down. Jake and Edgar followed it, half sliding to the bottom. Edgar raised the lantern high, and they carried the body across the ravine.

"They wanted my family to find me," Edgar said.

"Probably," Jake said. "Maybe they wanted them to see this, too."

They stopped at a toppled tree trunk six feet in diameter that had turned gray with age.

"This is where I had in mind," Edgar said, dropping his end. He set the lantern on top of the trunk and used his shovel to dig.

Jake shoveled one-handed. He moved half as fast as

Edgar but he contributed.

Thirty minutes later, they stared into a grave three feet deep.

"Keep digging," Edgar said. "I don't want this coming back on me."

They dug deeper.

"This is the second body I've buried for you," Edgar said.

"The difference is, this time you did the killing," Jake said. "Technically, I'm helping *you*."

"I killed you in self-defense."

"I killed AK in self-defense, too."

"I buried him all by myself. It wasn't all that different from what I'm doing now."

"I always hoped more people would attend my funeral. Thanks for showing up."

"This is deep enough," Edgar said at last.

They tossed their shovels aside, picked up their respective ends of the corpse, and flung it into the grave.

"Any last words?" Edgar said.

"Good riddance."

Edgar picked up his shovel, dug into the earth piled around the grave, and threw dirt onto the body.

Jake grabbed his shovel and did the same. "Definitely one of the more surreal moments of my life."

They buried the body in silence, then climbed the slope to the path in the woods. Jake's eye stung with perspiration, and he swatted mosquitoes out of his face.

"How are things between you and Joyce?" Jake said on the walk back to their vehicles.

"Good," Edgar said. "If things work out down here, maybe I'll marry her."

"You mean maybe you'll propose. She still has to accept."

"It would be good for Martin. What about you and Maria?"

"Things are good for us, too. Why wouldn't they be? She has a job; I don't. We're living rent free in Joyce's house, and she's fostering Papa Joe's daughter—it's domestication at its finest."

"Jake Helman with a Puerto Rican significant other and a black foster daughter. Who'd have thought?"

"She's not my foster daughter. Cute kid, though. Smart. Maria loves her. Life is full of surprises."

"Tell me about it. I didn't expect to see your ugly face here ever, let alone less than two weeks after I left the city."

"I'll follow you like a bad habit."

They reached the vehicles and Edgar turned to Jake. "This is where we part company."

"Don't you want to grab breakfast somewhere?"

Edgar shook his head. "This is the end of the road for us. We're all square, aren't we?"

"Yeah, sure. We've saved each other a bunch of times. Who's keeping score?"

Edgar held out his hand. "Take care of yourself, Jake."

Jake shook his hand. "You, too."

"Do me a favor. I'm trying to get my life back together down here. I'm asking you as a friend to stay away and keep your craziness in New York. Will you do that for me?"

Jake held Edgar's gaze. "Whatever you say."

"Good. Let me know you're all right when this is over."

"Yeah, we can be friends on Facebook."

Edgar got into the truck and started the engine. He did a three-point turn and pulled up alongside Jake. "Follow me out of here, then turn right. GPS will do the rest."

Jake watched him drive away.

.⁘⁙⁖.

The sun had risen when Jake returned the Escape to the car rental agency at Raleigh–Durham International Airport. Blisters had formed on his fingers, calluses on his palm. The airport looked smaller crowded with people yet larger with sunlight streaming through its windows.

He ate breakfast in an overpriced tourist trap and used his laptop to check the news in New York. He had to do a search to find Carrie's murder. The story rated three paragraphs and no photo. He was mentioned as Carrie's former employer but not as a suspect.

Geoghegan, he thought as he took out his cell phone and called Maria.

She answered on the second ring. "Where are you?"

"Never mind. I'm heading home in a little while."

"Is everything okay?"

"Things are in the air."

"Then this isn't over?"

He didn't want to be specific in case his phone was tapped. "Not yet. I think our larger houseguest should take you and our smaller houseguest on a sleepover just as a precaution."

"Already in the works."

"I need another rain check on that dinner."

Jake rolled his eye when he boarded the plane, another narrow air taxi. This time he was assigned to a window seat on the two-seat side of the plane. He felt crowded even before a woman sat beside him. She may have been fifty, with her short hair dyed blonde. She gave him a polite smile, which he returned.

"Sir, are you able to open the hatch if we have an emergency?" the flight attendant said to a man two rows ahead.

The man nodded.

At least they didn't put me there, Jake thought.

Sun blasted through the window. Unable to sleep, Jake flipped through a travel magazine. The photos of the United Kingdom and Ireland made him want to take a trip to Europe if his life ever returned to normal. He wondered if that would entail finding a regular job.

Sheryl had always proposed elaborate trips, and Jake had usually found a way to dodge them. He didn't want to make the same mistake with Maria.

The plane taxied onto the runway, and the flight attendant, a tall woman with her red hair pulled back in a ponytail, ran through safety procedures. Soon the plane took off, and Jake watched North Carolina shrink below. He saw more of the state from the air than he had while on the ground.

He felt sad that Edgar had ended their friendship, but he understood his decision. Having a normal life was an admirable goal, especially after what Edgar had been through.

The thought of settling down with Maria appealed to him. After her experiences on Pavot Island and during Hurricane Daria, she had become perhaps the only woman who could cope with his bizarre life. But did her willingness to have a relationship with him justify risking her life? Now that Shana had become part of that life, Jake felt trepidation.

The airplane climbed higher, and Jake nodded off, awakening only when the flight attendants distributed soft drinks midway through the flight. Sipping a diet cola, he imagined how it would have tasted with some Bacardi rum in it. The thought made him sigh. He had given up alcohol, just as he had given up cocaine before it. Now if only he could give up demons, angels, and vodou zonbies.

The thought of alcohol also led him to think of Black Magic. He had been subjected to the foul narcotic—created from the ashes of zonbies—twice now. Another exposure could transform him into a scarecrow, a junkie one step removed from being a zonbie slave. Thank God he had rid the streets of New York of the drug, reducing the chances of his coming into contact with it again. Even so, Lilith had sprung it on him. His eye twitched and he cracked his knuckles on his stump.

The woman next to him glanced at his stump.

"Sorry," Jake said.

She smiled. "That's okay. Would you mind if I asked how you . . . ?"

"I lost it in a war."

"Oh, I'm sorry. What branch of the military did you serve in?"

"I didn't but I used to be a police officer. I lost this in the revolution on Pavot Island. I was there as a civilian on vacation."

Her eyes widened. "That was last month."

"I still get phantom pain."

She held out her hand. "I'm Elaine Murich."

"Helman." He shook her hand. "Jake."

"What do you do now?"

"I'm a private investigator, but I'm considering getting into another line of work."

"How intriguing. A one-handed private eye."

With one eye, Jake thought.

"I work for the *New Yorker*. Would you be interested in . . . ?"

"Thank you, but no. I try to keep a low profile."

"Yes, you would, wouldn't you?" She glanced at her watch. "Twenty minutes to go. I can't wait to get back to Manhattan, even in the state it's in right now."

"I know what you mean."

"Besides, I hate flying." Elaine put on her reading glasses and took out an e-reader.

Jake rested his head on the back of his seat and closed his eye.

A male voice came over the speakers. "Ladies and gentlemen, we are now approaching LaGuardia Airport. Please fasten your seat belts."

Jake looked out the window and saw New York City stretching below him. Then the plane tilted, replacing his view of the city with clouds and sky.

Sky Cloud Dreams, he thought.

At the front of the plane, a man rose from his aisle seat.

A flight attendant walked over to him. "Sir, please sit down."

The man wore khakis and a pin-striped button-down shirt. His hair was shaved close to his head. "We're all going to die."

The hair on the back of Jake's neck prickled as passengers murmured around him.

112

"Sit down now," the flight attendant said.

The man shoved her, and she fell sideways onto a man sitting on the opposite side of the aisle. Someone to Jake's left moaned. Elaine looked up from her e-reader, her eyes alert. The woman sitting at the window beside the standing man stared at him with wide eyes.

The man glanced around the plane, searching faces. When his gaze settled on Jake, he smiled.

Jake gripped the buckle of his seat belt. "Everybody, duck!"

An instant later, the man exploded, showering passengers in blood, tissue, and bone fragments like shrapnel.

Jake flinched, then bowed his head forward. Screams erupted all around him. A hole the size of a small child opened up in the fuselage, sucking out pressurized air. Oxygen masks dropped from the ceiling, and Jake looked up just as a screaming flight attendant disappeared out the rupture.

Jake's ears popped, and he grabbed his mask and secured it over his face. Elaine flailed at hers and he assisted her. She took deep gulps of oxygen. The woman sitting next to the man screamed, then disappeared through the hole. Papers, cups, and soda cans spun through the air toward the vortex.

The plane dipped, then went into a spiraling nose-dive. Sharp screams pierced his ears. Jake's stomach clawed its way up his throat. Elaine pawed at his stump with both hands, and he clutched one of her hands while g-forces pinned him against his seat. Turning to the window, he saw clouds seeming to spin around them. He looked down and spotted distant houses and buildings spinning as well.

I've fought assassins, zonbies, and unimaginable monsters, he thought, *and this is how I'm going to check out— killed in some random act of violence, with no chance to save myself.*

He would have found it funny except for one thing: he wanted to live. He pictured Maria and even thought of Sheryl. His head tingled, and he swam in a sea of nausea. White light, so bright and intense he had to look away, filled the plane. At first he thought there had been another explosion, but everything outside the window appeared white as well, as if the sun had gone supernova.

Passengers seated before him—below him—turned still. Elaine's grip on his stump slackened, and he struggled to face her. She had lost consciousness but her head remained upright.

The white light intensified so he saw nothing but a blank page. Digging his fingers into the arm of his chair, he fought to remain cognizant until the moment of impact. Then the light seeped into his brain and everything stopped.

TEN

Darkness, floating.

The sounds of people crying, their weeping warbling as if underwater.

The stench of vomit filled Jake's nostrils and he gagged. His eyelid fluttered open, but he couldn't see anything. It closed and he fought the urge to vomit. Someone behind him wailed. He opened his eyelid again, an out-of-focus image filling his field of vision. He thought he would topple over until he realized a restraint held him in place.

Seat belt, he thought. *Plane.*

Had he and the other passengers somehow survived the crash?

Impossible.

Someone heaved the contents of his stomach somewhere in front of him. A baby cried nonstop.

What the hell had happened?

The magazine pocket on the back of the seat in front

of him came into focus. He ran his hand over his face, tracing his scars.

Elaine moaned beside him and he turned. She had doubled over in her seat and had thrown up on the floor. Jake pinched his nostrils shut and breathed through his mouth so he wouldn't vomit as well.

The plane had stopped moving. His head flopped to one side. Some people had risen from their seats. Others collapsed in the aisles.

"Help me." A woman four rows ahead flailed her arms. Pieces of bone protruded from her face, including her eyes. The human bomb had projected its remnants at her. The man across the aisle grabbed her wrists and tried to calm her down. Blood dripped from the ceiling and walls for at least the first six rows.

Through the window, Jake saw the airport in the distant background.

We landed, he thought. Somehow the pilots had saved their asses.

He unbuckled his seat belt and tried to rise, then swooned and collapsed into his seat. All around him, others tried to do the same thing, with similar results.

Elaine sat up and wiped her mouth on her sleeve. "I'm sorry."

"Don't be," Jake said. "Everyone feels the same way."

"What happened?"

"I don't know."

"I want to get off."

"So does everyone else." Jake rose again, and this time he stood on wobbly legs. "Can you walk?"

"I think so."

Jake held out his hand, which Elaine took, and he helped her stand. She reached for the overhead compartment.

"Forget your bag," Jake said.

Others managed to rise, and he squeezed past them, pulling Elaine behind him. The cockpit door opened and two uniformed men tumbled out. One vomited and the other staggered into the bathroom. Jake wondered if planes this size still had navigators and how the two men he just saw had defied gravity and saved their lives.

He moved into the wide space leading to the emergency escape hatch. The man who had agreed to open it if necessary blocked his way. He was on his hands and knees, vomiting. Jake pulled him upright and pushed him into the aisle. Bracing himself against the hatch door, Jake grabbed the lever and pulled it with all his strength.

A power source kicked on and opened the door, allowing fresh air into the putrid-smelling plane. Jake glimpsed the blue sky, then the slide chute shot out with a small explosion that caused other passengers to flinch. The slide inflated like a giant air mattress.

Taking Elaine's hand, he led her to the chute. "You first," he said.

She patted his chest in thanks, then took a breath

and jumped onto the slide, which bowed in the middle. Jake feared it would catapult her onto the tarmac, but she slowed to a stop at the bottom and climbed off.

Jake faced the passengers lumbering toward him. "Everyone! One at a time. Help each other. Don't trample."

He helped one person after another slide down the chute. Emergency vehicles raced toward them: ambulances, carts, police cars, and a fire engine. The pilots brought the woman with the bone fragments in her face over to him, and Jake helped her sit on the floor with her legs dangling over the edge.

"I can't see," she said, tears streaking the blood on her face.

"There are people down there waiting to help you," he said.

"Thank you, whoever you are." She pushed herself over the edge, and he held out his hand to make sure she didn't bang her head.

"You're next," the pilot said. The copilot stood beside him.

"How did you do it?" Jake said.

"We didn't do anything," the pilot said.

Jake measured the man before jumping onto the slide. His stomach lurched once more, then eager hands helped him onto the tarmac. People continued to cry and bleed around him, but at least they were off the damn plane.

"What the hell happened?" a man said.

"A UFO saved us," another said.

"No," a woman said. "It was angels."

A shuttle bus pulled over to the landing site. Those who were uninjured and able to walk boarded it. The rest were put in wheelchairs and on gurneys.

On the bus, Jake sat next to a woman who held the baby he had heard crying. The baby had recovered but now adults sobbed. Jake took out his phone. It was dead even though he had charged it at the airport.

"My phone isn't working," a woman said.

"Neither is mine," a man said.

All around the bus, people checked their phones and shook their heads.

Jake made eye contact with Elaine, sitting four rows back. She appeared more frightened now than she had been in the wake of the landing.

The bus circled the terminal and deposited them at an entrance where a cluster of men and women waited.

"Hello, everyone," the man said. "My name is Jon Keyes. I'm with the airport. These folks are with the Department of Transportation, the Aviation Bureau, and the Federal Aviation Administration. We know you've all undergone a stressful ordeal, and we're here to help. Please follow us inside, where you'll each be examined by medical personnel. We'll need to get a statement from each one of you, and we thank you in advance for your cooperation."

Mutters rose from the passengers, but they followed the officials inside, where one end of the airport had been closed off. Security officers and police stood around empty airline gates. Standing by were at least a dozen medics and airline personnel with clipboards.

"Ladies and gentlemen, please have a seat wherever you're comfortable," an older man said. "My name is Bill Brown, and I'm with the airline you just flew. We need to check your vital signs and ask you about what happened." He gestured to a group of men in suits. "They're with the Department of Homeland Security, and they'll be assisting us this afternoon."

Jake checked his watch. At least they had landed ahead of schedule, but he had a lot on his agenda.

"We just want to get out of here," a man said.

"This is a criminal investigation," Brown said. "I'm afraid we have to speak to each one of you before you can leave. We need to begin by taking attendance. When you hear your name . . ."

Jake found a seat and sat down.

The medic, a black man in his midtwenties, pressed the stethoscope against Jake's heart and listened. "You have

120

the heartbeat of a horse."

"I attribute that to healthy living," Jake said.

The medic glanced at Jake's scars. "Any dizziness? Nausea? Ringing in the ears?"

"All of the above while I was on board," Jake said. "Plus a tingling sensation. I don't feel any of them now. I feel perfectly fine. Can I go home?"

The medic returned his stethoscope to his bag. "That's not up to me."

While the passengers waited, flight attendants served water, soda, and lunch. Jake watched four men with a lot of shiny metal on their Air Force uniforms pass through the security station and enter an office.

Keyes began calling the names of people to be interviewed in alphabetical order. Jake blew air out of his cheeks.

Elaine sat beside him. "You were very brave back there."

"All I did was open a door. It's not like I crawled into the cockpit and landed the plane. Besides, I suspected something like this"—he nodded at the people receiving medical exams—"was going to happen. I wanted it to be inside and not on that plane."

"You make decisions very quickly."

"I just acted on instinct. I used to be a cop, remember?"

She looked around the airport. "The biggest story of my life, and I can't even file a report."

"Your magazine is monthly."

"But our website is daily. Have you been paying attention to the men and women going into that office? There are as many men in black as there are Air Force officials. If they think they can keep this quiet, they're crazy."

Jake studied the woman. He saw her attempt at conversation for what it was. "I already told you I want to keep a low profile."

Her smile did not seem friendly. "This is going to be a huge story, and you're part of it whether you want to be or not. You can't live in the shadows forever."

He looked away without saying anything.

"Helman, Jake."

Jake raised his head. His mosquito bites were driving him crazy. He had been sitting with his legs extended, his arms folded, and his head bowed, pretending to be asleep. Elaine had moved to another seat and spoke to an older couple.

He rose and crossed to Keyes, who led him into the office. As it turned out, an entire complex of offices. Keyes took him into a conference room where four stone-faced men and one stone-faced woman sat facing an empty seat across the table. He sat down without being told to do so. His inquisitors stared at his face.

"I'm Lyle Jeffman from the FAA."

"I'm Kevin Standers from Homeland Security."

"Corinne Waylund, FBI."

"Major Hughes, United States Air Force."

"Albert Rosen, Air Traffic Safety."

"You all know who I am," Jake said.

"This conversation's being recorded," Rosen said.

"Naturally."

Jeffman consulted his clipboard. "You live in New York and flew to North Carolina last night. You were only there less than six hours, all of them when most people are asleep. What was the purpose of your visit?"

"I was visiting a friend," Jake said.

"What's this friend's name?" Standers said.

"Does it matter? I was a passenger on that plane. Some lunatic put a hole in it, and I almost died. Somehow I'm alive. I don't know how. There was no air marshal on that flight. I had nothing to do with anything that happened, and I don't have any information that could possibly be useful to you. I'll answer any pertinent questions, and then I'll be on my way."

"Tell us what happened," Waylund said. "You're a private investigator. You must have an eye for detail."

"It was a beautiful morning. The sun was beaming and the angels were singing. Then we reached New York and this guy stood up. He said, 'We're all going to die.' A flight attendant tried to get him to sit down, but he pushed her aside. Then he blew up and took part of the fuselage with him. The flight attendant and the woman next to the nut got sucked out the hole, and the plane went into a tailspin. Then this bright white light filled the plane, and I passed out. When I woke up, we were safe on the ground. Beats the hell out of me how that happened."

"Did this man say anything else?" Waylund said.

"No, that was it."

"Did you see any explosives on him?"

"No . . ."

"Then how do you know he blew up?"

"Are you kidding me? Because I saw it. He went everywhere."

"Did you see any weapons?"

"Nope."

"Describe this white light," Major Hughes said.

"The plane was in a nosedive. The light filled the plane. Not light like from a lightbulb or even the sun; it was pure white, and it turned everything around it white. It felt like it came from the right side of the plane outside, but it grew so bright inside that can't be right. It was blinding."

"Did you hear anything in your head? A ringing?"

"Yes. I felt pressure squeezing my temples and my ears popped. Then my head tingled and I felt nauseous. I tried not to pass out, but I couldn't help myself. Then I woke up."

"Did you hear any voices in your head?"

Jake smiled. "No."

"Did you feel as if you'd been touched in any way?"

Jake held the man's gaze. Was he kidding? "No, there were no anal probes."

"What about any electronic devices?"

"I only had my phone, and it's as dead as everyone else's. I don't suppose the airline plans to reimburse me?"

"That's up to them," Standers said. "What happened on the ground?"

"I regained consciousness and the white light was gone. People were puking all around me. So I stood up and opened the emergency exit hatch so we could all get out of that crummy little plane."

"What about the pilots?" Rosen said.

"They stumbled out of the cockpit looking worse than the rest of us. I guess that's to be expected since they were staring down at the Hudson River the whole time."

"Did they say anything?"

"We didn't do anything," the pilot had said.

"I don't remember. I was busy helping people get off the plane."

Waylund and Standers looked at each other.

"Let's go back to the man you believe blew himself up," Standers said. "Can you describe him?"

"He was Caucasian, just under six feet tall, maybe thirty years old. He was in good shape, and his hair was shaved close to his head."

"Did he seem angry?"

"He seemed annoyed by the flight attendant who got sucked out the hole in the plane."

"Did he seem rational?"

Jake considered the question. "He said we were all going to die, then he tried to kill us and almost succeeded. I suppose you could say his declaration was a rational description of what he attempted to do."

"Is there anything else you can think of that might shed light on what happened up there?" Rosen said.

"I was hoping you could tell me," Jake said.

No one responded.

ELEVEN

The shuttle bus dropped Jake off at his car, he assumed to avoid any media attention. As soon as he started the engine, he plugged in his phone. Its screen lit up, but when he checked for messages and found none, he looked for his contacts and saw they had been erased. His record of calls had been wiped clean as well.

Modern technology, he thought.

Pulling out, he turned on the radio and switched to a news station.

Five minutes passed before the story came on. "Authorities are investigating the identity of a man they believe detonated a bomb on flight 3350. Eyewitnesses claim the passenger airplane spiraled out of control and say it's a miracle the pilot, Ken Calloway, was able to correct the plane's trajectory and land it safely. Two people were killed in addition to the alleged bomber. More on the story as it develops."

Much more, Jake thought.

He turned into the driveway at Maria's house—he hadn't taken to calling it home—and used the remote control to open the garage door. He didn't feel comfortable advertising his presence. As the door closed behind him, he stood in the driveway and scanned the cars parked along the curb, searching for Geoghegan's goons or worse.

Nothing aroused his suspicion, so he went inside and locked the door behind him. The house seemed empty without Shana and her cartoons. He went into the kitchen and used the landline to call Maria.

"Is everything okay?" Maria said.

"I'm fine but nothing's settled yet."

"Did you learn anything?"

"Let's not go through this again."

"Can you tell me where you went?"

"Not until this is over."

"When can I see you?"

"I'll let you know. I've got to go. I need to get busy detecting." Jake hung up and went into the basement, where he turned on his laptop.

Reaching into his back pocket, he took out the envelope Edgar had given him and opened it. Then he withdrew a piece of paper and studied the two fingerprints Edgar had taken from the corpse in North Carolina. He taped the fingerprints to the upper right-hand corner of his laptop.

Jake opened his documents on the laptop, selected

one identified as Personal, and scrolled through the files until he found what he wanted. An image of his own fingerprints came up on the screen. He enlarged the image until the prints were the same size as the ones Edgar had given him. He compared the curves and lines. The similarities were so strong that he searched for differences instead and came up empty-handed. He sat back in his chair. The prints matched.

"Jesus," he said in a low voice.

In a sense, he *had* murdered Carrie and attempted to kill Edgar. Leaving the fingerprints taped to the screen, he closed his file and went to the website for the *New York Daily News.* A single word comprised the headline above a grainy photo of Jake's plane sitting on the tarmac: *Miracle.*

He shut down the laptop, selected some clean clothes, and went upstairs with the intention of showering. Sunlight flooded the kitchen, and he entered the living room, where he recoiled at the sight of a man dressed in black standing near the front door. For a moment Jake thought he had been startled by his own reflection; the man had features identical to his own.

Both of them stood still, sizing each other up. Jake lowered his arm, allowing his clothes to fall on the floor. Seeing yourself in three dimensions can be unsettling. His counterpart had two hands.

Time stretched like molasses.

Jake moved to his right and so did the duplicate. Their movements were similar and fluid, maintaining the illusion of a mirrored reflection. Jake froze, then the duplicate, who wore a faint smile, froze. Jake charged across the polished wooden floor at the intruder. The duplicate charged at the same time, and they bore down on each other like jousting knights, swinging their fists and landing only glancing blows. Jake slammed into the stairway railing and spun around. The duplicate spun, too, and they stared at each other with greater intensity.

Jake wanted to beat his other self senseless, and he would be happy to kill him. There was room enough for only one Helman in the world.

The duplicate circled him with fists raised, assuming the position Jake had learned in the NYPD boxing league. Jake moved in the other direction, mimicking his double's motions even though he had just one hand to box.

The duplicate jabbed with his left, and Jake could only jab with his right. His doppelganger threw a right that grazed Jake's jaw. In the time it took for Jake's head to twist from the blow, the duplicate moved in with lightning speed, pummeling him. Jake fended off several punches with his forearms, but the duplicate landed more than one blow. The duplicate punched Jake's shoulders and biceps, breaking him down. Jake knew he would be unable to fight back if the onslaught continued. He moved his stump in a circular motion that deflected the duplicate's fists, then threw an uppercut that landed below the duplicate's jaw, shattering teeth with a loud crack. Jake immediately punched his attacker in the mouth, which caused the man's broken teeth to lacerate the flesh around his lips. Jake shook his hand, casting off the pain that burned his knuckles.

The duplicate spat blood and broken teeth on the floor, glared at Jake, then ran straight at him. Jake dropped low to the floor, wrapped his arms around the duplicate's legs, and stood up, throwing his head back at the same time. The duplicate flew through the air and crashed into the coffee table. He grimaced and Jake charged at him. The duplicate kicked Jake in the stomach, and Jake flew into the television stand, knocking the TV over.

Pain shot through Jake's ribs, and he cried out when he struck the floor. As he scrambled to get on his feet, his double advanced on him with fists poised to strike. Sinking back to the floor, Jake swung one leg, sweeping the double's feet out from under him. The attacker landed on the floor, and Jake pulled himself up with one hand.

Jake 2.0 rolled over, jumped to his feet, and moved out of the way as Jake rushed him. Jake slowed to a stop before hitting the wall and turned. Across the room, the double wiped blood from his ruptured mouth.

"Who are you?" Jake said, breathing heavy.

"I'm Jake Helman," the double said, his words

slurred by the blood and broken teeth.

Jake snorted. "The last time I checked my mail, *I* was Jake Helman."

The double moved forward. "You're an imposter."

Jake raised his stump. "This says otherwise."

"Liar!" The double snarled and swung his fists as he closed the distance between them.

Jake blocked a punch with his stump, then another with his right arm. The double landed the next punch with his right hand, then laid into Jake with a series of punches. Jake lashed out, driving the palm of his hand into his double's jaw, where he knew he could do the most damage. The double staggered backward and Jake followed him.

Jake drove his stump into his enemy's face. The blow inflicted no harm but kept the double off balance. He threw a roundhouse punch that connected with the unscarred half of the double's face, knocking him to the floor. Jake dove at his downed opponent, who raised his feet in a defensive motion. Jake landed on the raised feet just as his double kicked out, then flew backwards through the kitchen archway and landed on linoleum.

Spots of light flaring in Jake's eye obscured the silhouette of his attacker as he moved before him. Jake anticipated the man raising his right leg to stomp on his face. He lifted his hand, fingers outstretched. The impact of the stomp sent a shock wave of pain through his wrist. His elbow bent, and his hand grew closer to his face. He straightened his arm, throwing his shoulder into the movement, trying to push his double away, but the pain in his wrist prevented him from giving it his all.

Keeping his foot on Jake's hand, the double jumped in the air and drove his left foot down. Jake twisted to his left, and the rubber-soled shoe struck the floor with such force Jake felt the vibration through his body.

Pressing his stump above the double's heel for leverage, Jake twisted his opponent's foot until he heard a sharp crack. The double screamed and seized the frame of the door. Jake managed to sit up, but the double delivered a high kick that smashed Jake's nose and threw him to the floor. Numbness spread through Jake's face, and he rolled his head from side to side. He couldn't believe the double had managed to kick him while standing on a broken ankle. Blood filled his mouth and he coughed it out.

He won't stop, Jake thought.

Jake 2.0 dropped to his knees, sitting on Jake's stomach.

Neither will I.

Jake punched him in the jaw again, producing a soggy impact. The double punched Jake beneath his right eye, blinding him with pain. Jake drove his right knee into his assailant's tailbone, propelling him over his head and onto the floor. Jake wiped blood from his nose on the back of his hand and got on all fours.

The double crawled toward the counter, and Jake knew he was going for the silverware drawer. Jake dove forward, but the double rose on one foot, and Jake struck the floor where his nemesis had just been. The double hopped away, but Jake seized the man's bad ankle. The double cried out even before Jake thrashed the ankle and brought him back to the floor.

This time Jake succeeded in climbing on top of his double's back. The duplicate tried to push him off, but Jake braced his stump against the back of the man's neck and pushed down on his forearm, forcing the attacker's face into the floor. Then he released his grasp and punched the man in the back of the head, increasing the pain in his wrist. Both of them groaned.

The duplicate pushed himself up, and Jake lost his balance and toppled forward. For a second, his scarred cheek pressed against the duplicate's unscarred cheek. Jake raised his head, and the duplicate threw his own head back, smashing Jake's nose again. Pain exploded in Jake's head, and blood sprayed out of his nostrils. His body turned limp.

The duplicate stood. Jake felt too exhausted to get up. The duplicate steadied himself by holding the counter with his right hand and opened the nearest drawer with his left. The drawer of cloths, sponges, and serving spoons must have frustrated the man. He slammed it shut and reached for the next one. Jake inserted his legs between the duplicate's and scissor kicked. The duplicate growled as he crashed to the floor.

Gasping for breath, Jake and his duplicate got on all fours at the same time, facing each other like two junkyard dogs. Jake turned to the counter, but the duplicate grabbed the edge of the cabinet beneath it and slammed the door into Jake's face. Wincing, Jake was glad the cupboard door only smacked his forehead and not his nose.

Gripping the countertop, the duplicate got up on his knees. Four feet away, Jake grabbed the countertop with one hand. The duplicate raised one knee. So did Jake.

The duplicate stood on his good foot. With pain sizzling the nerves throughout his body, Jake stood, his knees threatening to give out. The duplicate jerked open the next drawer, fumbled inside it, and brought out a steak knife that he swung at Jake.

Jake stepped back and drew a steak knife from the storage block near the toaster. The duplicate swung his knife in the other direction. Jake swung his knife overhand and drove it through the duplicate's left forearm and into the countertop, pinning it to the Formica.

The duplicate screamed, his fingers turning spastic. He swung his knife at Jake. Jake blocked the advance and punched him in the face. The duplicate didn't drop the knife. Instead he drove it straight at Jake's face. Jake tilted his head, and the knife pierced his left ear.

Son of a bitch!

The knife hurt more coming out of the ear than it had going through it, its serrated blade tearing the wounded flesh like a saw. Jake moved closer to the duplicate, wrapping his arm around the duplicate's and using his elbow like a wing to prevent the knife from reaching him again. He jerked the knife he had buried in the duplicate's forearm free and punched the air beside the duplicate's face, slashing his throat with the knife in the process.

The duplicate's final scream turned into a gargling sound. He dropped his knife and clawed at his throat with his left hand, then fell to his knees.

Damn it, Jake thought. He had wanted to take him alive so he could interrogate him.

The duplicate looked at him with horror in his eyes, then toppled over, blood flowing from his throat.

Jake kneeled in his blood and removed the duplicate's hand from the gash in his throat. The wound reminded Jake of those made by the Cipher in his victims. He pressed his hand against the wound. "You're not who you think you are. Or *what* you think you are."

The duplicate coughed blood.

"Tell me who sent you here. Who used you?"

The duplicate went into shock. Then his eye glazed over. Watching him bleed out, Jake felt a chill.

Panting and aching, Jake stood, covered in blood. His nose and ear continued to bleed, and pain radiated from the center of his face with a steady throb. He studied the corpse, imagining he would look the same when his time came. Would Maria find him on the kitchen floor like this?

He waited for his other self's flickering soul to rise. The ability to see departing souls had been his for two years.

Nothing happened.

The other Jake Helman was not human. This did not surprise him. He had assumed the duplicate who killed Carrie had also attacked Edgar; now he believed he had just killed Carrie's killer. How many more were there?

TWELVE

Jake staggered into the bathroom and looked in the mirror. His right eye was swelling shut, something he could not allow to happen. Blood from his nose spattered his face like flower petals. A crimson slick from his ear congealed on his neck. He had to give himself credit: he had proven to be the most persistent opponent he had ever faced.

He located a razor blade for a shaver in the medicine cabinet and slit the swelling around his eye. His eyelid closed, but he forced it open, the blade out of focus. Blood spurted onto the mirror.

Jake set the bloody razor on the sink, then squeezed the swelling, forcing more blood into the sink. He wadded up tissue and pressed it against the wound. The tissue turned red, and he replaced it with another wad. Then another. When the bleeding slowed, he rubbed a healing gel over the gash.

Next, he tended to his ruptured ear. Between entry and exit, the steak knife had left a slit almost an inch high in the antihelix of the ear. It burned. As he cleaned the wound, he winced and sucked in his breath. He applied the gel to the slit as well.

He saved the worst for last. His nose was a mottled mess, and it turned to the right side of his face. Touching it with one finger, he cried out as pain flared through his face.

Broken, all right.

This time Laurel wasn't around to heal it. Pressing his stump against the side of his head to keep it from moving, he set his fingers over his right cheek. He took a deep breath, then drove his fingertips against the side of his broken nose, resetting it. Even as he screamed, he continued to apply pressure until his nose appeared to straighten. Then he collapsed to his knees, sobbing and cursing.

He splashed cold water on his face, both to numb the pain and wash away some of the blood. Stepping back from the mirror, he pulled his shirt off. Blood smeared his chest and stuck to his hair. He dropped the shirt in the sink, ran water over it, and massaged the garment. At least if Storm and Verila returned with a warrant, the only blood they would find would prove to be his.

Returning to the kitchen, he stared at the corpse. He had to get rid of it but how? New York City in broad daylight differed more than a little from the backwoods in North Carolina.

With his head aching all over, he stood on the

corpse's shoes, grabbed its wrists, and pulled it upright. His right wrist ached. Then he stood it like a giant puppet and allowed it to slump over his shoulder while he wrapped his arms around its waist. Groaning, he straightened his back, then carried his duplicate out of the kitchen and into the living room. At the bottom of the stairs, he gazed at the upstairs hall. He would need to keep his hand on his double's hip, so there was no using the railing for support.

No sooner had he started climbing the stairs than he slumped against the wall. He leaned against it all the way upstairs. At the top, he stumbled into the bathroom, where he threw the corpse into the bathtub. The thud was louder than he expected, the snapping of the corpse's neck nauseating him. He started the shower, then went downstairs for contractor bags, an electric carving knife, and a handsaw.

Jake laid a plastic tarp he found in the basement inside his car trunk, then carried each of the three stuffed contractor bags into the garage and deposited them in the trunk.

It took him an hour to mop the floors and stairs because he had to keep changing the water. When he finished, he washed the mop and bagged his bloody clothes. Then he went upstairs and scrubbed the tub and took a shower himself. The hot water caused his wounds to sting, and he cried out more than once. When he finished, he scrubbed the tub again, then showered. As he emerged from his second shower, his ear offered the sharpest pain. He bandaged his nose, which set off a new round of agony.

In the basement, he dressed in jeans and his old NYPD T-shirt. He went upstairs, where he put a Band-Aid over the self-inflicted gash in his eye and applied more gel to it and his ear wound. He was in the process of washing the bathroom sink when the doorbell rang. Even though he had been expecting this visit, his heart skipped a beat. If the police had a search warrant, it would extend to his car. Shutting off the water, he went into the living room and looked through the peephole.

Two men in suits stood outside. He couldn't make out their faces, but he knew they weren't Storm and Verila because they both had hair.

Screw them, he thought. *Just pretend you're not home.*

His phone rang in the kitchen.

Damn it.

He went into the kitchen and picked up his phone. He didn't recognize the number, but it had a 202 area code.

Washington, D.C. Maybe the president was calling him. He answered.

"Mr. Helman?" a male voice said.

"Who wants to know?"

"This is Adam Weissman. Do you remember me?"

Weissman and his partner, Bob Freeman, worked for the State Department and had interviewed Jake and Maria upon their return to Miami from Pavot Island.

"How could I forget?"

"My partner and I are standing outside your door. We know you're in there. Please open up."

Jake lowered his phone. What the hell did the State Department want with him?

They're following up on Pavot Island. Maybe they had learned the instrumental roles Jake and Maria had played in the revolution that overthrew Ernesto Malvado. He returned the phone to his good ear. "What's this about?"

"Not over the phone."

Thank God he had cleaned himself up. "Just a minute."

He ran into the living room, bent over, and pushed the wrecked coffee table across the floor and into the kitchen. Then he returned to the living room and set the TV on its stand. Taking a deep breath, he unlocked and opened the door.

Weissman and Freeman recoiled.

"Jesus," Weissman said. "You look worse than you did last time. What happened to you?"

"My girlfriend beat me up."

The two feds stared at him.

"I'm joking."

"Can we come in?" Freeman said.

"Can you give me a hint what this is about? I don't invite just anyone into my humble abode."

"You're not in any trouble," Weissman said.

"How I've longed to hear those words."

"We're here about flight 3350," Freeman said.

Jake tried not to react. He imagined his lumpy flesh would magnify any changes in his expression. He stepped back from the door and gestured to the living room with his stump. "Come on in out of the heat."

The men in black suits entered the house, and Jake closed the door.

"What took you so long to let us in?" Weissman said. "Were you hiding the bodies?"

Been there, done that. "I had to put my face on. Have a seat."

Weissman and Freeman sat on the sofa.

"Can I offer you a juice box? That's all we have at the moment."

"Pass," Freeman said. "Those things are loaded with sugar. I'm on a diet."

Jake sat in the easy chair facing the sofa. "You're a long way from home base, aren't you?"

"You don't know where our home base is," Weissman said.

"We travel a lot," Freeman said.

"What can I tell you about this morning's flight that I didn't already tell the other members of the alphabet?

And what's this got to do with State? I thought the guy who blew a hole in the side of the plane was a domestic terrorist. He didn't have an accent, anyway."

"It's no coincidence we're here."

"I figured. Did you get Geoghegan's message?"

"It was routed to us. We verified that we interviewed you and Vasquez."

Jake stared at them. "Routed to you by State? Because I also figure that's a smoke screen."

"Tell us about the bright white light," Weissman said.

"It was bright and white."

"Some of your fellow passengers claim to have seen a UFO."

"I heard others say it was angels."

"But you saw nothing?"

"Nothing but light, like staring into the sun. What did radar show?"

"A passenger taxi plummeting straight toward earth. Fifteen hundred feet from impact, it leveled off and landed on the runway."

"Only the pilots don't know how it happened. I know; I spoke to them."

"Have you watched television?" Freeman said.

"I've been preoccupied." Jake pointed at his face. "Private eye business."

Weissman took out his phone, the size of a playing card. He keyed in information, then handed it to Jake, who watched as the face of a movie star filled the screen.

"Recognize him?" Weissman said.

"Nico Graham," Jake said.

Graham had been the star of a police procedural show Sheryl had watched. Then the actor starred in a series of direct to DVD feature films based on the novels of the late science fiction author Campbell Bradley and produced by Bradley's son, Benjamin. Graham later became the celebrity spokesperson for Sky Cloud Dreams, and in the wake of Benjamin's death, Graham had taken a more active role in running the cult. Graham still had his looks, but his blond hair appeared as contrived as his dazzling white teeth.

"Graham gave a speech in the press room in the Dream Castle ninety minutes ago. Of course the Dreamers posted the video online, and it's gone viral. Tap the screen."

Jake tapped the phone and the frozen image attained motion. Graham stood at a podium, dressed in designer clothes. Two men and a woman stood behind. Jake recognized one of the men: Prewitt. He had been delivering a seminar in the Dream Castle when Jake and Maria stormed inside the auditorium and pulled Martin Hopkins out.

"Two weeks ago, Hurricane Daria almost destroyed Manhattan," Graham said. "Since then, we've heard nothing but scientific mumbo jumbo about how the storm was an impossible occurrence and religious declarations that

146

God was punishing mankind for his sins. Scientific extremism versus spiritual extremism, two polarizing views of one event. Now those same scientists are telling us the landing of flight 3350 was also an impossibility, and those same religious factions are saying that God—the same God they say punished us—performed a miracle and delivered those passengers to safety. I'm tired of scientists and religious leaders pulling people in different directions, forcing them to choose between an expanding universe and an all-powerful creator. Science and spirituality exist in the same universe. You just need to tune out the distractions and focus on truth."

Jake was familiar with the Dreamers' recruiting techniques.

"Daria wasn't an impossibility. It happened," Graham said. "Scientists can't explain it because they're limited by the rigid parameters they've set for themselves. Their laws are false laws, defined by man-made precepts. The same can be said for holy rollers. There are no miracles; there is only one truth, and it was laid out for us all by Imago."

"Here we go," Jake said.

"Imago spoke to Campbell Bradley in his dreams because Campbell was a visionary. In a short story Campbell wrote seventy-five years ago called 'Return of the Gods,' he prophesied this morning's events. Imago is the one true creator of us all, and he left our world so

147

we might evolve in his image. According to Campbell Bradley, Imago vowed to one day return to us, to show us the way to peace, love, and salvation. Imago knew flight 3350 would encounter difficulties, and he rescued its passengers from across time and space. Make no mistake, Imago is returning to earth! Now is the time to put aside your jealousies, your fears, and your preconceptions. Join the Dreamers today and pave the way to reality. It's not too late—yet. Visit the Dream Castle in person or log on to the Sky Cloud Dreams website. Learn from today and prepare for tomorrow."

Jake handed back the phone. "You came all the way out here to show me that? The Dreamers are capitalizing on a near tragedy to fill their coffers. That's nothing new."

"We couldn't care less what they do," Weissman said. "That's a matter for the IRS. But Graham has tapped into the zeitgeist. People are looking for answers, and today they're watching the stars. So are the FAA, the Air and Safety Transportation Department, and the Air Force."

"Space aliens," Jake said. "You guys aren't really from the State Department, are you?"

Weissman and Freeman looked as if they were straining not to glance at each other.

"Our State Department credentials are authentic," Freeman said.

"I bet you've got a lot of credentials, and your wallets are bulging with plastic," Jake said. "And not one of them identifies the government bureau you really work for, because the public doesn't know it exists."

The men stared at him, their silence addressing his speculation.

"So people on the street are waiting for the mother ship."

"Not just people on the street, people all over the world. We don't know if this is because Daria just happened, but the flight 3350 miracle is causing a stir the likes of which we've never seen."

"Why come to me?"

"Like I said, this is no coincidence. We know a lot more about what went down on Pavot Island than you think. And we know that your office is located smack-dab in the eye of Daria. Now you just happened to be on that flight this morning. We see a pattern."

"I don't believe in UFOs."

"UFO stands for unidentified flying object. How can you disbelieve something that hasn't been identified? Anything that can fly can be unidentified. Maybe it was a spacecraft or maybe it was angels."

"Do you believe in angels?" Freeman said.

"I'm open to the idea."

"But not aliens?"

Jake drew in a breath. "I believe in possibilities. After what happened this morning, I guess I believe in miracles."

"Do you believe in zonbies?" Weissman said.

This time it was Jake's turn to answer with silence. Weissman had surprised him by using the correct pronunciation for a vodou zonbie.

"You're up to your neck in this, whatever it is."

"I had nothing to do with whatever happened on that plane. I'm just glad to be here among the living to tell the tale."

"Did you have anything to do with Daria?" Freeman said.

"I can assure you I have absolutely no bearing on the weather."

"That's funny, because from where we're sitting, you're in the middle of a shit storm."

"You guys started out so friendly."

"We're not your enemies," Weissman said. "But we've got a job to do. Anytime some unusual phenomenon occurs and your name pops up, we receive a notification."

"And you hop on a plane?"

"If the unexplained phenomenon is alarming enough."

You're on too many people's radar, Jake thought. "What can I do for you to justify the time you've invested in speaking to me today?"

"Tell us everything you know about what happened to that aircraft."

"It's all in the statement I gave this morning."

"There must be more. Some detail you failed to elaborate on?"

"I gave those folks the full episode recap. There's nothing else to tell."

"We want you to consider being hypnotized," Freeman said.

Jake raised his eyebrows.

"It's a painless procedure," Weissman said. "Plenty of people claiming to be alien abductees have revealed startling details while under hypnotic suggestion."

Considering all the details of his life that would come out during hypnosis, Jake burst into laughter, eliciting daggers of pain throughout his face. He fought to control his laughter, then lifted his hand. "That is never going to happen, guys."

"What have you got to hide?"

Jake stood. "I know the secrets of Jack the Ripper and the Bermuda Triangle."

The feds remained sitting.

"We'd be interested in learning the answer to one of those," Weissman said.

"I wouldn't mind learning Jack the Ripper's secret," Freeman said.

"I can appreciate where you guys are coming from," Jake said. "Really, I do. But I don't know anything about Daria or what happened on that flight, and I will never consent to hypnosis. Banish that little item from your agenda right now."

Weissman stood. "We'll always have Pavot Island."

Jake ignored the comment. "I'm sorry I can't be more helpful, but I'm in a lot of pain, and I think I'll go spend six hours sitting in an emergency room."

Freeman got up. "You don't have to go to any ER. There are plenty of doctors who would love to treat a special patient like you. We'll be glad to take you to one."

Was Freeman kidding? "Thanks, but one of the reasons I became a PI was because I like to be independent. I have my own doctor, someone who respects my confidentiality. I can get to his place all by myself."

Weissman held out a business card. "I really wish you'd reconsider."

Taking the card, Jake glanced at it: State Department issue. "If I remember anything I haven't already detailed, you guys will be the first ones I call." Jake's phone chirped.

"Aren't you going to check that?" Weissman said.

He walked to the door and opened it. "I probably have an overdue bill."

Weissman and Freeman followed him.

"I hope you feel better," Weissman said.

Watching them step outside, Jake squinted at the sunlight. "Good luck," he said. Then he closed the door and ran to his phone.

THIRTEEN

Jake grabbed his phone. He had received an e-mail alert that his name had popped up online. Following the link, he discovered an article on the *New Yorker*'s website called "Miracle Flight 3350: A Survivor's Account." When he saw Elaine Murich's byline he knew what to expect: a minute-by-minute account of their flight together. What he didn't expect was to play such a prominent role in her story.

"Jake Helman is a private investigator after serving in the NYPD for a decade," she wrote. "He proved himself quick thinking and decisive and may have saved lives when he ordered the passengers to duck after the bomber's threat. When the plane depressurized and the oxygen masks dropped from their compartments, I struggled to catch mine. Helman affixed his own mask, then calmly collected mine and helped me put it on. As the plane spiraled to certain destruction, I seized his arm for comfort. Make that 'stump': Mr. Helman's hand was cut off during the revolution on Pavot Island, where he was vacationing.

"After our miraculous landing, Helman rose from his seat, helped me up, and coolly opened the emergency hatch, discharging the chute, while the passenger tasked with that job—and the pilots—were too sick to function. I can only conclude that Helman's instincts are as assured in his profession."

My first blurb, Jake thought. Clients would be knocking on his office door if they could get into the building.

He went down to the basement, strapped on his harness, and slid his Thunder Ranch and holster into a shoulder bag. He thought about packing a speed loader but decided against it. What was the point? He hadn't learned to use it with his mouth. Instead, he packed his backup weapon: a Ruger SR22. Like the Thunder Ranch, its lightweight, compact design allowed him to fire one-handed, but it had the added advantage of holding ten rounds over six. The next Jake Helman to come his way was getting a head full of lead.

He went back upstairs and rummaged through the cabinets. At the moment, his North Carolina mosquito bites irritated him more than the pain flaring in his face. He doused himself with bug spray, then swallowed three aspirins. After packing a latex glove, duct tape, and a contractor bag, he went into the garage, found a shovel with a long handle and a spading fork with a short handle, and put them in the backseat.

The garage door rumbled open, and he backed into the driveway and closed the door. Driving around the block, Jake glanced in his rearview mirror. No suspicious cars tailed him. He circled two other blocks. Triangles confused the Queens grid.

When he was sure he wasn't being followed, he merged onto I-496 West. Despite the anxiety of driving with the dismembered corpse of a duplicate in the trunk, he adhered to the speed limit; he didn't intend to take any chances getting pulled over. He got off on Thirty-fourth Street in Manhattan and took the Lincoln Tunnel into New Jersey.

"Authorities have identified the man who detonated a bomb on flight 3350 this morning. They haven't yet released his name or the identities of the flight attendant and passenger who were sucked out of the plane before it landed at LaGuardia Airport. So far, no explanation has been offered as to how the bomber snuck explosives aboard the plane. The greater mystery is how the plane managed a perfect landing after spiraling out of control in a nosedive.

"An undisclosed number of passengers sustained injuries. Several uninjured people credited the actions of New York City private investigator Jake Helman with getting them off the plane after the landing. The FAA and National Air and Transportation Safety Department are still investigating the claims of the pilot and copilot that they were unconscious when the plane landed."

Jake switched off the radio. His phone rang and he checked the display.

The *New York Times*.

A minute later, the phone rang again.

The *New York Post*.

A minute later, the phone rang again.

The *New York Daily News*.

He turned the phone off.

In total, it took Jake an hour to reach the South Mountain Reservation, a nature reserve covering more than two thousand acres. He drove alongside roads, scoping out unpopulated areas of the forest. He pulled into a clearing he assumed campers used and continued to drive into the forest as far as he could, rolling between trees. He parked the car behind dense bushes that hid it from the entry road.

Slinging his bag over his shoulder, he set out on foot, stopping every hundred yards to leave a piece of duct tape on a tree trunk as a marker. He passed a stream and a waterfall and discovered an impression eight feet in diameter, its center two feet lower than the ground around it. He checked the perimeter: no sign of people or vehicles, just layer after layer of dense trees.

Jake returned to the Plymouth and retrieved the

shovel and spading fork from the backseat. He located the impression and set about digging. Within minutes the humidity drew sweat from his pores, and mosquitoes swarmed around his exposed flesh. He applied another coat of repellent, stinging the cuts on his face and knuckles. Using his hook to support the shovel's handle, he dug deeper, piling dirt around the wide hole. His wrist ached, and he grew frustrated whenever he struck a rock or a tree root, which slowed his progress.

Jake didn't notice the droning at first, then identified it as a helicopter. Taking a break, he stood with his hand resting on the end of the shovel's handle, breathing heavy. The helicopter's roar grew louder. He moved behind a tree and watched the aircraft with two sets of rotor blades flying overhead. A military transport lacking military markings and painted white.

White River Security, he thought.

When the droning faded, he returned to work. By the time he had finished, he had dug four feet at the center. He tossed the shovel out of the pit, then scrambled up an embankment he had left for that purpose. Leaving the shovel and spading fork behind, he returned to the car and removed two of the three garbage bags and hauled them to the pit.

On his next trip to the car Jake noticed the silence. The birds had stopped making noise. He pulled the last bag from the trunk, swung it over his shoulder, and made his final trip to the grave. Every footstep seemed louder in the silence, the steady gushing of the waterfall the only thing audible. At the grave, he heaved the bag into the pit with the others and prepared to bury himself for the second time in twenty-four hours. He picked up the shovel and tossed dirt onto one of the lumpy bags.

A loud roar caused his body to turn rigid. The sound reminded Jake of a gorilla and an elephant combined and seemed to come at him from all directions at once, growing still louder before trailing off like a lion's growl. The rumbling roar echoed, and Jake's first thought was that a Tyrannosaurus Rex had been loosed in the reserve. Turning in a circle, he saw nothing. He tossed the shovel aside, leapt over to his bag, and removed his weapons. After tucking the Ruger into the back of his waistband, he clicked off the safety on his Thunder Ranch and stood ready.

Jake was familiar with the tales of the Jersey Devil. The versions he had heard as a child described a creature—the thirteenth child of a witch—with the body of a kangaroo, the head of a goat, and bat-like wings. The legends claimed the monster stalked the Pine Barrens, and southern New Jersey's proximity to Queens, where he had grown up, made the beast more tantalizing than Bigfoot, the yeti, or the Loch Ness Monster. But the South Mountain Reservation was not the Pine Barrens.

So what? If it has wings it could have flown here. He looked to the sky, where he had seen the helicopter.

He had never believed the stories, but if the Jersey Devil did exist, why wouldn't it come after him? Every other monster under the sun had.

Off to his left, sunlight streaming through the tree branches intensified. Colors coalesced, and a man with brilliant blue eyes and long golden hair stood before him. The man wore a white cowboy hat and a duster. He waved at Jake, with panic etched on his features.

"Abel?" Jake said.

He had not seen Abel since teaming up with the agent from the Realm of Light and his brother Cain, emissary from the Dark Realm, to defeat the monstrous Avademe and his followers. He had never expected to see the agent of Light again; neither Abel nor Cain had responded to his calls for help during the crisis on Pavot Island.

Abel did not speak to him now, either verbally or telepathically. He faded into the sunlight as if he had never stood there. Jake felt shortchanged.

Then the creature, whatever it was, bellowed again. Jake found himself unable to move while the roar engulfed the forest. The thing sounded angry this time, and the hair on the back of Jake's neck stood on end.

Less than a quarter of a mile away, green foliage, brilliant in the sunlight, darkened. A massive shadow appeared and small trees surrounding it swayed.

What the hell? Jake tightened his grip on the Thunder Ranch.

The creature roared and the foliage exploded. A beast as large as a rhinoceros thundered in his direction.

Jake flinched and almost dropped his revolver. At first he couldn't discern details of the approaching monster's appearance because its green skin blended with its environment. But as it galloped forward, kicking up branches and clumps of earth with its massive hooves, he catalogued the massive body of a bull supported on long legs, like those of a horse only more muscular. Its head had an equestrian configuration minus the long neck, so it resembled a giant armadillo, but it had a muscular trunk instead of a shell. On either side of the creature's skull, long, fleshy tendrils flopped behind it like dreadlocks. Jake thought they were ears until he saw them coiling and uncoiling in a rhythmic pattern and realized two tentacles had grown from where the horns would be on a bull.

Jake bent his knees but there was nowhere to run. Climbing a tree one-handed was out of the question. The creature bore down on him with incredible speed for its size, and as it drew closer he noticed thick scales covering its hide. Bracing himself, he aimed the Thunder Ranch, pressing his hook against the back of his wrist for support.

Mother-father!

The creature roared as it closed the distance between them.

Jake fired, the recoil paining his wrist. He was certain he had delivered a round to the monster's skull, but no wound opened up and the beast continued charging. He fired two more rounds with similar failure, wincing at the pain. By now the creature was so close that even if it dropped dead it would crush him beneath its weight. The monster launched itself into the air. Jake waited until the last possible second, then dove out of the way.

The creature landed headfirst in the pit. Rolling over, Jake hoped the gargantuan beast had broken its neck until he remembered he had seen no neck on it. Roaring with animalistic rage, the monster righted itself and turned around, its back an undulating mass of muscles. Jake pumped three shots into its back and glimpsed the monster's scales absorbing the rounds.

The monster reared back on its hind legs, bringing its head over the ridge of piled dirt with such speed Jake flinched. Its jaws parted like those of an alligator, revealing serpentine teeth that glinted in the sunlight.

Steel teeth, Jake thought.

The tentacles atop the creature's head lashed out with lightning speed, ensnaring Jake's ankles. Before Jake could react, the monster dragged him feetfirst over the piled dirt, its jaws opening wider. Tossing his Thunder Ranch aside, Jake clawed at the ground, but his efforts did not slow the speed with which the monster pulled him toward its waiting mouth.

Rolling to his left, Jake reached behind him and drew the Ruger from the waistband of his jeans. He knew the monster would not bite his feet or shins with its tentacles wrapped around his ankles, so he was safe until the second when it had a clear path to his knees and thighs. Sitting up, he aimed the handgun, waving his stump for balance, and opened fire.

The monster swallowed three rounds. It clamped its jaws shut, its tentacles releasing Jake, then opened its jaws to cough, blood slicking its teeth. Jake fired three more shots inside the crimson maw, and the beast lunged at him, its eyes glowing red. Its jaws just missed Jake's legs. Jake shot out one of its eyes, which exploded jelly, and the monster shook its head and snorted. Jake shot out its other eye. Blinded, the monster opened its mouth and roared.

Jake had only one round left, so he had to make it count. He shoved his hand inside the open mouth, warm blood and saliva pouring over his wrist. If it closed its jaws, he would lose his other hand. He squeezed the trigger, firing a round through the roof of its mouth to where he calculated the monster's brain to be. The monster's roar warbled and its body quivered. Jake jerked his hand out. The monster's head slammed onto the dirt pile, exhaling red mist through its gaping nostrils. Then it slid back into the pit, dragging its tentacles with it.

Jake kicked the ground with both feet, driving himself

away from the pit's edge. Glancing at the empty Ruger, he stood and collected his Thunder Ranch, then went to his bag. He ejected the Ruger's magazine, set the weapon on the ground, stepped on the gun, and pressed a replacement magazine into its grip. Then he deposited the empty magazine and the Thunder Ranch into the bag. Still holding the smaller gun, he walked to the edge of the pit and looked down at the dead monster. Its carcass covered the remains of his duplicate. He scanned the terrain for signs of additional creatures and saw none.

"Jersey Devil my ass," he said.

This beast had New York blood.

He slid the Ruger into his waistband, then resumed shoveling. Since the beast filled most of the hole, he didn't have to return all the dirt to where it had originated. He filled the pit and the impression that had been there upon his arrival, then dragged fallen tree limbs and branches to cover it. He searched the ground for shell casings, collecting as many as he could find. He wasn't worried about being connected to his duplicate's corpse: he had pulled its teeth and chopped off its fingertips and toes, a trick he had learned from Dawn Du Pre.

After slipping the strap of the bag over his shoulder, he gathered the shovel and spading fork and headed back to the car. The forest remained quiet, and he wondered if anyone had been close enough to hear the gunshots. The adrenaline coursing through his system caused his knees to wobble, but he managed to walk faster anyway. When he saw the Plymouth, he broke into an awkward run, the handles of his gardening tools bouncing against his shoulder.

He backed the car up without removing the camouflage he had laid over it. Some of the branches fell off when he pulled out, some fell off when he stepped on the brakes, and some fell off when he accelerated.

When he had driven for five minutes, he stopped to punch coordinates into his GPS. Then he tried different roads to the highway, knowing the GPS would correct his course. Checking his phone, he saw he had received twenty-one calls, most of them from media outlets, several from television stations, and three from Maria, who had by now learned everything that had been made public about flight 3350.

Jake drove to Manhattan. On East Twenty-third Street, he parked the Plymouth in a lot near First Avenue. A medical helicopter flying overhead reminded him of the military chopper he had seen earlier. He took the guns from his bag and hid them beneath his seat.

Exiting the car, he took the bag with him and headed west. Construction vehicles took up the street, and a wooden fence had been erected around Ground Zero One, where Lilith's waterspout had toppled buildings. The shattered windows of Laurel's first-floor psychic parlor and the windows in Jake's office had been replaced, and dust already covered them. The rubble that had spilled out into the street and blocked the entrance to the building had been removed, and a metal framework had been erected from the sidewalk to the top of the fourth floor.

Jake entered the lobby. The place reeked of rotting wood. Signs of water damage streaked the walls and floor. He knew better than to take the elevator to the basement office, which still must have been flooded. He took out his phone and entered Jackie's number from memory.

"Krebbs," Jackie said.

"I'm in the house," Jake said. "Where are you?"

"In your office, as a matter of fact."

"I'll be right up."

Jake climbed the stairs. Darkness shrouded each dark, dirty, and unoccupied level. On the fourth floor, he entered his office and faced the desk where Carrie had sat. The floor had buckled and humidity caused him to sweat. He went to the windows and looked at the ruins across the street. Cranes and power shovels scooped up debris and deposited them into waiting dump trucks, and men wearing orange vests and yellow hard hats pushed wheelbarrows.

"It's some sight, isn't it?"

Jake turned to face Jackie, who had been the building's engineer before Laurel had willed him the building. They hadn't known she had owned it until Jake had rescued her from Lilith's upstate estate. Laurel had also allowed Jake to keep his office and her parlor for one dollar a month for twenty years.

"Jesus," the little man with the drooping mustache said. "What the hell happened to you? The storm is over."

"Not for everyone. How's the landlord business?"

"I'm sure Laurel thought she was doing me a favor leaving me this place, but it hasn't worked out for me. Tenants don't pay rent on office space they can't use. People are funny about wanting electricity and cable. Dealing with the insurance companies is a nightmare. I can't even start real repairs until the utilities are back on." He jerked a thumb toward Jake's office. "Come into your office, which is temporarily my office."

Jake followed Jackie past his ruined kitchenette and into his office. The floors had been destroyed by water, but his desk looked okay. Several plastic totes stood along one wall.

"I saved most of your records," Jackie said.

"Thanks. I appreciate it. I just don't know what to do with them."

"Any luck finding that dwarf?"

"Someone else found her first. She's dead."

"Karma's a bitch."

"You can use the parlor for an office if you want."

"You think that's better than this?" Jackie snorted.

"Then hang on to this one for as long as you need it. Let me know when the power comes back on, and I'll give you a hand with the place. Any mail for me?"

"Upper drawer."

Jake opened the drawer, pulled out a handful of sealed envelopes, and dumped them on the scarred desktop.

"Nice hook," Jackie said.

"Thanks." Jake looked through the mail. There was no letter from Carrie. Had she lied? "I have to run. You've got my number. Stay in touch."

"You, too."

Jake walked out of his office, grateful to escape the memories. On the sidewalk, he turned left and continued west. The wooden fence prevented him from seeing the damage on Madison Avenue, but he had seen plenty of footage of the destruction on TV. The Flatiron Building loomed overhead, and he passed the front entrance to the Tower. The fountains had been shut off, but lights glowed in the lobby, although the two-story statue of a DNA strand did not rotate.

Generators, Jake figured.

He took out his phone and snapped a photo of the distinctive skyscraper, then uploaded it to the cloud. He also forwarded a copy to Edgar, which he knew his friend would appreciate, then crossed the street and circled the mammoth building.

When he reached the security entrance in the rear,

he pushed through the revolving door without bothering to take a deep breath. Inside, nightmarish images assailed his mind. This was where the ghost of Shannon Reynolds had melted all over his hands and where he witnessed the demon Cain murder two security guards by smashing their heads against each other.

Two new security guards, their faces illuminated by the monitors before them, stood behind the desk. They looked at him like he belonged on the street.

He approached the men with a purposeful gait. "My name is Jake Helman. I'm here to see Kira Thorn."

FOURTEEN

The guards regarded him with unimpressed expressions.

"Am I supposed to know who that is?" one guard said.

"Save the stupid act for the rubes. I know she's here and she'll want to see me."

"I still don't know who you're talking about." But he picked up the phone.

"Sure you do."

"Jake Helman is here," the guard said into the phone. "He says he wants to see someone named Kira Thorn."

Jake watched him.

"Just a minute, sir."

Thirty seconds passed, then the guard hung up. "You can go on up. Take one of those elevators—"

"I know the routine. I used to work here." Jake grabbed the electronic clipboard on the desk.

"You don't need to sign that."

Jake signed in. "Yes, I do. I want every possible record that I was here." He took out his wallet, removed his driver's license, and set it before the talkative guard. "I'll take a visitor's badge."

The guard sighed. "That really isn't necessary."

"Humor me. I know the protocol."

While the guard scanned his license and printed a visitor's badge, Jake glanced at one of the domed security cameras watching him.

"Here you go." The guard handed him the printed badge.

Jake peeled off the sticker and stuck it on his shirt, then slid his license back into his wallet. "Has a seven-foot-tall demon with a volcanic temper been through here?"

The guards stared at him.

"You're lucky." Jake turned his back to the guards and aimed his phone at himself. "Smile."

"You shouldn't be taking photos in here," the other guard said.

Jake snapped the selfie. "Too late." He uploaded the image to the cloud and forwarded it to Edgar. "It's in the clouds now, no retrieving it."

He crossed the floor, his muddy sneakers squeaking. Standing before three gold elevators, he waved his pass at a scanner mounted on the wall. One door opened and he boarded the car. The door slid shut and the elevator glided upwards. Because he didn't have an authorized key card, the elevator headed straight to the fiftieth floor. Jake stared at the domed camera looking down at him. Every event that had occurred over the last two years had built to this moment. He took another selfie and uploaded it to the cloud and forwarded it.

The elevator slowed and stopped, and when the door opened a Japanese man in a black suit stood staring at Jake with his hands folded behind his back. He appeared to be just a few years older than Jake. Two men in Tower Security uniforms stood behind him, their hands on the butts of their Glocks.

"Mr. Helman," the Japanese man said, "I'm Robert Hanaka, director of security for the Tower. Will you submit to a search?"

Jake stepped off the elevator. "Sure."

He raised his hand and hook in the air. Hanaka's gaze darted to the hook, which made Jake smile. One of the guards frisked him.

"We'll need to search your bag as well," Hanaka said.

Jake lowered his arms. "Not happening."

"I insist."

"Nobody looks inside my bag. But I understand your position; after all, I used to have it. You need to make sure I'm not waltzing in with a weapon. Don't worry. I'm not here to assassinate anyone. This is purely a social call."

"There are no exceptions."

Jake shot a questioning look at the security camera.

Hanaka's phone beeped, and he fished it out of his

pocket. He read a text, then nodded to one of the other guards, who waved a handheld metal detector over Jake's body. It emitted an electronic whine when it passed over his hook but did not react when passed over his bag.

"See?" Jake said. "No guns, knives, or hand grenades."

"Please follow me," Hanaka said.

Jake followed him, and the two bruisers brought up the rear. Someone inside the security bay unlocked the door from the central security station. Jake half expected to see Simon Graham, his old colleague, but he had been replaced by a black woman whose light blue contact lenses gave her an icy stare.

The security bay had not changed. It still resembled the bridge of the Starship *Enterprise*. A corridor wrapped away from the entrance to the left and right like coiled tentacles, and Jake's old glass-faced office overlooked the station. Triggered by an electronic eye, the wide double doors opened.

A woman stood silhouetted in the doorway, the deep office behind her flooded with sunlight shining through the floor-to-ceiling windows along the back wall.

Jake's pulse quickened at the sight of her.

She stepped into the security bay, the overhead fixtures casting light over her perfect features. Raven hair spilled over her shoulders like part of her anatomy. She wore her blazer unbuttoned, revealing ivory cleavage. A tiny waist curved into rounded hips, and her short black skirt showed plenty of leg. In her heels, she was as tall as Jake.

Almost two years ago, Kira had been Jake's supervisor when Nicholas Tower hired him to be the director of security at the Tower. She had seduced him and had ordered Marc Gorman, the Cipher, to murder Sheryl and steal her soul. Jake discovered she was one of Tower's Biogens: a biogenetically engineered weapon. After he had caused Tower's death, Kira had come to his apartment to kill him. She transformed into a hideous spider creature, but Jake threw her into a bathtub full of alcohol, which had dissolved her flesh and bones.

"I didn't expect to see *you*," Kira said.

"I bet you didn't." Jake's voice tightened. "But I've been waiting for you to come back."

"You look a lot worse than you did the last time I saw you." This seemed to please her.

"You look a lot better than you did the last time I saw you." *When I rinsed your remains down the drain of my bathtub.*

Kira gestured behind her. "Come into my office and let's catch up."

"I thought you'd never ask." Jake followed her inside her spacious office.

The doors closed behind him, and Kira walked over to her desk, turned around, leaned her ass against its edge, and raised one knee in a provocative manner. She teased him with a half smile. "Have a seat."

He approached her but stopped at the chairs facing her desk. The view outside her window revealed the Flatiron Building below. The Tower dwarfed it. "I'll stand."

"You really should have called ahead. I would have prepared a proper welcome for you."

"I've been coping with your hospitality for twenty-four hours."

"Judging by your face, you had your hands full. Sorry—make that *hand*. I had no idea."

"Obviously." Jake unzipped his bag, removed his duplicate's left hand, its wrist spotted with dried blood, and tossed it onto her desk.

Kira glanced at the hand, then returned her gaze to Jake.

"I know that looks like mine once did, but I believe it belongs to you, unlike my heart."

Making a quiet snort, Kira circled her desk. Jake couldn't help checking out her hips and buttocks; she had been created with an increased level of pheromones that attracted men to her. Once upon a time, just standing in her presence had given him an erection, but having seen her vagina in an agitated state, he now felt only revulsion. He pictured slick teeth snapping shut like those of a steel trap.

Kira sat in the throne-like leather office chair behind her desk. "What brings you here, besides tossing your hand on my desk?"

"Not my hand. My duplicate's hand—my clone's. I killed one; Edgar Hopkins killed the other. You underestimated both of us."

She gave him a smile as mysterious as the Mona Lisa's. "What can I do for you?"

"Answer one question for me." He moved closer to her desk. "Where's Old Nick?"

"Nicholas Tower is dead. You caused his death almost two years ago."

"According to the media, he died of natural causes."

"You and I know better."

"I want to see him."

Kira crossed her legs. "What makes you believe he's alive?"

"Not him—another clone. Or a Biogen like you. I know he's behind all this."

She cocked her head. He couldn't decide if it was a human motion. "What makes you think so?"

"Because he likes to play games. You don't. You would have gone straight for the kill. Only he would orchestrate mind games involving artificial life-forms for his own amusement."

"Am I artificial?"

"You were developed in a petri dish. That makes you unnatural."

Her smoky eyes cooled. "It makes me superior."

Jake forced a bored expression to mask his impatience.

"Produce the old man."

"Or what? You're in no position to make threats. You're *unarmed*. I humored you by bringing you in here, but I could easily have your replacement throw you to the curb."

Making a fist, Jake pressed his knuckles against her desktop and leaned on them. "You came at me once before. I wasn't armed then, either, but I took care of business."

She narrowed her eyes, which appeared curious, not angry. "How did you do it?"

"Let's just say it wasn't pretty. Now I'll ask you one more time: Where's Nick?"

"I'm right here, Jake."

The commanding voice caused Jake's body to jerk.

A tall, muscular man, perhaps twenty-two years old and clad in a red sweat suit, stood behind him. Jake had seen the younger version of Nicholas Tower residing in a metal cylinder connected to an artificial respirator in Tower's Soul Chamber. That clone had been created as a vassal for Old Nick's mind in Tower's scheme to gain a second lifetime. Jake had put a stop to that plan.

Tower skipped across the office and clapped Jake's arm. "My God, you're a sore sight for eyes."

Jake was not accustomed to the spring in Tower's step, the twinkle in his eyes, or the firmness of his grip, let alone the dark hair that swept back from his forehead in a widow's peak. He wondered if he could bury his hook in the man's forehead.

"Well," Tower said, "isn't this something? The three of us back together again. Incredible. You have a way of defying the odds."

"My survival is far from the most curious aspect of this meeting," Jake said.

Tower touched his shoulder. "I suppose you're right."

"I'm not used to seeing you in the sunlight or outside your lair."

"What do I have to hide from? The higher powers have no interest in me now. I was watching your conversation while I was working out in my gym, and I couldn't resist popping in." He made a muscle with his right arm. "Feel that. Rock hard."

"I'll take your word for it."

"Healthy living. You should try it." Tower stared at Jake, then shook his head. "What's happened to you? I don't mean the injuries . . ." He turned to Kira. "You see it, don't you?"

"I do."

Tower turned back to Jake. "Underneath those bruises and that mottled flesh." He sucked his teeth. "It's a damned shame."

"What are you talking about?" Jake said.

"There's a shallowness around your eyes, a drawn-in look to your cheeks. I know that look. You've ingested

Black Magic, scarecrow."

Jake felt dirty. "Not by choice."

"If you say so." Tower joined Kira behind her desk, and they stood side by side. "Kira didn't tell you the grand news: we're married."

Kira extended her left hand, revealing a sparkling diamond ring. "I'm now Kira Tower."

"They'll never ask her to testify against me now." Tower winked at him.

"Congratulations," Jake said.

Tower gestured to the lounge area, where four elegant chairs surrounded a square coffee table. "Let's sit." He moved toward the lounge, then stopped when he realized Jake had remained still. "Come on. There's no point in us standing toe-to-toe like boxers; we're not going to climb into the ring. Let's be comfortable. I'm sure you have as many questions for me as I have for you."

Tower sat in the lounge. Following him, Jake eyed the wall of security monitors displaying images of offices and corridors. He sat across from Tower, and Kira slid into a seat between them.

Tower narrowed his eyes at Jake, then pointed at Jake's glass eye. "That one. A useless hunk of old-fashioned glass. You could have had a new one therapeutically cloned if you hadn't provided the ACCL with that video footage of my Biogens. Ironic, isn't it? Have you ever considered how many people's lives could have been improved if you hadn't interfered with this company's plans?"

Jake resisted the urge to drum his fingers on the arm of the chair despite the surreal nature of the conversation. "Isn't this the part where you brag about how brilliant your schemes are?"

"I don't need to impress you. The fact that Kira and I are even here is impressive enough."

Jake crossed one leg. "Aren't you impressed I'm here, too?"

"Yes and no. You crippled my domestic empire. If you'd gone down like a sucker after that, it wouldn't say much for me, would it? I found myself almost rooting for you to survive everything I threw your way. When I hired you, you were my patsy. Now you've evolved into a worthy opponent, like my old associate Karlin Reichard."

He suspects I crushed the Order of Avademe. "I know you're dying to tell me, so . . ." Jake gestured at Tower. "How? Or, more importantly, why?"

"You're the private eye. You tell me."

"You and Kira aren't clones per se. You're Biogens. Previous models of Kira existed before I killed the one that came after me. What's one more? You grow them full size. Maybe you had one ready to go. The replica I saw of you in the Soul Chamber the night the real Nicholas Tower died was also a Biogen: a fully formed adult duplicate."

Tower raised one finger. "Old Nick didn't die. You killed him. Just as you killed the duplicate of him you saw that night. I should be angry, but as far as I'm concerned, I never died. And now I have this perfect form. I look pretty good for a seventy-eight-year-old, don't you think?"

Jake stood and circled the lounge. He wanted them to feel like he was in command. Maybe that was the truth but he doubted it. "Again, what's one more? But you're both more than reproductions. You've retained the memories of the original, or previous, models."

"Programmable DNA," Kira said with pride. "Patent pending. It will revolutionize life as we know it."

Tower grunted. "Imagine a world in which people can guarantee that their memories, ambitions, and dreams live on after they've expired. Everyone on this planet will live forever, in a manner of speaking. They'll be able to fulfill every goal they've ever had, if not themselves, then their duplicates. Reproduction will cease to be the only form of continuing lineage. Of course, the world isn't ready for this now, but it will be someday—perhaps during my second lifetime."

"We'll hold the patent on the one thing everyone on earth will want," Kira said. "And they'll pay through the roof for it."

"I'm the first of my kind," Tower said. "A perfect reproduction, created in my own image, with my memories and knowledge intact. I'm the second Adam."

Jake looked at Kira. "When Old Nick had his heart attack earlier that day almost two years ago, you drew his blood."

"I remember everything that happened until that moment," Tower said. "But I've had to rely on Kira's memory of that night in the Soul Chamber to fill in the blanks."

Jake remained focused on Kira. "Likewise, you must have drawn your own blood before you came to my apartment to kill me, or you wouldn't remember you'd planned to eat me alive. The fact that you awakened in a metal cylinder told you that you'd failed." He gestured at Tower. "Around the same time, you must have activated Nick's Biogen."

"I took longer to initiate," Tower said. "Even though we'd been creating duplicates of Old Nick for years, harvesting them for organs to keep him alive, we'd never activated his—my—memory cells before. Seven decades' worth of experiences is a lot of data."

"The world knew you were dead," Jake said, "and that Kira had disappeared soon after becoming the head of Tower International, so you couldn't just magically reappear. When I summoned Cain here, you said in preparation for him transplanting your living consciousness into the younger model of yourself, you'd already created a history and paper trail for Nicholas Tower Jr., an unknown heir to your throne. The US was too hot for you because of the footage I sent to the ACCL. The government's antitrust suit against Tower International complicated things further. You have a lot of holdings in Europe, so you must have gone there to lay the pipe for your comeback, operating in secret while maintaining the illusion of a disabled company in the States. You could have stayed there indefinitely, but you couldn't stand that I'd outmaneuvered you."

Tower offered Kira a triumphant smile, as if he had won a wager. "You see? I told you, you don't give him enough credit."

"Yes, Daddy."

Jake circled the lounge again. "You've held a grudge against me for obvious reasons and kept tabs on me. You could have sent assassins to kill me anytime you wanted—at least, they could have tried—but that solution offered no satisfaction to your ego. So you bided your time until you could return. Besides, I had Afterlife and you wanted it back. Carrie didn't decide overnight to stab me in the back. You must have been working on her for a while."

Tower's expression turned into one of fading interest. "You were in New Orleans, then Miami, then Pavot Island, then back in Miami, and then you drove all the way back here."

They traced my credit card activity, Jake thought. "Carrie was a college dropout with student loans to repay, and I wasn't paying her a fortune. It probably didn't take a lot of persuasion to convince her to rob my safe if the opportunity presented itself."

Tower smiled.

"Hurricane Daria provided her with an opportunity she couldn't refuse. When I went outside, she sent her boyfriend with me, the poor sap. When I made it back to my office she was gone, and so were my files. Sometime during the next two weeks, you returned. My guess is Carrie had second thoughts, so you had her killed. But you couldn't just send your new director of security or some other lackey to do your dirty work. That wouldn't satisfy your twisted urges. So you sent me—a version of me, anyway.

"When I worked here, there was a DNA scanner in the anteroom leading to your office. A needle jabbed the back of my hand when I stuck it in the scanner. Even though you didn't make me provide you with a hair follicle sample when you hired me—that would have screwed up everything, because I never would have passed a drug test—you had my DNA. You sent the first duplicate of me to kill Carrie just to punish her for reneging, and as an added bonus, you tried to frame me for her murder."

"Hanaka made the initial contact with Miss Scott. She didn't know who he represented. Once she told us she had Afterlife in her possession, she failed to make second contact. And we'd already traveled back here."

Jake's voice softened with regret. "You had a backup copy of Afterlife all along, didn't you? You just couldn't stand that someone else had it, too, especially if that someone was me."

"Of course. I funded that project. It's mine. Why should I share the information it yielded with anyone? Jonas Salk was a fool."

"What I don't understand is why you sent the second duplicate to kill Edgar," Jake said. "He knows nothing about what went on here or what you could be up to now."

"I know you killed Ramera Evans, aka Dawn DuPre, who did research for Afterlife. She never would have brought Black Magic and its zonbies to New York if you hadn't killed my former incarnation. By impeding my empire, you made hers possible. And in the middle of that calamity, your friend Hopkins disappeared. What did she do, turn him into a rat?"

Jake tried to hide his amazement at Tower's deductive reasoning. "A raven, actually."

"I know the significance of Pavot Island. I just never cared about it except as a historical curiosity. The people are nothing but a bunch of Kalfu worshippers. Men like Ernesto Malvado are a dime a dozen; they have no sense of what real power is. You and Detective Vasquez helped topple his regime, and in return, Miriam Santiago restored Hopkins to human form. I admire your loyalty. I've honestly never met anyone who would go to the lengths you did for your friend. It stands to reason he feels the same loyalty to you. So he had to go."

"Why did you send my second duplicate to off him? It didn't appear you were going to frame me for that."

Tower shrugged. "Call it a devilish streak. I wanted to imagine the horror he would experience when he believed you were beating him to death, and I knew that somewhere along the line you would feel guilty for his death. The more you suffer, the better."

"Too bad I'm not the only one you underestimated."

"I'm still astonished he beat your duplicate. He's older than you by a decade."

"That's easy: Edgar's really Edgar, and those duplicates weren't really me. They haven't experienced what I have since you pushed me into this insane world you inhabit. I'm not the same man I was then. Plus, you must have erased some of my duplicates' memories when you programmed them to kill Carrie and Edgar, or they never would have followed your orders. I'm not programmable."

"That's why experiments like these are necessary."

"You monitored my phone activity, so you knew Edgar beat your puppet. You also monitored my credit cards, so you knew I flew out there, which gave you time to implement a backup plan: that human bomb on the plane, another Biogen, grown from the cells of a suspected terrorist."

Tower smiled. "Tower Satellites, hard at work. Information is always a valuable commodity."

"I assume the explosives were in his DNA, and he triggered them mentally."

"Assume what you like."

"You tried to kill all those passengers just to take me out."

Tower's smile faded. "And then the impossible happened . . ."

"We'll get to that in a minute. Because your attempt to blow me out of the sky failed, you sent the first duplicate to finish me off when I got home. Like I said, he wasn't me."

"It looks like he came close," Kira said.

Jake didn't care to admit how close. "That was strike two. Maybe it was all the knocks I took, but I was too slow to realize I should have left my phone behind. You tracked me all the way to New Jersey and sent that monster to kill me. Strike three."

"This isn't baseball," Tower said. "It's hardball. Once we came here, the clock started ticking for a public announcement. I couldn't allow you to interfere with that."

"I always knew the possibility of Kira returning in some form existed. I chose the office I did so I could keep my eye on this place. I wasn't counting on Daria displacing me. When this stone started rolling yesterday, I still wouldn't allow my mind to accept it. I looked at the organizations run by your old pal Reichard and the other members of the Order of Avademe."

Tower rose, his eyes gleaming with excitement. "You did it, didn't you? You took them all out."

Now Jake had his interest. "I was sure it had to be one or more of them. Maybe some sequel group. The heirs to the thrones should have been happy those gee-zers were gone, but if they knew about me, they would view me as a continuing threat."

"In a manner of speaking, you were right. With my former associates out of the picture, I spent much of the last year acquiring a controlling interest in their companies—all but Sky Cloud Dreams. What would I do with a cult that worships space aliens? Mr. Hanaka came to me from White River Security. While the government was breaking my monopoly on genetic engineering, I increased my hold on international shipping and weapons manufacturing."

"I figured that out after I killed the beast you sent after me. I saw a military transport helicopter before that thing tried to make pork chops out of me. It belonged to White River Security. You used it to transport that Biogen to South Mountain Reservation and set it loose to find me. It knew my scent, because you provided it with the scent of the duplicates."

"I had an understanding with the order once I resigned from it." Tower's voice turned sad. "Their deaths freed me from that bargain. Now I'm far wealthier and more powerful than I was. For that, I'm indebted to you."

"I killed Avademe."

Tower's eyes grew bulbous. "Impossible."

"I didn't do it alone. I had a little help from my good friends Cain and Abel."

"You expect me to believe the Reaper and the Messenger are your allies?"

"Believe what you want, but the three of us took

down that monster and its scaly offspring."

"Those two would never work together."

"I admit it was touch and go, but I was the lynchpin that held the partnership together. The only reason the authorities didn't find the slimy corpses of that giant mutant octopus god and its amphibious children was because Cain took them to the Dark Realm with him."

Tower snorted. "Not only are you a master survivor but a master fantasist."

"I couldn't make this stuff up. You mentioned Adam a minute ago. Cain and Abel helped me because Avademe was their father . . . and their mother."

Tower's facial muscles relaxed, his eyes filling with realization. "Adam and Eve . . ."

"Don't feel bad. None of your peers knew it, either. Abel spelled it out for me."

Tower spoke with awe in his voice. "I remember the first time I saw Avademe. I believed it was God. But I came to realize otherwise. What god depends on human beings for secrecy and protection? Still, it was godlike and beautiful."

Jake glanced at Kira. "You and I have different definitions of beauty." He gazed at Tower. "UFOs didn't rescue my flight this morning. Abel and the agents of the Realm of Light did. I have angels and demons in my corner."

Kira stood and looked at Tower with concern in her eyes.

"That's not possible," Tower said.

"Listen to the accounts of the other passengers. Most of them say the same thing: angels saved the day. And I couldn't have stopped the Biogen in the woods if Abel hadn't warned me it was coming. He gave me the edge I needed. Are you sure you want to keep coming after me?"

Now Tower circled the lounge. "I have nothing to fear from the Realm of Light or the Dark Realm. I have no soul, remember? Neither side has a claim on me."

"Aren't you full of yourself? They're not interested in you; they're interested in *me*. They want to keep me alive."

"What makes you so special?" Tower said.

Jake walked over to the floor-to-ceiling windows behind Kira's desk. "Come here."

Tower's face turned passive, as if he wrestled with his temper. Beside him, Kira's expression darkened. Tower crossed the office with Kira following him.

That's right. You come when I call you, Jake thought.

Tower and Kira stood beside him, and the three of them gazed at the city below. Jake had forgotten what it was like to stand in the clouds. Tower glared at him, waiting.

"What do you know about Hurricane Daria?"

A mischievous smile returned to Tower's lips. "I know what's on the news all day, every day."

"I think you know more than that."

"Our neighborhood is Ground Zero One."

"Be more specific."

189

"The exact eye of the storm was that building."

"Lilith occupied the top floor."

Jake could see Tower struggling to show no reaction.

"Lilian Kane was the Storm Demon?" His voice quivered with excitement.

"Funny you should put two and two together just like that."

Tower drew in a breath. "If you have something to say, spew it out."

"Like you said, information is a valuable commodity. If you want to know what I know, open the gate."

Despite his smile, rage swirled behind Tower's eyes. "I became aware of a power source occupying this neighborhood before I built the Tower. It's why I chose this spot. I had reason to believe this force was more powerful than Avademe. I hoped to tap into it when I secluded myself in here. Unfortunately, I was never able to solve the mystery."

"But you know who Lilian Kane was?"

"She's been in the news of late, hasn't she?"

"And you know Lilith was known as the Storm Demon."

"I'm well versed in lore, you know. The entire world knows that hurricane was caused by a powerful spiritual or supernatural force. And now"—he spread his hands apart—"the power is gone, apparently washed away with the storm."

Jake moved closer. "Because of me. I made that happen."

Tower swallowed, a sign of fear that surprised Jake. "You're the Romance Killer?"

He smiled. "I'm Jake the fucking giant killer, and Cain was pretty damned happy to collect the soul I sent his way."

"Did you kill Bill Russel on Pavot Island?" Kira said.

Jake fixed her with a one-eyed stare. "Like he was a cockroach."

Something changed in Kira's expression. Was it attraction to Jake? He had never looked more pitiful, but she had been programmed to lust after power; that glitch in her DNA had caused her to turn her back on Tower when Jake had summoned Cain for their summit. Maybe Jake had something after all, something he could use to turn her himself, even though the thought repelled him.

"I really have underestimated you," Tower said. "You have powerful friends in high places."

"And low ones. If I wore your shoes, I'd call off this war you've declared on me. Leave me and mine alone."

Tower moved closer as well. "I can't. You know too much—*more* now—and we both know you'll never leave *us* alone. You can't. We had your wife murdered."

Jake's spirits dampened. Tower had called his bluff.

"But what I can do is bring you into the fold."

Jake studied the younger man. "I'm not interested in

being your director of security again."

"I don't mean I'll make you an employee. I'll make you a partner. I'll give you your own company. How about White River Security? You'll never have to get your hands dirty again. Go buy an island and live there in peace."

"Pardon my skepticism, but why would you make such a generous offer?"

"To guarantee my safety and my agenda. And because of my fascination with the occult. You're probably the leading expert now. Your experiences outweigh your lack of historical knowledge. I need to know everything you've learned, beginning with Lilith."

"Talk money," Jake said.

"Ten million a year, plus stock options."

"You promised me those once before. They never materialized."

"You're a different man, Jake. You said so yourself. So am I. I have my extra sixty years. I have no desire to negotiate with heaven or hell again. I don't need to. But you could be my special consultant on the supernatural."

"That's a lot of cake," Jake said.

"You'll never have to set foot in that dingy office again. And you'll never have to worry about the people you care about. Isn't that what really matters to you?"

Jake had revealed his weak spot to Tower. "I need time to think about it."

Tower stared into his eyes. "You have twenty-four hours. After that, all bets are off the table."

"You said you were indebted to me for taking down the Order of Avademe. I'll give you a chance to honor that debt. Whatever happens from here on between you and me"—he looked at Kira—"or her stays between us. You leave Maria and Edgar and their families alone. They pose no threat to you."

"I don't let anyone tell me how to conduct my business."

"If you harm either one of them, I'll bring this building down around your ears."

"I admire your bravado," Tower said. "Accept my offer, and nothing will happen to any of them. Decline and we'll see how *they* fare against my creations."

Tower offered his hand and Jake shook it.

FIFTEEN

Seated at her desk in the squad room, Maria keyed in her report on a DOA she had investigated on the west side earlier in the day: a homeless man had been discovered on the docks with his head caved in. She had no leads, no suspects, nothing to go on, and no one would care.

Bernie had taken a couple of personal days to watch over Shana and Paolo in the Bronx, so Maria had found herself working alone, which she did not mind.

Her phone vibrated in her pocket, and she took it out. The display identified the New York State Office of Children and Family Services, the agency that had allowed her to foster Shana.

"Maria Vasquez," she said into the phone, ignoring the activity of detectives bustling around her.

"Detective Vasquez, this is Miss Shilo."

Maria liked Rita Shilo, the caseworker who had been helpful to her. "Hi, how are you?" She hoped the agency didn't plan to visit the house to check up on Shana so soon.

"I'm fine. How are you?"

Maria knew small talk was a delaying tactic. "I'm well and Shana is doing great."

"I'm glad to hear that. I'm calling because I have good news."

I could use some, Maria thought, waiting.

"Callie Robbins got in touch with me. She's Shana's aunt on her maternal side."

"Oh?" Maria said, her spirits sinking.

"Ms. Robbins filed for custody of Shana."

Maria closed her eyes. "Shana's mother took up with a drug dealer whose entire family has been engaged in illegal activities." The words came out harder than she had intended.

"I know this is hard, but as I said, Ms. Robbins is from Shana's maternal side of the family. I've vetted her and she's no criminal."

"Where was she when Shana's parents were killed? Why did Papa Joe's sister Alice get custody of her?"

"I don't know what factors played a role in her decision not to seek custody then, but Ms. Robbins lives in Colorado and works for a nonprofit devoted to helping children with asthma. She's been in Thailand setting up a clinic and just learned of Alice Morton's death last week. She's Shana's closest living blood relative, she can provide Shana with a good home, and she wants custody of her niece. I know you've grown close to Shana, but please put her best interests first. Foster situations are always intended to be temporary. This is what we call a happy ending."

Maria regulated her breathing. She couldn't argue that she could give Shana a better home than her mother's sister. She had brought Shana into Joyce's home, and now the little girl was hiding out in the Bronx because Jake couldn't stay out of trouble. Shana would be safer far away. "When?"

"Ms. Robbins arrives tonight. She's already filled out the necessary forms, and she and Shana will be leaving in the morning."

So fast. "So Shana can stay with me one more night?"

"That's right."

"May I take her to the airport tomorrow morning?"

"No, you'll have to bring her to my office. But there's nothing preventing you from seeing her off at the airport. I'll e-mail you the information."

"Thank you."

"You did a wonderful thing for that little girl, especially in your situation. You should feel proud of yourself. Please see this for what it is."

Choking back tears, Maria hung up. She stood and went into the ladies' room, where she dabbed at her eyes and fixed her makeup.

I'm not going to cry. Not here.

Cops didn't cry.

She crossed the squad room to Mauceri's office and knocked on the door.

He waved her inside. "Did you finish up on that homeless DOA?"

"It's in the system."

"Good. I've got something else for you." He tossed a file folder onto his desk.

"I'm off in an hour, L.T."

Mauceri chuckled. "Look around. Do you see anyone working bankers' hours?"

Maria gestured to the chairs in front of the desk.

"Please," Mauceri said.

"I need to take tomorrow morning off."

"Do tell. And may I remind you that your partner just requested two days off? Things are more than a little chaotic around here, and I need all my detectives on the floor."

"Shana's aunt is taking custody of her. Tonight is my last night with her, and I need to take her back tomorrow."

Mauceri's features softened. "I'm sorry to hear that."

"I'd like to see her off at the airport, too. I should be in before lunch."

"Sure, sure. I understand. Silver lining and all that, right?" He nodded at the folder. "But you're catching now. Take Thacker with you. Tell him I said he's the primary, so you don't get stuck with the paperwork."

She picked up the folder and exited the office. By the time she returned to her desk, her vision had blurred.

Jake fought to exit the Tower at an even keel. He knew Tower and Kira were watching him on monitors, and he could not exhibit an ounce of fear. Although he believed he had bought himself some time, he couldn't help but wonder if some elaborate trap would manifest itself and dispatch him to a violent death.

Emerging outside, he took a deep breath of humid air. He craved a cigarette and wished he was packing a gun. Hurrying along the sidewalk, he didn't breathe easier until he escaped the shadow of the Tower. He found himself standing in the center of a triangle formed by the Tower, the Flatiron Building, and Jackie's building. For weeks he had sensed there was no coincidence that Lilith and Old Nick had been neighbors, and by electing to set up shop close enough to keep an eye on the Tower, Jake had brought himself within Lilith's sphere, courtesy of Laurel.

Moving along the plywood barrier that surrounded the work zone, he took out his phone, dropped it on the ground, and stomped it until it shattered. Then he picked up the broken pieces and flung them over the fence. Backtracking, he went the long way around the block, passing beneath the Flatiron Building's shadow. Not long ago, he had waded through water on this same strip. He passed the ramp of the garage he had swum into to reach his car, still submerged in dirty water.

"Beware the devil," a preacher standing on an apple box said at the corner. "For he walks among us."

Jake passed the man.

"Turn your back on evil at your peril!"

Thanks for the advice.

When Jake reached East Twenty-first Street, he made his way to Detective Bureau Manhattan. Climbing the steps, he no longer felt uncomfortable returning to his old stomping grounds. Any old wounds incurred by the circumstances of his resignation from the force had scabbed over.

Inside the squad room, he saw the same flurry of activity he had expected: detectives answering calls, clerks hurrying back and forth, all over the dull din of generators. He approached Maria's desk, facing Bernie Reinhardt's desk. Two years earlier, it had been his desk facing Edgar's. Homicide had moved on without them.

"Feeling nostalgic, Helman?"

Jake turned to Mauceri, who stood with his sleeves rolled up. Air conditioners were not permitted during the blackout. Of course, the Tower had a more sophisticated backup system.

"Feeling old," Jake said.

Mauceri recoiled at the sight of him. "Jesus, what happened to you now?"

"I tangled with some ruffians."

"I'll say you did. Where's the other guy, six feet

under?"

Jake smiled. *And pinned under the carcass of a genetically engineered monster.* "Is Maria around?"

"I sent her out on a call." Mauceri gestured at Jake's face. "Did this happen since Geoghegan pulled you in?"

"Teddy doesn't mess around. Just joking." He wanted to change the subject. "Do you mind if I leave Maria a note?"

"If that's better than calling her."

"My phone died."

"Suit yourself. Did you see a doctor?"

Jake slid Maria's notepad across the desk and plucked a pen from a pencil cup. "No time, I'm a little crazed."

"*Make* time. Your nose looks broken."

Jake wrote on the pad. "It's on my list."

"How's that hook working out for you?"

"It'll be a while before I can do much with it."

"Good seeing you," Mauceri said in a puzzled tone. "Take care of yourself."

> *Babe,*
> *No phone. I'll be in touch. Stay safe.*
> *Jake*

Jake tore the note from the pad and taped it to the desktop. Then he left.

Jake returned to the Plymouth and slid behind the wheel. A layer of dust covered his legs and arms, and when he looked in the rearview mirror he saw dust on his face as well. He returned his guns to the bag in case he needed them in a hurry.

As he drove through the streets of Manhattan, he looked forward to getting out of the city. Every twisted lamppost, shattered window, and food line reminded him of Lilith and her fury. He needed to put her wrath behind him and worry about Tower and Kira. For close to two years, he had been beset by supernatural forces that stemmed from his time with the evil pair. He visualized a chart tracking each villain and creature he had battled and imagined a solid line connecting them to Tower. He wondered if defeating the enemy who had thrust him into the world of the occult could once and for all break the cycle.

Maybe he could lead a normal life with Maria. They could take a page out of Edgar and Joyce's book and get out of Dodge. Would Maria even consider leaving New York City with him? Maybe, if it was the best thing for Shana. Right now, the thought of retiring to some island had its appeal, just not at Tower's price.

Nothing was going to be easy, especially with Geoghegan hot for his blood and whatever government agency Weissman and Freeman worked for aware of Jake's movements. Jake would have to watch his step around Hanaka from White River Security. Maybe a bullet between the eyes would be the best way to deal with him.

He checked the dashboard clock: an hour had already passed since he made his deal with Tower. That left only twenty-three hours to take the man down, assuming Tower honored their deal.

Why would he if I'm not going to?

Navigating the streets of Jackson Heights, he watched for a tail. As far as he could tell, no one followed him. He wondered if Tower believed anything he'd said. Jake had exaggerated his relationship with Cain and Abel. They weren't his friends or even reliable antagonists. On Pavot Island Jake had called on Cain and Abel for help, and they ignored him. But Abel had appeared to him at South Mountain Reservation. Why hadn't the agent of the Realm of Light spoken to him? It made no sense.

Something troubled him more. He had lied when he told Tower the angels had rescued the plane. No evidence suggested that was the case, and he had no idea what had really occurred. For all he knew, Nico Graham was right, and space aliens had rescued the passengers. But he couldn't accept the miracle was unconnected to Tower's Biogen self-exploding.

Pulling into Maria's driveway, he opened the garage door and parked the Plymouth inside, then entered the house and set the bag on the kitchen counter. He popped a couple of aspirins for the pain in his face and slipped into the bathroom to examine himself. The dust made it difficult to see his injuries, so he went upstairs and took a shower, which caused him to scream at the pain even warm water inflicted.

After drying himself, he looked at the mirror. The "good" side of his face had turned purplish black. He reapplied a healing gel to his flesh and pressed a bandage over his nose.

The doorbell rang.

Dressing, he wondered which of his interrogators paid him a visit now. He took his time descending the stairs, then leaned close to the peephole. A woman with dark hair stood outside, her back to him.

Kira?

He went into the kitchen, removed the Ruger from the bag, and tucked it into the rear waistband of his jeans. Returning to the living room, he opened the door. The woman faced him, fading sunlight highlighting her hair.

"Jake?" Sheryl said, her eyes widening. "My God, what happened to you?"

SIXTEEN

A jolt of surprise lanced Jake's brain. Sheryl's reaction told him she was not the spirit of his late wife, who had ascended to the Realm of Light and taken up with Abel. The beautiful woman who stood before him was a *thing*—a monster. Yet she spoke to him in the same loving voice he had missed since her murder.

He made a fist, and when she reached for his face, he swatted her hand away with the base of his hook. Seeing it, she shrieked, a look of horror in her eyes, and staggered back. She lost her balance on the edge of the step and landed on the sidewalk.

Jake scanned the immediate area. Children on skateboards, old men sitting on lawn chairs, and women chatting in foreign tongues all stopped what they were doing and turned in the duplicate Sheryl's direction. Jake needed to get her inside before anyone came over to offer assistance.

Forcing a look of worry onto his face and wondering if anyone could tell beneath his scarred and discolored flesh, he pulled the tail of his shirt out so it covered the butt of the Ruger and rushed down the concrete steps to the sidewalk, where he helped Sheryl to her feet. "Are you all right?"

"Yes, I think so. But your hand . . . " Her voice grew shrill.

With his good arm around her shoulders, he helped her up the stairs. "Don't worry about that. I'm fine. Let's just get inside."

"Don't tell me you're fine. *Your hand is gone.*"

"Is she all right?" a man across the street said.

Jake turned and waved his hook. "Yes, she's fine. Thanks!"

The man, who had tufts of white hair on the side of his head and allowed his belly to hang out through his unbuttoned shirt, blanched at the sight of Jake's face and hook.

Maybe that wasn't a good idea, Jake thought as he guided Sheryl inside.

"I'm not fine and neither are you," Sheryl said. "What happened to your hand? What happened to your *face?*"

Jake waved to the people outside, this time with his hand. Then he closed the door and turned the locks.

"Answer me. I want to know—"

Jake slapped the creature hard across the face. Then he grabbed her hair, jerking her face close to his, and pulled the Ruger and held it beneath her left eye. Both her eyes showed white all around her irises, and blood trickled from the corner of her mouth.

"Let's get something straight," Jake said through clenched teeth. "You're not Sheryl Helman. You're not my wife. You're not even human."

Terror spread across her face and tears filled her eyes. "What are you talking about?"

Once, he had touched her with love. Once, he had touched her and she had melted into multicolored light. Once, her soul had passed through his heart.

"What did they send you here to do?" he said.

"Who?"

"Nicholas Tower and that biogenetic bitch Kira Thorn."

Sheryl knitted her eyebrows together. "Old Nick? Your boss? Why would he—?"

He backhanded her, then forced his forearm against her throat and leaned close. "I don't have time for games. I've had enough games to last a lifetime. If you're going to explode and take me with you, do it. If you're going to transform into some hideous she-creature, do it. Let's just get on with it."

Her face turned scarlet. "You're hurting me . . ."

"I'll kill you if you don't start talking." He meant it.

"What do you want me to say?" she said in a ragged voice.

"Tell me what you want."

Her lips quivered, and then she drove her forehead

straight into his nose, detonating an explosion of pain that threatened to pop his good eye out of its socket. The pain was so intense that Jake felt nauseous.

Sheryl grabbed the barrel of his Ruger and pointed it away from her, then stomped on his left foot. He had taught the real Sheryl this move in case any man tried to attack her. As soon as he realized what had happened, she yanked the Ruger from his hand, twisted away, and aimed the gun at him with both hands, in the proper stance of a police officer.

Jake staggered back, blood flowing from his nose. Tower had made a shrewd move, sending Jake's dead wife to assassinate him.

"Stay back," Sheryl said, her face contorted. "I don't understand anything that's going on, but if you lay a hand on me again I swear I'll pull this trigger."

Gasping, Jake wiped blood from his lips onto his sleeve. "All right, the ball's in your court. What do you want to do?"

Her lips quivered again, and he thought she was going to bawl. "I want to know what's happening to me, what's happened to us, what's happening to the whole world."

Jake didn't want to think of her as a feeling human being, let alone a copy of his wife. That would make it harder to kill her. But he had no choice. Like it or not, the construct standing before him had Sheryl's memories and emotions. But did that mean she had her thoughts as well? "Okay, I know you're confused. Take it easy."

"*You* take it easy. You're my husband. Why the hell did you hit me?"

He kept his hand raised so she could see it. "That was a mistake. My emotions got the best of me."

"The emotion you feel when you see me is to beat me? What happened to begging me day and night to take you back?"

"I can explain everything. Just put the gun down. You don't need it."

"Says the man who almost crushed my windpipe."

"I'm . . . sorry."

"You don't sound sorry."

"This is a difficult situation for both of us. You'll understand when I explain."

Sheryl's gaze darted to the living room, then back to Jake. "So get in there and start explaining."

Lowering his hand, Jake walked into the living room. "Can I take care of my face? I need ice for my nose." Maybe he could get his hands on a kitchen knife.

"No." The flat tone of her voice told him she had made up her mind. The real Sheryl had sounded like that the night she had ordered him to leave their apartment.

Jake gestured to the sofa. "Here?"

"Sure, why not." It wasn't a question.

Jake sat on the sofa, and Sheryl entered the living room with his gun aimed at him.

"Aren't you going to sit, too?"

"I don't think so," Sheryl said.

She's—it's—not making this easy, Jake thought.

"I remember this house. It's Joyce's. We came here for Martin's birthday one year. This is where you live?"

"Temporarily."

Sheryl relaxed her grip on the Ruger. "Why aren't you at the Tower?"

"This would be easier to explain from the beginning."

"Tell me what happened to you."

"From the beginning."

Sheryl swallowed. "All right, go ahead."

"Why don't you tell me the last thing you remember?"

"I remember having a bad day. This creep came into the store and gave Kelly and me a hard time, so I acted like a cop's wife and got rid of him. Then another creep tried to feel me up on the train ride home. I remember walking home from the station. Then I got inside, and the lightbulb in the living room blew out, so I was going to change it. I went into the kitchen and heard footsteps behind me." She stopped for a moment, collecting her thoughts. "When I turned around, it was you. You were stinking drunk, and you kept babbling about a demon and monsters . . . some insanity about your job. I sent you into the bedroom to sleep it off until dinner."

"What happened then?"

"I went out for a walk to get my head together."

"And?"

She shook her head. "I can't remember."

Had shock prevented her from remembering her own death, or had Tower erased part of her memory? "What *do* you remember next?"

"I was standing on the sidewalk a few blocks away. I don't remember how I got there, but I knew I had to find you, knew you were here. I didn't recognize the house until you brought me inside." Her eyes brightened as a thought occurred to her. "Where's Joyce?"

Jake had been afraid of this: the creature aiming a gun at him remembered everything Sheryl would remember. He wanted to hate her but he couldn't. "I think we'd better take a drive. I want to show you something."

"Where?"

"It isn't far. You won't need that gun, but you can hang on to it if you want."

"It makes me feel better," she said.

Jake had spoken those same words to Old Nick and Kira once. Did he and Sheryl—and now her duplicate— just share the same attitude and sense of humor, or had Tower and Kira programmed her to say that?

"I understand," he said, rising. "Let's go into the garage."

"What for?"

"That's where my car is parked."

"Since when do you have a car?"

Since when do I have only one eye, one hand, and half a face? "It's Edgar's. He's letting me use it."

"I have a better idea. You get the car, and I'll go out the front door and wait for you in the driveway."

Jake gestured to the front door. "After you."

Sheryl backed toward the stairs. "Don't move until I'm outside."

"Don't worry."

When she reached the door, she picked up a purse Maria had left near the stairs. She unlocked the door and opened it, then slid the gun inside the purse and stepped outside, shutting the door behind her.

．❖❖．：

The garage door rumbled open, and Jake started the Plymouth's engine and backed into the driveway, where Sheryl waited. Leaning across the passenger seat, he opened the door for her. She pushed the seat forward and climbed into the back, where she would have a better chance of shooting Jake if that became necessary, he reasoned. He got out and locked the front door of the house, then got back in and pulled out of the driveway.

Sheryl turned on the air-conditioning. "It was November when you came home to see me. Now it's summer. Have nine months passed? A year?"

"You'll understand everything in fifteen minutes," Jake said.

"Why can't you just tell me?"

"I need visual aids."

He drove to the Long Island Expressway, which he followed onto the stretch known as the Cemetery Expressway because it bordered so many cemeteries, and got off at the exit. He drove into the cemetery and switched off the engine. Through the windshield, he watched the sun set.

"What are we doing here?" Sheryl said.

Jake opened the door and got out. He had not been here in a while.

Sheryl got out and made a show of slamming her door. "Hey, I'm calling the shots, remember?"

"So stay in the car and live the rest of your life in a cloud of confusion. Or shoot me for acting on my own impulse. Either way, you'll never learn what's happened to you."

Sheryl looked around. "I don't like cemeteries."

She never had.

Jake started walking.

She fell into step behind him. "Talk to me, damn it."

Jake ignored her and kept walking. He knew the way by heart.

"If you're trying to scare me more than I already am, you're doing an excellent job," she said.

He wondered if he was trying to scare her. Was he punishing her for what she was?

When they reached their destination, he saw the Manhattan skyline across the water beyond the cemetery. It only occurred to him that he had been hurrying when Sheryl caught up to him.

"Is this it?" she said, gazing across the gravestones gleaming in the fading pink light.

He nodded at the stone at her feet.

With dread forming on her features, Sheryl looked at the stone he had indicated and turned still. "No, no, no. That isn't me. It can't be." She turned on him. "I'm *alive*." She pounded on his chest. "I'm *alive*, goddamn it!"

He seized one of her wrists, but she continued to flail at him with her free hand.

"I'm alive!" she shrieked, and then she fell sobbing to the earth.

Jake couldn't help but feel sorry for her. Crouching on one knee, he reached out and set his hand on her back.

She continued to wail and crawled upright, draping herself over his outstretched leg, and clung to him. He massaged her back.

City lights gleamed in the darkness as Jake drove Sheryl into Manhattan. She sat slumped in the front seat, staring out the window.

Jake drove to the Upper East Side, a few blocks from the apartment where they had lived, and they walked to Carl Schurz Park. Both of them remained silent until they arrived at the aqueduct below the walkway running along the East River.

Sheryl stared inside the aqueduct, illuminated by lamps around the park. "I came here because it was always my favorite place in the neighborhood." She raised her gaze to the upper level. "I walked along the river, thinking about you—about us—and then it started to rain, so I came down here to stay dry. That's when he arrived. I recognized him: the creep who harassed me and Kelly at the shop. I knew right away he must have followed me. I saw in his eyes that he wanted to hurt me. I stood paralyzed, and he took out a camera and snapped my photo. And then he had a knife in his hand, this long dagger, and he lunged at me. I tried to fight him, but he covered my mouth and nose with one hand and cut my throat . . .

"I fell to the ground, and I couldn't move or talk, and I heard the rain hitting the ground and felt my blood along my neck. He opened a bag and removed a strange-looking oxygen mask with a plastic bag attached to it, and he put the mask over my mouth and nose. He looked down at me, chanting in some language I'd never heard before, and all I could think about was what you were going to think when you woke up. You'd never know that I wanted us to get back together."

"I knew," Jake said.

"How?"

"This story is just beginning. Let's go back to the car."

"Is he still alive?"

"No, I killed him."

"When?"

"The day after he killed you."

"How long ago?"

Jake didn't want to tell her the truth, but he did. "Almost two years ago."

SEVENTEEN

In the car, Sheryl took Jake's Ruger out of Maria's purse and held it out to him. "Take it back," she said.

"I didn't bring a holster. Keep it in the purse for me." Jake started the engine and pulled away.

"What am I?" Sheryl said.

"The reason I went home to our apartment that day almost two years ago was because I discovered Tower International was conducting illegal experiments. They were creating new forms of life: biological weapons they were selling to countries in political turmoil. I saw some of their creations. I saw other things, too, and I bolted from that place. The Cipher worked for Old Nick. He was like his personal assassin. Nick wasn't just financing experiments straight out of a dime-store science fiction novel; he was a fervent believer in the supernatural. The Cipher killed people and stole their souls."

Sheryl did a double take. "Come again?"

"At first I didn't believe it, either. But when I took

off, Tower and his assistant, Kira Thorn, sent the Cipher to kill you and steal your soul . . . and he did."

"Why would they do that?"

"To keep me under Tower's thumb."

"I'm not buying a word of this."

Jake knew he had revealed too much. "You remember the Cipher attacking you . . . killing you. Sheryl Helman's body is in that grave I showed you."

"*I'm* Sheryl Helman."

"You're a clone fabricated from Sheryl's DNA."

Sheryl stared at him. "Clones grow in a womb and age at the same rate as anyone else."

"Tower calls his creations Biogens—biogenetic life-forms. He manipulates their DNA, grows them outside wombs, and brings them into the world fully grown. I saw one of them with my own eyes . . . and I've seen as many as six since then." He pointed at his face with his hook. "One of them gave me this black eye."

"If I was a clone, I wouldn't be Sheryl Helman inside. I wouldn't have my memories or anything else that makes me who I am."

"Biogens retain their original DNA source's genetic memory. They remember everything up until their last conscious moments when their DNA was extracted."

"You've told me what you think I am. Now tell me why you think I am."

"I caused Old Nick's death. I saw him die. Kira

Thorn came to our apartment to get revenge. I killed her, too."

"Jesus . . . Jake."

"But Tower is back as a biogenetic clone. He has the body of a twenty-four-year-old, and he's going to pass himself off as his own son. I've been working as a private investigator, and he had a biogenetic duplicate of me kill my former assistant. He sent another one to kill Edgar in North Carolina, but Edgar killed it instead. Then he sent the first clone to kill me."

"What happened?"

"I'm sitting here, aren't I?"

"I don't recognize you. Not on the outside and not on the inside."

"He needs to kill me because I know too much. But he wants to do it slowly, to screw with my mind and keep me off balance. It's not enough for him to kill me. He needs me to suffer. Deep down he's a psychopath."

"So he created me? You're saying I'm just a human pawn?"

"As far as he's concerned, we're all pawns. Who could screw with my head more than my murdered wife?"

"If you're right, there has to be more to it than that."

"Maybe he sent you to spy on me or kill me. You could be a sleeper agent with a trigger mechanism, or maybe you're playing me for a fool."

"What are you going to do with me?"

"That's the ten-million-dollar question."

"I don't have anywhere to go."

"Tower's counting on that."

"I don't have any money, credit cards, or identification."

"You'll have to stay with me tonight. We don't have any other choice. Tomorrow night is another story."

"What aren't you telling me?"

"I still have a lot to spill."

"What aren't you telling me that affects *me*?"

"When I freed Sheryl's soul, it went to heaven."

"How do you know?"

"Because I had contact with her spirit and she told me so."

"You're shitting me."

"I visited that grave regularly for over a year, and then in the middle of a case I was working, she appeared to me several times. I learned she had become . . . involved . . . with another angel, so I had no choice but to move on."

"You're seeing someone." The declaration had an air of accusation about it.

"Maria Vasquez. She replaced me as Edgar's partner. She even investigated your murder."

Sheryl stared straight ahead. "Is it serious?"

"As serious as my life allows. She's actually the one who's staying at Joyce's right now. I'm just displaced because a hurricane destroyed my office two weeks ago."

"Where does that leave me?"

"My wife was murdered almost two years ago. Her spirit has moved on and so have I."

"Do I have a soul?"

Jake hesitated. "No."

"Thank you for being honest with me."

Jake parked the car in the garage, and they entered the house.

"Take your clothes off," he said.

Sheryl stared at him.

"I need to examine you head to toe."

"For what?"

"With Tower, you never know."

Sheryl stepped out of her shoes, then turned around. Jake unzipped her dress down to her waist, then he moved back and sat on a chair. Sheryl wiggled out of the dress and turned around, then unclasped her bra, revealing perfect breasts. Despite his best intentions, Jake found his heart beating faster.

Do you believe in true love?

With her eyes focused on his, she hooked her thumbs in the waistband of her panties and dropped them.

Jake lowered his gaze to the strip of pubic hair between her legs. Feeling a twitch in his own loins, he stood. "Turn around."

Sheryl turned.

"Put your hands against the wall and spread your legs."

Sheryl obeyed him.

Crouching on the floor, he scrutinized the soles of her feet, then the spaces between her toes. He slid his hand over her ankles, up her calves, and around her thighs. Turning her around, he saw tears in her eyes. He inspected her breasts and felt nothing unusual in them, then opened her mouth and looked inside. Satisfied, he bowed her head and examined her scalp. As far as he could tell, she was human. But Kira had seemed that way when he had fucked her. Then her teeth had come out.

"Get dressed," he said.

Holding his gaze, Sheryl pulled the garments on. "Are you hungry?"

"Starving."

"So am I. Let me see what you have in the house, and I'll fix us something. Why don't you put some ice on your face? It looks painful."

Jake opened the freezer and took out an ice pack.

Sheryl crouched beside him and searched the contents of the freezer.

Sheryl cooked steaks with a side dish of fried potato. They ate in the kitchen. Jake had never imagined he would have the opportunity to enjoy her cooking again.

"It's delicious," he said.

"Maria will be upset when she finds out."

"Yes."

"Where's she staying?"

He looked at her. If Tower had been able to track his cell phone, he could do the same with Maria. But he didn't want to take any chances. "Somewhere safe."

"You don't trust me."

"I can't trust you. Nothing will change that."

"You must care about her."

"I never thought I could care about anyone again after you—I mean, after Sheryl—was murdered."

"Do you love her?"

He offered a noncommittal smile. "Maria's been through a lot, just like I have. But I live a dangerous life. Even though she's proven herself more than capable of handling herself—she may be tougher than me—I don't know if it's fair for me to keep exposing her to these situations. There's someone else now, too. A little girl."

"She's a mother?"

"She fostered a girl she got close to during a case. The girl's parents were killed."

"I always wanted us to have a baby."

Stop talking like you really are Sheryl. "I know."

Sheryl rose and took a bottle of red wine from the top of the refrigerator and selected a glass from the cupboard. "Do you want some?"

"I don't drink anymore."

"What about your other bad habits?"

"Clean and sober."

"Do you mind if I have a glass?"

Each of Tower's Biogens had a built-in Achilles' heel or control factor. Kira's had been alcohol.

"Go ahead," Jake said.

Sheryl filled the glass, sat back down, and sipped the wine. Her flesh did not percolate. She sighed. "That's good. Why do you have wine in the house if you stopped drinking?"

"It must have been Joyce's."

"How do you like being a private eye?"

"I've had my share of successes and failures, but it's a way to help people."

She sipped her wine. "That's why you became a cop in the first place."

"But now I'm my own boss, and I can choose which cases I take."

"Will you tell me how you got those scars on your face and what happened to your hand?"

He considered the question. Tower had expressed an interest in learning what Jake had discovered about the supernatural. "No."

"You know my secrets."

"Maybe."

"And there's your left eye. I didn't notice it at first."

"The rest of my face must have distracted you."

"What's on the agenda for tomorrow?"

Jake gave her a look that said, *Don't ask*. "It's been a long day. Why don't we go to bed? My body could use the rest."

"I should do these dishes first."

"I've got them."

"You have changed."

"There's a child's bedroom upstairs. It used to be Martin's, and now it's Maria's foster daughter's. You can sleep in there. The green toothbrush in the bathroom is mine."

Sheryl stood. "Jake?"

"Yeah?"

"I could really use a hug."

He stared at her. "I'm sorry, but I think that would be a bad idea."

"You don't trust yourself?"

He shook his head.

"Good night."

He watched her leave. "Good night."

Jake lay in his bed in the basement, listening to traffic sounds outside, his glass eye resting in a glass of cleaning solution. He had planned to make a trip as soon as he got home from the Tower, but the sudden appearance of Sheryl's duplicate had thrown his plan off course.

That was Tower's intention, he thought.

Now it was too late. He would have to leave tomorrow instead, which meant he would miss his twenty-four-hour deadline.

Damn it all.

The basement door squeaked open, and a shaft of light fell over the steps. Sheryl descended the stairs, silhouetted and wearing a robe. She crossed the basement to where he lay and untied the sash of her robe, which she dropped on the floor.

Jake discerned her body through the nighty she had found. His pulse quickened. He glanced at the glass eye on the bedside table. He realized how ridiculous it was, but he didn't want her to see his socket.

"I'm afraid. I need you to hold me." Sheryl climbed into bed and crawled into the crook of his arm.

"No other touching," he said.

"Okay. Just hold me."

Sliding his left arm around her shoulders, he held her with his stump, but he reached beneath his pillow with his hand and closed his fingers around the grip of his Ruger.

EIGHTEEN

Jake awoke with sunlight on his face. He had slept on his back all night, with his hand on the Ruger. Sheryl had gone upstairs. Rising, he fished his glass eye from its cup of cleaning fluid and pushed it into his socket. He grabbed clothes from his dresser, then retrieved the Ruger and climbed the stairs. Not for a moment did he think Sheryl had left the house. Where would she go? She had been sent here.

The door at the top of the stairs was open, and he smelled bacon cooking before he entered the kitchen. Sheryl stood before the stove just as Maria had two days earlier. She wore her dress again.

In another life, it would have been perfectly normal for him to slide his hands around her waist and kiss her cheek. He couldn't help but remember when she had dissolved in his hands back at their apartment, just after Marc Gorman had murdered her. He reminded himself the real Sheryl had ascended to the Realm of Light, where she had taken up with Abel.

"Good morning," Sheryl said in a fragile-sounding voice.

"Good morning," Jake said.

They faced each other, an awkward silence hanging between them.

"Sit down. Breakfast is almost ready." Sheryl turned back to the stove.

Jake sat at the table, and Sheryl poured him a cup of black coffee and set it before him.

"Thanks," he said.

Small talk with my dead wife, he thought. *But she isn't my wife.*

Jake sipped the coffee and Sheryl served eggs Benedict. He stared at his favorite dish.

"It feels like just yesterday that we ate together," she said.

Not for me. But he did remember their last meal together, breakfast the day his life fell apart. They had discussed Sheryl's desire to have a child. Ninety minutes later, he and Edgar stared at the corpse of Shannon Reynolds, one of the Cipher's victims. Before the day had ended, Jake shot dead two thugs attempting to rob a tavern, suffered a drug overdose, and resigned from the force. And then Sheryl told him to move out of their apartment. For Sheryl's clone, a day had passed since then while his life had been a living hell for almost two years.

Jake sampled the eggs. Feeling her gaze, he met it.

"How do you like them?" she said.

"They're great, just like always." He regretted the words as soon as he spoke them.

"I'm glad."

Jake ate so he wouldn't have to speak.

Sheryl studied him. "What are we going to do?"

Jake took a moment to gather his thoughts. He didn't intend to tell her any more than necessary. "You'll find out when we do it."

He could tell she was fighting her emotions.

"Why are you treating me this way? Don't you understand how horrible my situation is?"

His body stiffened. "Your situation isn't my fault."

"You won't even say my name."

"It isn't your name. My wife is dead."

"I'm Sheryl Helman. I know where I grew up and how we met, and I remember our wedding and our honeymoon and our anniversaries. That's me. I did those things. Your . . . activities . . . were a betrayal that hurt like a fresh wound. But I decided to take you back. Now I learn I'm a duplicate of a woman who was murdered, our marriage is over, and you're with someone else. Fine, I'll cope with that. How am I supposed to survive in this world? I have no place to live. I can't get a job." She held up one hand. "I have Sheryl Helman's fingerprints because *I am Sheryl Helman*."

Goddamn her for making me care. "We don't know anything yet. Tower and Kira had a reason for bringing you back. When we know their plan, we'll deal with your future. One thing at a time."

The front door opened, and Jake and Sheryl traded alarmed looks.

Someone crossed the living room. Jake recognized Maria's footsteps. Exhaling, he rose from the table, and Sheryl's gaze darted to the basement door.

Maria entered the kitchen and froze, her look of fatigue collapsing like a demolished building. She registered Sheryl, and Jake saw a delayed reaction before recognition set in. Jake knew how fast that resignation could give way to anger. Maria turned to Jake. "Why can I see her?"

Jake had told Maria that Sheryl's spirit had revealed to him the secret by which Edgar could be restored to human form.

"She isn't an angel," Jake said.

Maria looked at Sheryl again. "Then what is she?"

"She's a Biogen."

Maria had encountered other Biogens on Pavot Island. Revulsion spread over her features. "Then why is she sitting at my table?"

Sheryl stared at her plate.

"I hoped to keep this from you," Jake said.

"Then you shouldn't have brought it into my home."

"I didn't think you'd come back here yet."

"Obviously. How convenient that you told me to

stay away. What did I interrupt?"

"It isn't like that."

"What's it like, then?"

"I'm trying to protect you by keeping you out of this."

Maria glanced at Sheryl and grunted. Then she turned and walked out of the kitchen.

"Stay here," Jake said to Sheryl.

Jake made it to the banister of the stairway just as Maria reached the top of the stairs and moved out of sight. He followed her into Martin's bedroom, where she opened dresser drawers and removed Shana's clothes.

"We're leaving now," he said. "This should all be over in another day. You don't need to take so many clothes."

"What happened to your face this time?" Maria said in a forced casual tone.

"Old Nick is back in a younger body. Kira Thorn is back, too."

Maria stopped and faced him. "I'm not sure who it says more about, you or me, that I don't even question that statement."

"My double in that security footage was a Biogen. They sent him to kill Carrie and take Afterlife from her. They sent him to kill me, too."

Emotion stirred within her eyes. "And?"

"No one will find his body."

"That's a great way of helping yourself."

"What am I supposed to do, go to Mauceri or

Geoghegan and tell them this story? Tower's a Biogen, and they're painting him as his own son. They've got billions of dollars to cover up what they're doing. I can't afford to get stuck in the system. None of us can. I have to act quickly and decisively so you don't end up like Sheryl. Shana isn't safe, either."

"You won't have to worry about Shana. An aunt has claimed custody of her."

Jake was getting used to having Shana around. "I'm sorry. Isn't there any way—?"

"I can fight it? Why should I when she's obviously safer elsewhere?" Maria returned to packing Shana's clothes.

"I'm sorry if I made her staying here worse."

"Don't be. It isn't your fault; it's mine. I should have known better."

"Meaning it's my fault . . ."

"Meaning I made the decision to have a relationship with you."

"I had something to do with that decision."

"What happened on the airplane?"

"Depending on who you believe, we were saved by divine intervention or UFOs."

"Who was the terrorist? I know you know."

"He was another Biogen. Tower was willing to blow up the plane to get rid of me."

Maria threw some books, a game, and a stuffed animal into the suitcase. "You can never have a normal life, and neither can I as long as I'm with you." She zipped the suitcase.

"Do you want to break up?"

"I don't know what I want. Scratch that. I do know what I want. I just don't think I can have it." She swallowed. "Did you fuck her?"

Jake frowned, which caused his face to hurt. "*No.*"

"You had a hard time letting go of her before. Now she's back. Why should you settle for me?"

"In the first place, that isn't my wife downstairs. In the second, she isn't even human. Tower and Kira sent her to me to . . . I don't know what. Spy on me. Kill me. Throw me off my game."

"You think she could kill you, and yet you brought her home."

"I didn't bring her here. She just showed up, like the duplicate of me they sent to kill me."

"When did she show up?"

"Yesterday around dinnertime."

"So she stayed here?"

"Yes." He didn't like the direction Maria was heading.

"Where did she sleep?"

"I didn't touch her."

"Where?"

"In the basement. I had to keep my eye on her. I had my hand on my gun the whole time."

"I'd slap the shit out of you, but I don't think you

could take it in your condition."

Jake maintained a reasonable tone. "Listen to me. I don't have any feelings for that thing downstairs. *Nothing* is going to happen between us."

"Says the man who had an orgy with a coven of witches."

"You're never going to forget that, are you? You're going to hold it against me forever."

"I think I've been pretty damned understanding."

Jake cupped his hand around her arm. "I don't know what their scheme is with her. She says she doesn't know anything."

"And you believe her?"

"I don't know what to believe. Tower said these Biogens retain the personalities and memories of the people they duplicate. According to her, only a day's passed since Gorman killed her."

"So she believes she's the real Sheryl?"

"Yes."

Maria snorted. "And you think you don't have any feelings for her?"

"I think I can use her to turn the tables on them."

"You poor, stupid son of a bitch." Maria took the suitcase off the bed.

"When does Shana leave?"

"I'm on my way to pick her up. I'm taking her to the agency, then I'm seeing her off at JFK."

"What's the flight info?"

"American, departing at 10:00 a.m. Why?"

"I'd like to say good-bye."

"Looking like this? Don't bother. You'll just scare the hell out of her."

"Are you going back to work after that?"

"I don't have any choice if I want to keep my job."

"I think you and your mother should stay at Reinhardt's place tonight, not at your mother's."

"Anything else?"

"Leave your phone at work. Tower can track it with one of his satellites."

"You know what's funny? You're staying in my place, and me and my mother have to shack up with Bernie." Maria carried the suitcase out of the bedroom, leaving Jake alone.

NINETEEN

Aldous Severn awoke at dawn and prayed for one hour. When he finished and rose, his aching knees snapped. His fifty-eight-year-old body did not suit his spiritual will. He fixed himself a light breakfast of toast and eggs, which he ate alone in the kitchen.

He kept his apartment free of modern conveniences such as television and radio, so he didn't know what calamities might have rocked the world while he preached the word of God on the street all day. He listened to the sounds outside his apartment: traffic, chatter, brakes squealing. Everything seemed as normal as it could be in the wake of Hurricane Daria and the miracle of flight 3350.

After breakfast Severn washed his dishes, then flagellated himself with a cat-o'-nine-tails until blood trickled from his shoulder blades. He had bought the tool as a sex toy during his days as a heroin addict and dealer; since then, he had thrown away the rest of his leather.

In the shower, he screamed as hot water stung his fresh self-inflicted wounds. It was all part of his daily routine.

Dressed in gi karate pants and slippers, he walked shirtless into the living room, which also served as his painting studio. Scores of canvases on wooden frames littered the room, making it seem smaller. Each painting bore an identical image: a self-portrait in varying shades of gray.

Standing before the easel in the center of the room, Severn scratched the gray whiskers on his chin and stared at his work in progress: another self-portrait. Beyond the easel, his reflection in an upright mirror on a stand gazed at him. He studied his reflection, then the painting. After picking up a long brush, he set to work on the crow's-feet beneath the eyes of his painted self. The shadows around the eyes needed to be darker, always darker, and by the time they matched those of his reflection, the self-portrait depicted a man driven wild by paranoia.

"I am damned!" He hurled the brush across the room.

Severn regarded his self-portraits as measurement of his penance and redemption. So far, they left a lot to be desired. He would allow his most recent effort to dry, then store it with the others.

He went into the bedroom and changed into his preacher's outfit: black slacks and a black tunic with a white clerical collar. Maybe another long day of preaching to disinterested souls would save his soul.

Two years earlier, Severn had been known as Professor Severn, aka the Needle Man. He had peddled dope to support his own habit and worked as a tattoo artist in this very apartment.

Then Knapsack Johnny had come to him with an unusual proposition: he wanted Severn to tattoo faces onto his chest. Severn enjoyed body art even though he had no tattoos of his own, and he liked the concept of a collage of faces. Once or twice a week for several months, Knapsack Johnny brought photos of the subjects he wanted embroidered into his flesh. Each face exhibited terror. Even in his drug-induced haze, Severn had recognized something fiendish about his client, but he was fascinated by the challenge of reproducing fear in those faces and went along with the project.

Knapsack Johnny stopped coming, and Severn discovered the man he had been inking was Marc Gorman, the Cipher. A victim or a vigilante had cut the serial killer's throat and ended his reign of terror. The media made much of the tattoos covering Gorman's torso: the terrified countenances of his victims. Investigators speculated Gorman had photographed the men and women just moments before slaying them.

Severn realized he had been a willing accomplice to Gorman's crimes and closed down his guerrilla tattoo business the next day. In a fit of depression, he overdosed and almost died. He stopped dealing and using one month later and found God a month after that. It wasn't until Hurricane Daria ravaged Manhattan that he took to preaching, which consisted of bellowing at passersby on the sidewalk. God had punished the city for his sins and the sins of others, and he would make his fellow citizens see the light. Yesterday's miraculous salvation of flight 3350 had been a sign from God that his efforts were paying off.

Then why haven't I been forgiven?

He crossed the living room and opened the door.

A man stood in front of it. "Hello, Professor," Marc Gorman said in his Knapsack Johnny guise.

TWENTY

Jake drove to JFK and parked in one of the massive lots. Sunlight caused the windshield to gleam. He had put on his harness before leaving the house.

"Shall I wait here?" Sheryl said.

"No." He switched off the engine. "You're coming with me."

"I don't think your girlfriend will like that. I can wait here. I'm not going to run away."

"You're coming with me," he repeated.

He got out and so did she, and he locked the doors. A breeze blew in his face, and the sound of planes landing and taking off carried across the lot. They boarded a crowded shuttle.

"Did you sleep all right?" Sheryl said.

I slept with one eye open, Jake thought. "About the same as usual."

She nodded, a hurt look in her eyes.

They got off at the American Airlines terminal and

went inside. The airport seemed as busy as Times Square to Jake. For five minutes, he searched for Maria and Shana.

"There she is," Sheryl said.

Jake followed Sheryl's sight line to where Maria and Shana stood with a tall, slender black woman dressed in a skirt, matching blazer, and blouse. It made him uncomfortable that Sheryl had spotted Maria with such ease. A wife's intuition or something more diabolical?

"Come on." He made his way through the bustling commuters with Sheryl at his side.

Maria spotted them and said something to Shana's aunt, who turned in their direction and blanched.

Jake approached the woman and Maria gestured to him. "This is Jake Helman. Jake, this is Shana's aunt, Callie Robbins."

"Hi," Jake said.

Callie couldn't take her eyes off Jake's face, but she extended one hand anyway. "How do you do?"

Polite, Jake thought as he shook her hand. "I promise you I've seen better days."

Callie turned to Sheryl.

"This is my late wife's sister," Jake said.

Sheryl held out one hand. "Lisa DeCosta."

Maria glared at Jake.

Callie shook Sheryl's hand and said hello.

"I'm sorry about *your* sister," Jake said to the woman.

"Thank you."

Jake got down on one knee before Shana and stroked the tip of her nose. "Hey, Purple People Eater, I hear you're going on a trip."

"What happened to your face?" Shana said.

"Private eye business. I can't go into detail, client confidentiality and all."

Shana shook her head. "You should get a job you're better at."

"Yeah. Anyway, I'm sorry to see you go. I was looking forward to taking you out on stakeouts with me. But Maria tells me you're going to a beautiful home and your aunt is very nice. You've been bouncing around like a basketball, but now you'll be with family, and you can stay put. You'll have a great time in Colorado."

"Will you and Maria visit me?"

Jake stood and glanced at Maria, who swallowed. Then he turned back to Shana. "I promise at least one of us will get out there." He slipped his hand into his pocket and removed two business cards. "One is for you, and the other is for your aunt. If either of you ever gets into trouble, call me or send me a message and I'll come running. Do you understand?"

She nodded.

"And if you ever just want to talk to someone handsome, you have my number now."

She smiled.

"I have something else for you." He removed a

bronze amulet from his pocket and handed it to her. "Remember our talk about monsters?"

Holding the amulet, Shana nodded again.

"This is called an Anting-Anting. It's from a country called the Philippines, and it's hundreds of years old, so be careful with it."

"Is it worth money?"

"It's worth far more than money. This will keep you safe. If you ever run into one of those supernatural monsters, this will protect you. It will even keep most nightmares away."

"Is it real?"

"Swear to God and hope to die. It's worked for me, and I want you to have it." Taking the amulet from her, he hung it around her neck. "You'll have to remove it when you go through security. But after that you can wear it whenever you want, as long as your aunt says it's okay."

Shana threw her arms around Jake and held on to him. It was the first time they had shown each other such affection, and he imagined it would be the last. Despite everything she had been through, she smelled fresh, unspoiled.

Innocent, he decided. Sighing, he let go of her. "You be good out there, you hear? Because your aunt can always call me, too. Study hard in school. Be friends with people you can trust, and stay away from troublemakers. If anyone teases you, turn the other cheek."

Leaning closer, he whispered, "But never let a bully push you around."

"Well, we'd better be going now," Callie said, facing Maria. "Thank you so much for everything. You're welcome in our home anytime."

"Thank you," Maria said.

Shana moved to her and hugged her hips. Maria bent down and put her arms around the girl, squeezing her.

Jake leaned close to Callie. "I know that amulet's ugly, but it really is an authentic artifact, and I think it will stop her nightmares. Please let her keep it."

"I will," Callie said.

Maria's eyes glistened. "Oh, I'm going to miss you so much. Thank you for keeping me company. I know you're going to love it out there. You're going to make new friends and have fun."

Tears streamed down Shana's cheeks. "I'm going to miss you, too."

Jake saw Maria wrestling to hold back her own tears.

"No crying, you're a big girl. There's nothing to be sad about. We'll see each other again." Maria held Shana's head to her bosom, then kissed her cheek. "I love you."

"I love you, too," Shana said.

"Listen to Aunt Callie, okay?" Maria straightened.

Rubbing the tears from her eyes, Shana nodded.

"Thank you again," Callie said. "Good-bye."

"Good-bye," Maria said.

Callie held her hand out to Shana. "Let's go home."

They moved toward the security line and Shana glanced over her shoulder. Maria waved. Then they melted into the crowd.

Maria turned to Jake. "That was nice of you. You've always got a surprise up your sleeve. Did you have to bring her with you?"

"Yes," Jake said.

"I'm sorry," Sheryl said. "I didn't want . . ."

Disgust filled Maria's face. "Don't talk to me. I really can't deal with that."

Sheryl lowered her eyes.

"Come here." Jake pulled Maria aside and turned her back to Sheryl so he could still see her. "I understand you're feeling emotional right now . . ."

Maria shrugged his hand away. "Don't do that." She raised one finger. "Don't tell me what I'm feeling."

Jake kept his voice low and reasonable. "Okay, I won't. I'm sorry. And I'm sorry Shana left. But I can't let Sheryl out of my sight."

"I see you've started calling her by her name."

"I have to call her something."

"What are you going to do now?"

"I'm taking the fight to Tower. I bought myself a grace period by telling him I'd consider an offer he made me. We're all safe until about five o'clock."

"And then?"

"Watch your back. I mean it."

"Do you need my help?"

He shook his head. "I told you, you're out of this."

"But I have to worry about them coming after me?"

"Yes."

"Because of our relationship?"

"Unfortunately."

"Then it seems to me I'd be safer with you."

"I won't be in the city until tonight. Do you want to call in sick?"

"That isn't possible."

"Then I'll let you know when I'm back. If you don't hear from me by tomorrow, you probably won't."

"What do I do then?"

"I'll take every step I can to make sure you're safe."

"But I'll be on my own in more ways than one?"

"That's the long and short of it."

"I really hope you know what you're doing."

"Trust me."

Maria gave him a long, hard look, then strode over to Sheryl. "If anything happens to him, I'll find you and make you wish you'd stayed dead."

Sheryl remained passive, and Maria disappeared into the tide of commuters.

"I told you I should have stayed in the car," Sheryl said when Jake joined her. She had always been fond of saying I told you so.

"Don't start."

"She reminds me of you," she said.

"Let's get one thing straight: this day will be much more tolerable if you don't mention Maria again."

They headed for the doors.

"What did you give the little girl?"

"You don't need to know."

With his hook resting on the steering wheel, Jake drove to a storage facility in Long Island City. Twenty-one months ago, on the same night the Cipher had murdered Sheryl, Cain had tortured Jake in an abandoned factory just a block away until Jake agreed to help him acquire Nicholas Tower's soul. Jake hoped the real Tower was suffering now. He parked the Plymouth and led Sheryl to the entrance.

"What are we doing here?"

"Stop asking questions," he said.

He entered a code into a security keypad: Sheryl's name broken down into numerical digits. The door opened, and he showed his ID to a security guard sitting behind a desk. The man checked a roster and then nodded.

Jake grabbed a dolly and led Sheryl to the elevator. On the third floor they prowled the steel doors protecting individual storage units until he found the one he desired. He entered another code into a keypad next to the door, this time Sheryl's maiden name, DeCosta. The lock on the wide door clicked, and he opened it.

Inside the windowless storage unit he switched on overhead fluorescents, which hummed to life. Black canvas bags of different sizes occupied the metal shelves. Jake picked up one and loaded it onto the dolly. When he turned around, Sheryl held a sword in both hands. He had used the blade to disable the demon Kalfu on Pavot Island and to decapitate Lilith.

"Put that back," he said.

Sheryl slid the sword into its scabbard and returned it to the shelf. "I didn't know you had any interest in swords."

"That counts as a question." Jake grabbed a military footlocker with a padlock on it and set it on the dolly. Surveying the storage unit, he grabbed a plastic tote and a cardboard box wrapped with packing tape and set them beside the other items. "We're done here."

They stepped outside the unit, and he turned off the light and closed the door, which locked.

"How long have you had this storage unit?" Sheryl said as he pushed the dolly back to the elevator.

"What difference does it make?"

"I just want to know if it was another secret you kept from me while we were married."

Jake palmed the elevator call button. He had leased the storage unit after he had defeated Tower and Kira. At first he had needed it to store his and Sheryl's belongings when he gave up their apartment, but over the next several months he had found other uses for it. He didn't tell Sheryl's duplicate that, though.

Back outside, with the dolly behind the Plymouth, he loaded certain items into the trunk and others into the backseat. Then he pushed the dolly out of the way. "Let's go."

Sheryl circled the car to the passenger side. "Where to?"

"You'll see when we get there."

TWENTY-ONE

When Maria reported to Detective Bureau Manhattan, she saw Mauceri speaking to David Totty, a senior detective with silver hair. Mauceri nodded to her and Totty turned around, so she knew she would be hitting the pavement soon. The prospect of something taking her mind off Shana and Jake pleased her.

Mauceri led Totty over to her. "Everything okay?" Mauceri said.

"I'm good," Maria said.

"Totty caught a DOA downtown, something ugly. You're his wingman today."

Totty had been a floater since his partner had taken a leave of absence after Daria. Maria liked his easygoing demeanor.

"Let me clock in and I'm ready to roll," Maria said.

Mauceri returned to his office.

"Just grab me at my desk when you're ready," Totty said.

"I'll be right over," Maria said. She unlocked the top drawer of her desk and took out her Glock.

Totty jingled the keys as he and Maria entered the bureau's parking lot. "You mind if I drive?"

"I prefer it," Maria said.

They got into the unmarked car, and Totty started the engine. "Do you care which way we go?"

"Whatever you want."

Totty pulled into the street, and dust settled onto the windshield. Maria glimpsed the top of the Tower rising from the skyline ahead. Debris from Daria littered the sidewalks.

"Traffic still hasn't returned to normal," Totty said.

"Maybe it never will."

"Nah, New York always bounces back." He turned onto Park Avenue South, which became Union Square East.

Maria ran through a checklist of questions she could ask to pass the time. "You married?"

"Eighteen years, same number I've been on the job."

"Retiring when you reach twenty?"

Totty chuckled. "What, and sit home with my wife all day? I'm going to stay in the game until the bosses won't have me. Besides, I've got two kids to put through college. They'll have to pry my shield from my cold, dead fingers. How about you? You plan to get hitched anytime soon?"

By now everyone in the squad knew she was seeing

Jake. "Not likely."

"It's not my place to say but . . . never mind."

"I like my job. I don't need to have kids to know I'm a woman."

"Fair enough."

Hundreds of people crowded Union Square, waiting for food rations. Police and armed National Guards stood at attention, waiting. Children with dirty legs ran on the asphalt surrounding the park while grim-faced adults chatted in the line.

"Welcome to the third world," he said.

"They've got to do a better job feeding these people," Maria said.

"Or move them somewhere distribution is easier."

They drove down Broadway, where scaffolding had been erected before buildings on either side, and workers replaced windows. On Eighth Street, water gushed out of a fire hydrant, and scores of people fought to fill jugs, thermoses, and other containers. Vehicles with blown-out windows occupied the parking spaces along the curbs.

A double-parked police cruiser came into view on St. Mark's Place, and Totty parked behind it. Maria and Totty got out and crossed the sidewalk. A PO stood at the top of a half flight of stone steps.

"Maria Vasquez and David Totty," she said.

The police officer recorded their names on a clipboard.

"Down here?" Maria said.

"Yes, ma'am," the fresh-faced PO said.

The rookie made Maria feel old. She descended the steps to a bloodred door with a window hatch set in it. "This can't be good."

They pulled on latex gloves and shoe covers.

Inside the apartment, the first officer stood near the door.

"You're a cadet, aren't you?" Maria said.

"Yes, ma'am," the young man said. "They pressed us all into service."

"During our time together, feel free to call me Detective."

"Yes, Detective."

Jenkins, a tall black man with a shaved head, and his Detective Area Task Force partner walked over. They wore short-sleeved shirts with ties but no jackets. "This isn't just a homicide, young blood; it's a special homicide. That's why they sent Special Homicide Task Force to pick up our slack."

"Feeling squeezed?" Maria said. She and Jenkins had known each other as uniforms before either of them had been promoted to detective.

"I'm just wondering what you and Totty can do with this case that we can't. Oh, this is my partner, Steve somebody."

"Steve Papper."

Jenkins snickered. "I just love to hear him say that."

Totty cocked his head. "Do you guys want to show us the crime scene and give us the particulars, or do you want to keep yacking?"

"I love yacking," Jenkins said.

Papper held up his notepad. "The vic is Aldous Severn, age fifty-eight. He was identified by the building super. According to him, Severn was a street preacher who used to be a guerrilla inker."

"That means he operated an illegal tattoo parlor out of this apartment," Jenkins said.

"I know what it means," Maria said. "I smell paint."

Papper led them into the next room. Scores of paintings leaned against the walls. Another rested on a wooden easel. "This is a self-portrait."

Maria studied the maniacal face in the oil painting. "He didn't think much of himself."

"According to the landlord, Severn was a recovering doper and used to be a dealer."

"His aliases were the Professor and the Needle Man," Jenkins said.

Totty moved along one wall, studying the paintings below him. "These are *all* self-portraits."

"You see that?" Jenkins said to Papper. "They *are* good. Real good."

Maria suppressed a smile. "Is there a body, or is that another mystery we're supposed to solve?"

Jenkins pointed to the doorway. "You can't miss him."

Maria moved into the next room and stopped.

Totty followed her. "Jesus H."

Aldous Severn lay in a barber's chair with its back lowered. His nose had been ruptured, and a tattoo needle attached to a tube connected to an inking machine protruded from one eye socket. Blood and tissue covered his face, neck, and torso. Flies buzzed around the gore.

"We suspect foul play," Jenkins said behind them.

Maria circled the chair. Severn appeared as tortured in death as he had in his self-portraits. "Got an estimate on the time of death?"

"Crime Scene Unit hasn't arrived yet," Papper said.

"As much as I enjoy this witty repartee, you fellows are free to go," Totty said. "We can hold down the fort until CSU gets here."

"Thanks but we'd like to stay," Jenkins said. "Maybe we can pick up some pointers watching some real detectives work."

Maria entered the kitchen. Dishes overflowed in the sink, trash overflowed in the wastebasket, and empty cans overflowed in the recycling bin. Spaghetti sauce caked on the ancient-looking oven had petrified.

Stained linoleum tiles buckled as she walked into the musty bedroom, where a filthy depression in the bed suggested the sheets had not been changed in months—possibly years. Framed paintings filled the room—they rested against the walls, on top of the bureau and armoire, and spilled out of the closet and from beneath the bed. "David, get in here."

Totty joined her. "He needed a bigger boat."

"Let's start going through these paintings."

"What do you hope to find, a butterfly?"

Maria flipped through canvases: one painting of a giant eyeball after another. "I have a feeling . . ."

"She has a feeling," Jenkins said to Papper in the kitchen. "Can we help you in there?"

"There isn't room for anyone else," Maria said. She went through a series of paintings of what appeared to be a human brain.

"Guy was seriously into toes," Totty said, looking through another series.

Maria opened the closet door wider and rifled through the paintings there: blood drops.

"I've got a dead cat on a sidewalk now . . ."

"I don't think he had time to paint a portrait of his killer," Jenkins said.

Maria got down on the dusty floor. "You never know." She pulled six canvases out from under the bed and turned them around for a better look. "David."

"They look familiar," Totty said.

Maria stared at a collage of terrified human faces. One belonged to Sheryl Helman. "You saw them in the newspapers almost two years ago. These were the victims of the Cipher."

"Holy . . ."

Jenkins and Papper crowded the doorway.

"Say what?" Jenkins said.

"We never found out who tattooed their faces on Marc Gorman's chest," Maria said.

"I remember now," Totty said. "L.T. had the whole squad checking out ink parlors. But all this painting says is that Severn copied one of the photos that made the papers."

Maria set the painting aside, revealing an almost identical one beneath it. She set that one aside, revealing another almost identical painting. Each canvas under the bed told the same story. "He was as obsessed with those victims as he was with his other subjects."

"That was your case, wasn't it?" Totty said.

"Gorman, yeah. My first homicide. I never put it down." *But I know who did him.*

"Congratulations. At least you've solved one mystery."

TWENTY-TWO

As the George Washington Bridge receded in the rear-view mirror, Jake squinted in the sunlight. "Do me a favor and put my sunglasses on me."

Sheryl took his shades from the visor.

"Careful with my nose," he said.

With a pained expression on her face, she eased the sunglasses into position. "How's that?"

"Good, thanks."

She settled into her seat and lowered her visor. "Are you going to tell me where we're going now?"

"No, but I will tell you we'll be on the road for four and a half hours if we don't stop for lunch."

Sheryl switched on the radio. "I'm already hungry."

"We'll stop in an hour. I need coffee anyway. It's my sole remaining addiction." *Except maybe for Black Magic.*

"I'm impressed. I knew you could stop drinking and . . . the other thing, but I thought it was beyond you to stop smoking."

The spirit of the real Sheryl had something to do with that. When Jake had freed the thirteen captured souls from Tower's Soul Chamber, Sheryl's had passed through his body, cleansing him.

"I have to start preparing for middle age," Jake said. "Nobody lives forever, and I'm likely to have a shorter life than most."

"Don't say that."

"Look at me: you know it's true."

"Stop being a private eye."

"It's more complicated than that. This thing with Tower and his monsters isn't the only problem I've gone up against. There are other dimensions out there—the Realm of Light and the Dark Realm."

"Heaven and hell."

"They know I know they exist. That knowledge has made me a marked man."

"I never thought I'd see the day you accepted the existence of God. When I think of the trouble I had getting you to agree to have our wedding in a church . . ."

"Don't make any assumptions about what I believe. I can't deny the beings I've encountered, but they all evolved from human beings. I'm more inclined to believe in a creator now, but I have yet to cross his path. Trouble has a way of finding me, and I don't need to go looking for it."

"Do you want me to do some of the driving?"

"No, I'm good. I usually drive with only one hand anyway."

"You're going to be tired by the time we get wherever we're going."

Jake knew she was right. "Maybe so but we'd be in a difficult situation if we got pulled over and you were driving. I don't have your license, and if you gave them your real name . . ."

"They'd learn I'm dead and think I was an imposter, which would only create more suspicion."

"You're catching on."

"I've been married to a cop for three years." She paused. "Sorry."

"I'm not a cop anymore. If I was, I could show a state trooper my shield, and he'd probably let us go without running a check on you."

A commercial came on the radio, and Sheryl switched the station.

"It's a volatile day on the stock market with the unexpected announcement that Nicholas Tower Jr. has assumed leadership of Tower International and its subsidiaries," a newscaster said.

"Leave it there," Jake said.

"Until today, no one knew there was an heir to the throne," the newsman said. "Tower International is the largest privately owned company in the world and is the parent company of DNAtomy, Genutrition, and other entities focused on the development of genetic engineering. Following Nicholas Tower's death almost two years ago, the US government broke up the corporation's monopoly on the genetic frontier, and the company diversified its interests, acquiring controlling shares in Reichard Shipping, White River Security, and several defense contractors. The announcement that Tower Jr. is now in the driver's seat has caused stocks in competing companies to plummet. He is expected to lay out his plans for the company's future in a press conference later today. I expect the question of the day will not be 'Where's Old Nick?' but 'Where has Young Nick been?'"

"That didn't take long." Sheryl switched to a soft rock station.

"I wish I could be a fly on the wall at that press conference," Jake said.

"We could turn back," Sheryl said.

"No, the busier Tower and Kira are, the less time they have to worry about me. The time to strike is now."

The song on the radio ended, and a new one came on, causing Jake's heart to clench: Van Morrison's "Have I Told You Lately That I Love You?" He and Sheryl had always considered it their song. Despite the Plymouth's speed, Jake let go of the steering wheel to change the station.

Sheryl covered the radio with one hand. "Leave it."

Jake returned his hand to the wheel.

Sitting at her desk in the Special Homicide Task Force

squad room, Maria conducted a search on Aldous Severn while Totty keyed in his preliminary report. Severn had graduated from New York University with a master's degree in fine arts and had held a string of teaching jobs for over two decades. Then he had been busted for heroin possession and later for dealing. He hadn't had a job of note for eight years.

Checking the time on her monitor, she took out her phone and called Bernie.

"Talk to me," Bernie said in a jovial tone.

"How's it going over there?"

"Your mother keeps beating me at pinochle. This is some vacation. If this keeps up, I'll have to come back to work just to make up for the dough I've lost."

"How is she?"

"She's good. But she won't stop cleaning my bathroom. It's making me self-conscious. I was planning to cook dinner, but she insisted on doing it. Looks like I'm getting some authentic Puerto Rican food."

"Did she make you go shopping?"

"Don't worry. I've got it covered."

"You weren't supposed to leave your apartment."

"She twisted my arm. What was I supposed to do, put her under house arrest? She's about as easy to manage as you are."

Across the room, Totty glanced up from his keyboard and did a double take.

Male detectives around the squad room looked up from their work and focused on the doorway behind Maria.

Maria turned in her seat, and her heart caught in her chest. A striking woman with long dark hair and perfect curves emphasized by a red dress stood in the doorway: Kira Thorn. Maria had interviewed the woman after Old Nick's death. Kira had provided an alibi for Jake regarding the execution of the Cipher, a murder Jake had confessed to Maria.

"Are you there?" Bernie said.

"I have to go. I'll see you later." Maria hung up.

Kira crossed the squad room, her gait exuding cool confidence. She didn't look like the spider-human hybrid Jake had described killing.

Maria stood, prepared to pull her Glock if necessary.

Kira stopped before her and smiled. "Detective Vasquez? I'm not sure if you remember me—"

"Of course I do, Ms. Thorn."

"It's Mrs. Tower now." Kira held out her left hand. "I married Nicholas Tower Jr. He's taking charge of the family business."

Good Lord. "Congratulations. I didn't know there was a Nicholas Tower Jr." *Keep this game going.* "You're supposed to be missing."

"That's why I'm here, to explain my absence."

Maria gestured to the chair beside her desk. "Please sit down."

"Could we do this somewhere more private?" Kira said. "Every man in this office is staring at me, and it's making me uncomfortable."

Then maybe you should conceal those curves instead of emphasizing them, Maria thought. But according to Jake, Kira had been engineered with enhanced pheromones designed to make her even more alluring.

"Certainly. Follow me." Maria led Kira across the room. "Would you like some coffee?"

"No, thank you."

Maria walked down a corridor and opened the door to an interview room. "After you."

As Kira passed her, Maria caught a whiff of her perfume, which she found subtle and yet somehow exciting.

"Which seat shall I take?" Kira said.

"Whichever one you like. You're not being interviewed about a crime, so it doesn't matter. We're not being recorded." But Maria had felt safer in the squad room, surrounded by her colleagues.

Kira sat with her back to the door, signaling to Maria she had nothing to fear, and Maria sat opposite her. She followed the curves of Kira's exposed cleavage through the opening of her dress. Swallowing, she looked back up, and the amusement in Kira's dark eyes made her feel guilty.

Science or magic? she wondered as she spread her hands apart. "So?"

"The last time we spoke, my employer, Nicholas

Tower Sr., had just died."

"I remember."

"That was the beginning of a turbulent period for our company. After I talked to you regarding our director of security, Jake Helman, I flew to Europe to oversee our operations in numerous countries there while Daryl Klemmer, the CEO of Tower International, handled matters on the home front. When the Department of Justice brought suit against us alleging we'd violated antitrust laws, I remained there."

Maria held the woman's gaze, fearing that to do otherwise would be a show of submission. "As I recall, there was also an investigation into illegal genetic engineering."

Kira stared straight into Maria's eyes. "Allegations that were proven unfounded."

You lying bitch. Maria reminded herself Kira was not human, just like Sheryl. "This explains where you were and why you were there, but it doesn't explain why you never got in touch with me when I made follow-up inquiries."

A faint smile formed on Kira's red lips. "Tower International never filed a missing person's report, and since I was raised in an orphanage financed by the company, I have no family that would have done so. I simply carried on with business as usual, albeit discreetly and on foreign soil."

"So no one could serve you with a subpoena?"

Kira raised one eyebrow. "International business can be complicated. In the meantime, Daryl ran the company here and complied with all edicts from the Department of Justice. We're compliant in every way, and there are no current investigations into our operations as far as I know."

Maria clasped her hands. "So it was safe for you to come home."

"I've never felt unsafe."

"When I contacted your company, I spoke to Mr. Klemmer. He denied any knowledge of your whereabouts. But that can't have been true if you were acting on the company's behalf in these other countries."

"Our European and continental US holdings are separate entities. I can't testify as to what Mr. Klemmer may or may not have known, and unfortunately, the dear man suffered a fatal heart attack last week, which is the reason my husband and I returned to Manhattan."

"And why exactly did you come to see me?"

"As a courtesy to you—to tie up any loose ends from our previous meeting."

"That's very kind of you."

"I don't want any outstanding business with the New York Police Department."

"Well, you're obviously not missing, and since there's no actual missing person's report, I don't think there's anything else to discuss. Thank you for coming in."

Kira rose. "My pleasure. It's nice to see the woman who gave Jake something to live for."

Maria felt a stab of fear, followed by a sharper pain of anger. She intercepted Kira at the door. "You don't get to come in here and threaten me."

"No one's threatening you, dear. Nicholas is holding his press conference right outside the Tower at four thirty. Why don't you stop by?"

Kira opened the door and walked out, and Maria clenched her fists.

TWENTY-THREE

Jake took an exit off I-287 North to look for someplace to eat. He wanted a truck stop, not fast food. Sheryl never ate fast food.

He spotted a family diner and parked in the lot. They got out and he popped the trunk. Rifling through the contents of a tote, he removed a small leather case. Sheryl watched him take out ten one-hundred-dollar bills from the case, which he returned to the tote before closing the trunk.

"You must be hungry," Sheryl said.

"We have to pay for everything in cash, so Tower can't trace us. I hope this will be enough. Until the insurance company pays me for my car, which is currently submerged in a parking garage, this is all the money I have left in the world."

"How do you afford rent on your office?" she said as they walked toward the entrance.

"I started my business with the money I got from my signing bonus from Tower and your insurance policy," Jake said. "Then I cut a deal with my landlord for reduced rent in exchange for building security. Now I don't pay anything but my office is useless." He opened the door for her.

"Free Manhattan office space? That landlord must be some friend."

Jake followed her into the diner. He didn't feel like discussing Laurel or how he had come by his rent deal. A sign said Seat Yourself, and they chose a booth away from the windows. Jake faced the door in case any surprises came his way.

A middle-aged woman wearing a sky-blue smock came over to their booth. "Hi, folks. Something to drink?"

"Coffee and keep it coming. I think we're ready to order."

"Shoot."

"I'll have the turkey burger deluxe, and she'll have the grilled chicken salad." Jake looked at Sheryl. "Right?"

"Right," Sheryl said. "Light Italian dressing on the side."

"Coming right up," the woman said. "You kids been married long?"

"Three years," Sheryl said.

"Newlyweds." The woman winked and walked away.

"Remember our honeymoon?" Sheryl said.

Jake nodded. "Good times. The best."

"Then what happened?"

Jake shrugged. "Life. Death. The job."

She stared at him with sadness in her eyes. "You should have quit before you didn't have any choice."

"I know. That just isn't in my DNA."

"None of this would have happened. The other me would still be alive, you two would still be together, and I wouldn't be sitting here. Neither one of us would have been in this predicament."

"That's true." But then the Dark Realm would have claimed the other twelve souls Marc Gorman had claimed for Old Nick, and, according to Abel, hell would have ruled heaven. Katrina's zonbies might still be walking the streets of Manhattan. Avademe and Lilith would still be alive. Ernesto Malvado would still be ruling Pavot Island. "We all make choices."

"Do you regret yours?"

"Sometimes."

"Are you going to tell me what happened to your hand, eye, and face?"

"It doesn't matter. That's in the past."

"Like me?"

She always read him like an e-book. "My past has a way of keeping up with me."

Sheryl rubbed her arms. "It's cold in here."

"I have some warmer clothes in the car. We can go get them if you want."

"That's okay." Her eyes turned shiny. "Do you plan

271

to kill me when this is over?"

Jake saw the server returning so he didn't answer.

"Here ya go." The woman set their coffees down. "You folks from the city?"

"How did you know?" Jake said.

"You don't look like small-town people is all."

Jake snorted. "I bet we don't."

"I'll be back with your food in a few minutes." The woman walked away.

Sheryl stared at Jake, waiting. She appeared to be on the verge of tears again.

"Look," he said, lowering his voice as he leaned forward. "I know you didn't ask for any of this. And I know that in your mind you're still my wife. But, honestly, even in that case, you'd be my estranged wife. You threw me out."

"You gave me good reason. I couldn't believe anything you said after all those lies."

Jake raised his hand. "I know. Let's not dig all that up again."

"I wanted to take you back . . ."

"For you, it was yesterday. For me, it was almost two years ago."

"Nice to know you waited."

"I didn't see anyone for more than a year."

"And then you jumped at the first slut who shook her ass."

"There were two women before Maria, not to mention a Biogen in woman's clothing. Is that what you want to know? She isn't a rebounder."

Sheryl sipped her coffee and set it down. "I don't want to hear about your sex life."

"Then why did you ask me? Jesus, it's like we're still married."

"We are."

"The real Sheryl got all trippy when she reached the Realm of Light and took up with an angel. She waited less time than I did."

"Well, good for her. But that wasn't me."

"Exactly my point."

"You don't even know what point you're making."

Jake exhaled. She had a way of driving him crazy.

"I want to know if you intend to kill me."

He leaned back. "I don't see how I can." Did she believe him? He didn't know if he believed himself. "Besides, I'm the one who has to worry about you killing me, not the other way around."

Sheryl's face grew animated, her voice louder. "You're being ridiculous. I don't kill people."

"Sheryl Helman didn't kill people. But just because you like Van Morrison and grilled chicken salad doesn't make you Sheryl Helman. You're her memories made flesh and blood. But what else are you? I wish I could X-ray you to see if Tower built some special features into your body."

Sheryl glared at him.

"Remember *The Manchurian Candidate*? All Laurence Harvey had to do was see the queen of diamonds to become a political assassin. I could say the wrong word right now, and it could trigger a program in your DNA. You could cut my throat with that knife."

Sheryl unfolded her napkin and picked up the steak knife. "This one?"

Jake nodded.

"Something tells me you wouldn't let that happen."

"I left my gun in the car."

"So? I'm still the same woman, but you're a different man, and I mean on the inside. You've improved yourself in a lot of ways, but you've also become a killer. I see it in your eye. If I tried to use this"—she brought the knife close to his face—"I'm the one who wouldn't walk out of here alive."

Jake drew in a breath. "If you were the same woman, we wouldn't be having this conversation."

She set the knife down. "Which brings us back to my question."

He could see she wasn't going to let him off the hook. "If we both come out of this alive, and I'm still relatively in one piece and you haven't turned into a giant praying mantis or something, I promise to help you. And I never go back on my promises."

"Help me how?"

"Obviously you can't stay in the country. But so what? You always said you gave up your dream of living in Paris when you married me. This could be your chance. I'll help you set up a new identity and relocate. As long as you're careful, you can start over and live a happy life without anyone connecting you to my dead wife."

Sheryl swallowed. "You said that all the money you have in the world is in your pocket. How am I supposed to start over with that?"

"Don't worry about money. There are people I can borrow money from if I have to." *Like Miriam Santiago.* "All you have to do in return is help me with what I have to do."

"Which could get me killed."

"That's right. But if you're sincere about your intentions, I don't see that you have any choice."

"If I do get killed, will you mourn me?"

Damn her. "I've already done that." But he knew that whatever else happened, the death of his duplicate wife would reopen deep wounds.

TWENTY-FOUR

Sitting in the backseat of the stretch limousine as it cruised through Brooklyn Heights, Kira scanned her iPad for news about Nicholas Tower Jr.'s assumption of control of Tower International. As expected, all outlets treated Nicholas like a man of mystery, and she grew tired of seeing "Where's Young Nick Been?" in the headlines. The media were so predictable, especially those on Tower International's payroll.

The press release she had issued earlier this morning had created the desired buzz: *Forbes* and the *Wall Street Journal* had bumped the president's reelection announcement far down the pages.

The limousine slowed to a stop.

"We've arrived, ma'am," the chauffeur said. "Shall I come up with you?"

"That won't be necessary."

"Are you sure? My orders from Mr. Hanaka . . ."

"You take your orders from me, not from Mr.

Hanaka." The nerve of this man, who had been provided by White River Security. He had no doubt seen combat in several Middle Eastern countries, but no one could protect her better than she could protect herself.

"Yes, ma'am."

"I don't know how long I'll be."

"I'll double-park for as long as I can, but if I'm not here when you come out it's because I'm circling the block."

What a nuisance. Parking in New York City was a pain in the ass, even in Brooklyn and even for the rich. She looked forward to bringing Mayor Connie Krycek under her control in the near future, which would simplify such matters. Mayors were good for taking care of parking.

The chauffeur opened the door for Kira, and she got out. The muscular man had the battle-hardened features of a security contractor but lacked the class of someone meant to be ornamentation. She wore a long raincoat and sunglasses in an attempt to minimize the attention she drew on the street, but his eyes bulged and she sensed the speed of his breathing increase. Without thanking him, she crossed the sidewalk to the entrance of a stout apartment building.

A man to her left whistled and she kept walking.

As Kira opened the outside door, she glimpsed the reflection of the chauffeur in the glass. He glared at the man who had whistled. Inside the foyer, she pressed a buzzer button.

Seconds later, the inside door buzzed and she entered

the lobby, her heels clacking on the polished floor. After palming the elevator call button, she waited a full minute before the car rumbled in the shaft. She was a long way from the high-speed elevators of the Tower.

On the fifth floor, she crossed the corridor to the appropriate door, which opened before she could ring the bell. Marc Gorman stared at her, lust and excitement in his eyes. Perhaps without meaning to, he licked his upper lip.

Kira strode into the apartment, and he closed the door behind her so hard the slam echoed in the hallway.

"What took you so long?" he said.

Always the same question.

Facing him, she gave him the patient look only a teacher could summon . . . or a mother. "You know I have a lot on my plate right now."

He clenched his fists and squeezed his eyes shut. "But I've missed you so much." He opened his eyes.

"Unclench those fists this instant, Marc Gorman."

He uncurled his fingers and they twitched at his sides.

"How do you like your new apartment?"

"I liked living in Manhattan better."

"Doesn't everyone? But it's safer for you here. There's less chance of someone recognizing you. You're famous now. And people think you're dead. We have to make sure they go on believing that."

He said nothing.

She moved closer to him. "I saw an interesting report

on the news today. Can you guess what that was?"

He lowered his gaze. She supposed he meant to look at the floor but wound up stuck at her crotch. "No," he said.

"*Look at me.*"

Gorman raised his eyes to hers.

"Tell me what I learned."

"I killed Professor Severn, the Needle Man."

"Why, for God's sake? He's nothing but a broken-down heroin addict. He didn't even know we brought you back."

"I went to see him as Knapsack Johnny. He recognized me so I had no choice. I did it for us."

"Why did you pay him a visit in the first place?"

He didn't answer.

"Unbutton your shirt."

Biting his lip like an insolent child, Gorman unbuttoned his short-sleeved shirt.

"Take it off."

He shrugged off the shirt, revealing gauze bandages taped all over his chest. She didn't need to count them to know there were thirteen.

"You fool."

He looked at her, and for the first instance in all the time she had known him, she saw anger lurking within his eyes.

"Don't you realize those are as good as a signed confession?"

"You brought me back without them. I wanted

them. I *earned* them."

Kira slapped him across the face. "You don't kill anyone unless I tell you to."

He turned back to her, one side of his face red. "It was self-defense."

She cocked her head. "Tell me about it."

"I made him do all thirteen faces. He kept sweating and his hand shook. I asked him what was wrong, and he told me he'd kicked but needed a fix. But I knew better. When he got to the last one—Helman's woman—he tried to stab me with the needle. I got the better of him and took it to his face and then his brain. But I made sure I cleaned up after myself before I left."

Kira caressed the side of his face she had struck. She loved him as she expected any child loved a stupid dog that had to be put down for acting on his own instincts. She reached into her coat pocket and took out a color printout. "I want you to kill this woman tonight."

Gorman studied the picture. "She's pretty. Who is she?"

"Helman's new woman. Her information is on the back."

He studied Maria Vasquez's features. "Am I stealing her soul?"

"We can't do that anymore. We don't have souls of our own."

"I liked the chanting."

"It's a waste of time."

"Can we do it now?"

Stepping back from him, she opened her raincoat and dropped it around her ankles. She wore stockings and a leather corset. "Do you want to fuck me?"

Gorman stepped forward. "More than anything . . ."

"Stop."

He obeyed her, and she wondered if he understood he had been programmed to do so.

"You can't have me," she said.

"Why not?"

She removed her gloves, which she wore to prevent getting fingerprints on the printout of Vasquez, and showed him her engagement ring and wedding band. "I'm a married woman now."

Gorman's features contorted into a mask of shock. "Who?"

"That doesn't matter." Kira gestured around the apartment. "He's a very powerful man, and he made all of this possible. He brought you back; you owe him your life."

"I don't care. You belong to me! Tell me who he is and I'll kill him."

Kira shook her head. "You can't do that. He won't let you. *I* won't let you. He gave you life and he'll take it away. Do you understand me?"

He nodded.

"Tell me you understand."

"I-I understand."

282

She slid her fingers down her thighs. "You can never have this again."

Tears formed in his eyes and he blubbered.

"I want you to think about that when you kill Helman's woman. Think about how much you want me and how you can't have me because I belong to someone else."

Gorman made fists, held them before his face, and roared, his face turning red and spittle flying from his mouth. "I want to kill Helman for what he did to you, for what he did to me."

"You'll get your chance, I promise. *After* you kill his bitch."

TWENTY-FIVE

Jake and Sheryl drove through Utica, which had seen brighter days. It possessed a different form of melancholy than Manhattan did: an older one, rooted in long-term economic depression. The buildings were old and had a crumbling texture matching that of the potholed asphalt.

Sheryl stared out her window. "This is our destination?"

"Not exactly," Jake said. "This is just a pit stop."

He parked at the curb of a street lined with small shops. He plied a meter with two quarters and led Sheryl into an Internet café decorated in a faux bohemian style with subdued lighting.

He handed Sheryl a ten-dollar bill. "Get me something fancy. Something with caramel and whipped cream."

"Why don't you just tell me to get your usual black coffee and wait by the door so you can work the computer in private?" Sheryl said.

"That'll do," he said with a smile.

Sheryl walked to the counter, and Jake sat before a computer. He went to a site and checked a company directory. After confirming the identity of an employee, he took a flash drive out of his pocket and connected it to the computer, then copied a photo to it. When Sheryl walked to the door he disconnected the flash and joined her.

"Let's go," he said.

They went outside and got into the car, and Jake drove out of the city. Thirty minutes later, as they drove along a wooded stretch, he pulled over to the side of the road overlooking a deep valley. A long driveway led to a security booth with a gate, then continued to a complex of modern brick buildings with tinted windows.

"What's this place?" Sheryl said.

Jake pointed to a rectangular blue sign with a white logo. "Home to both DNAtomy and Genutrition, two of the companies Tower International held on to after the Department of Justice broke up its monopoly on the genetics industry. Genutrition is where genetically enhanced foods are designed and produced in the US; there are similar factories in other countries. Most of the buildings in this complex are Genutrition. DNAtomy is the low, hexagonal building in the rear. That's where they make the monsters."

"You mean that's where they . . . grew me?"

"That's right."

"Do you think I'm a monster?"

286

"I don't know what you are."

.•✣•.ᐧ ᐧ•

Circling the valley, Jake turned onto a side road. They passed a field and a farm, and then a hill rose on the right. A large brick house with a two-car garage sat atop the hill.

"That's where Andrew Jaeckel lives," Jake said.

"Who's that?" Sheryl said.

"Tower's Dr. Frankenstein. Sixteen years ago, he won the Nobel Peace Prize for his research on genetic engineering. Fourteen years ago, Tower hired him to do private research. His work over the last twelve years has been top secret. When the government investigated the experiments being conducted at Tower—after I anonymously sent evidence of Tower's illegal activities to the ACCL—Jaeckel testified in closed-door senate hearings, and the company was ultimately cleared."

When the house was out of sight, a small police car, parked on the side of the road, came into view.

"Private police force," Jake said.

"You're kidding me."

"You may not have noticed, but we're in the village of Terry. Three thousand men and women work at those two companies, and all of them are required to live within ten minutes of the industrial park; the executives and scientists must live within five minutes of the complex. The private police force is like human resources at any company: it appears to exist to serve the employees, and in this case, the public. But in fact, it's there to protect the company's interests. Terry has a low crime rate, though."

"How do you know all this?"

"It's public information, and I've been researching the company ever since I quit my job at Tower. I drove up here a couple of weeks later to scope the place out."

"So you became obsessed with it."

Jake grunted. "I appointed myself the company's watchdog." He glanced at her. "Was I paranoid?"

"No," she said in a quiet voice.

.·✦·。 : ·

Using his GPS, Jake located a megastore he despised outside of town and drove there.

"What have we come to?" Sheryl said as they entered the gargantuan store.

"I want you to get a gray skirt and matching jacket, with a blouse, shoes, and a purse."

Sheryl arched her eyebrow. "You do realize I consider myself a fashionable woman, right? And that I managed and purchased for a high-end boutique?"

"You're not playing Sheryl Helman tonight."

"Then who am I playing?"

"I'll tell you later. Get shopping. I'll meet you in half an hour to pay for your haul."

"Oh no. If I have to lower myself to do this, you're suffering with me."

Jake rolled his eye. "You know I hate shopping with you. You take forever."

"This will be different, I promise. Usually I can't make up my mind what looks best. In this case, I'll be lucky to find something that doesn't make me vomit."

.᠅⦂ ⦂

Jake found a motel outside Terry and parked in its dirt lot. Only three other vehicles occupied spaces.

"Come into the office with me."

Sheryl followed him inside.

A bearded man with silver hair looked up from the television behind the counter. He stiffened at the sight of Jake. "Can I help you?"

"We'd like a room," Jake said.

"ID?"

Jake took out his wallet and handed a fake driver's license to the man.

He pushed his bifocals up on the bridge of his nose. "New York City, huh?"

"We're on our way to Vermont. We just need to stop for a few hours, maybe the night."

The man smiled. "You look like trouble."

"We're not."

"I don't mean the lady, just you."

"I got jumped outside a bar in Brooklyn. If I was trouble, I wouldn't look like this."

"What happened to your hand?"

"Afghanistan. Regular army."

"Let's see your tags."

"I gave them to my nephew. He wears them every day."

"How about a veteran's card?"

Jake slid a piece of plastic out of his wallet bearing the Department of Veterans Affairs logo, his alias's name, and an ID number. He handed it to the man, who studied it as if he knew what to check for authenticity.

"Seventy-five dollars in advance." The man returned the phony benefits card.

"Will cash do?"

"Does the government deduct too much taxes from me?"

Jake handed the man a hundred-dollar bill. "Keep the change."

"I like a credit card to keep on file as a security deposit."

"I don't have a credit card. I don't believe in them. You start using those, and the next thing you know you're an indentured servant."

"Ain't that the truth. How about your lady friend? I bet she carries plastic."

"We're married. I won't let her have one."

The man looked Sheryl over. "Married, huh? How

did you manage to land her?"

"It's the other way around," Sheryl said. "I landed him."

"How long have you two been together, if you don't mind me asking?"

"Five years but it only feels like half that long."

The man took a tagged key from a rack on the wall and set it on the counter. "Room two. Cable and Wi-Fi are free, and the vending machines are at the far end of the building. If you want a decent place to eat, my brother-in-law owns a bar and grill less than ten minutes away. There're coupons for 10 percent off in the room. Checkout's at 9:00 a.m."

"Thank you," Sheryl said.

Jake scooped up the key. "Have a good night."

"You, too."

Outside, Jake popped the Plymouth's trunk.

"It's scary how well you lie," Sheryl said.

"You stretched the truth yourself. I had to chase you to get you to even go out with me." He handed her the room key and lifted one of the totes. "Close the trunk, please."

Sheryl closed the trunk. "Do we need the shopping bags?"

"Just the one with the towels, paper towels, and water bottle."

Sheryl removed the bag and skipped ahead of Jake to unlock the door.

Jake entered the moldy room first and set the tote on

the queen-size bed. Sheryl closed the door, turned the lock, and slid the chain lock into place, then followed him. Jake switched on the air conditioner, which rattled to life.

"It's been a long time since we were in a hotel room together," Sheryl said.

Jake unpacked the items from the tote and arranged them on the bureau. "I never took you to a dump like this."

"Thank heaven for small favors." Sheryl examined a human face draped over a Styrofoam head. "What is this?"

"A silicone mask I had made when I found myself an unemployed director of security."

"Dr. Frankenstein?"

He turned on all the lights, making the room as bright as possible without opening the ugly floral print curtains. "You're catching on."

"Who am I supposed to be, Elsa Lanchester or Igor?"

"One thing at a time." He pulled the chair from the desk, set it before the bureau, and sat facing the mirror. "Wrap a towel around my neck, then fill the spray bottle with water."

Sheryl wrapped the towel around his neck. "I don't think I like you giving me orders like this. In fact, I know I don't."

"It's part of our deal."

Sheryl took the water bottle into the bathroom and filled it.

Jake had no choice but to stare at his reflection. His black eye and the purple swelling around his broken nose looked worse than the deep scars.

Sheryl returned with the water bottle. "Now what?"

"Plaster my hair down with gel, then stretch the bald cap over my head."

Sheryl scooped gel out of its jar and ran her fingers through Jake's hair, triggering an involuntary wave of excitement through his body.

"I see a white hair," she said.

"Just one?"

Once she had gelled his hair to his scalp, she pulled the bald cap on with an elastic snap. "This is you in thirty years."

"If hair loss is the worst I have to worry about for the next three decades, I'll die a happy man. Get a wet paper towel, and wipe the silicone inside and out to get rid of any dust. Don't rub it. The appliance is prepainted, and if that paint starts peeling I'm going to be in a lot of trouble."

Sheryl picked up the silicone and made a face. "It feels disgusting."

"I went with silicone because it's durable and long lasting. Latex decomposes like real skin."

Sheryl wiped the appliance with tender care. "There. It's probably cleaner than you are."

"Lay it over my face."

Holding the appliance in both hands, Sheryl stood between Jake and the bureau. "How do I do it without hurting you?"

"You don't."

Taking her time, Sheryl laid the appliance over Jake's face. The silicone felt cold and did not conform to his features.

"That's not right," he said. "Move it around until it settles over my features and won't move anymore."

"That's going to hurt like hell."

"I can take it."

With trepidation on her features, Sheryl wiggled the appliance in search of the perfect fit.

Pain radiated from Jake's nose, wrapping itself around his skull like tentacles. Clenching his teeth, he suppressed a scream that escaped as a strangled growl. He dug his fingers into his knee but swung his hook into Sheryl's midsection.

She jumped back against the bureau, knocking the Styrofoam head over.

"Sorry," they said at the same time.

"That looks right," Sheryl said. "How does it feel?"

A tear filled Jake's right eye as he worked his jaw in a circular motion. The appliance's lips and chin held snug to his real ones. "Better."

She stared at him. "That is so damned creepy. I don't know if you look like a mad scientist, but you definitely look like another man. It's so real."

Wiping the tear from his eye, Jake gazed at his reflection. He had worn the appliance only once before, as a test conducted by the special effects makeup artist who had created it. He knew that once he wore the gray wig, he would become Dr. Andrew Jaeckel.

"Time for the wig?" Sheryl said.

Jake shook his head. "That's the final step. We still have a long way to go. See that little bottle? That's the adhesive. You have to glue this whole thing on centimeter by centimeter."

"But your cuts—"

"Glue it."

Swallowing, Sheryl grabbed the bottle and read its label. "How does it come off?"

"The remover is in the other bottle."

"How long is this going to take?"

"If you stop asking questions? A couple of hours. Get started."

Sheryl unscrewed the cap on the bottle and picked up a brush.

TWENTY-SIX

Maria knocked on Mauceri's office door.

"Are you going to dazzle me with the identity of the perp in the Severn case?" Mauceri said.

"I'm afraid not."

Mauceri remained focused on his monitor. "Then get out."

Maria entered the office. "I need to take an hour."

"I didn't hear that."

"I'll stay late to make it up."

"You're staying late anyway."

"I'll stay later."

Mauceri looked at her. "What's the crisis now?"

"No crisis. I just want to attend that press conference outside the Tower."

"Really? I didn't know you were a journalist, too."

"Call it a hobby of mine."

"Can't you just watch it on TV? You'll probably have a better view of the self-appointed king."

"I want to see him in person."

"The crowd's going to be insane, especially with the cleanup going on over there."

"I'm a cop, remember? I'll use my influence."

"Oh yeah, I keep forgetting. I wonder why."

"Can I go?"

Mauceri waved her off. "Bring me back a candy bar."

"You're on a diet." Maria turned and walked away.

Maria had just exited Detective Bureau Manhattan when her phone rang. Remembering Jake had warned her about her phone being traced, she felt anxious as she checked the display. It was the district attorney. She continued to walk as she took the call. "Detective Vasquez."

"Detective Vasquez, I like the sound of that," said a familiar voice.

Maria smiled. "Assistant District Attorney Delgado, what can I do for you?"

"I happen to have two tickets for the mayor's ball tonight, and I was wondering if you'd like to be my date," he said.

Maria shook her head. Arturo Delgado had asked her out a couple of weeks ago, and she told him she didn't date cops or ADAs. "Don't you think I'm a little too uptown for the mayor's ball?"

"So am I. That's the point."

"You're a lot more polished than I am. I'm sure you fit right in with all those political operatives."

"Now that you mention it, I do. And I consider this event an important networking opportunity. I have high ambitions."

"I'm sure you do."

The Tower rose behind the buildings across the street.

"A lot of important Latino leaders will be there tonight."

"And you'd like to have a Latina on your arm?"

"That's only part of the reason why I want you to go with me. The man of the hour is supposedly going to be there."

"Who's that?"

"Nicholas Tower Jr."

Maria's muscles tightened. "I'm on my way to his press conference now."

"I'm sure I could wrangle a meet and greet for my date."

That would go over wonderfully. "I don't have anything to wear, and I have to work late tonight."

"Are you sure it isn't because of that PI you've been seeing?"

"There's him, too."

"I heard he's looking even rougher around the edges than usual."

"Where did you hear that?"

"I have my sources. I also heard Geoghegan brought him in for questioning about the murder of that dwarf who used to be his assistant."

"They're called little people now. You should learn that; every future vote counts, doesn't it?"

"Helman sounds like bad news to me. You deserve better."

"Like an ADA with high ambitions?"

"Exactly."

"Thanks. I'm flattered but I'm involved." But was she?

"All right, be that way. I'm going to keep trying, though. Maria Delgado has a nice ring to it."

"I'm sure my mother would like that."

"I'd like to meet her sometime."

"Maybe she could be your date tonight."

Arturo laughed. "Your quick wit is one of the things I like about you."

"You'd better hang up and start looking through your little black book."

"I don't have one of those, but I'd better get moving. Talk to you soon."

"I'm sure."

Arturo hung up, and Maria returned her phone to its holder on her belt.

When she reached Twenty-third Street and turned the corner, she saw hundreds of people crowding the street and sidewalks, surrounded by uniformed police officers, some of them mounted on horseback. She also spotted members of the mayor's security detail stationed around the plaza leading into the Tower.

As she made her way through the crowd, she waved her shield in the air, and a PO admitted her into the front, with a prime view of the plaza.

The citizens around her buzzed like attendees at a rock concert waiting for the main act to take the stage. Maria counted dozens of photographers and eight different television news crews set up in the same line where the officer had put her.

"I see them," a woman said.

An Asian man and three men wearing Tower Security uniforms crossed the sunlit lobby of Tower International, followed by members of the mayor's security detail, Mayor Connie Krycek, her aides, Kira Thorn, and a tall, fit man with handsome features and a widow's peak.

The crowd cheered and roared.

You idiots, Maria thought.

The security officers and featured speakers assembled near a podium surrounded by tall speakers. Mayor Krycek spoke to Tower, and Kira scanned the audience, her gaze settling on Maria. The woman smiled in her direction, then continued to search the crowd.

The cheering continued for several minutes before Kira stood at the podium. Her welcoming expression bore little resemblance to her demeanor both times she had spoken to Maria. "Thank you all for turning out on such short notice. I am not a public figure. When I worked here two years ago, I was the executive assistant for the most commanding person it's ever been my privilege to know: Nicholas Tower Sr.

"For ten years, Nicholas hid from the public eye in the Tower. But he never wavered in his commitment to expand the scientific frontier for the betterment of mankind. Those efforts made him a target for religious extremists and domestic terrorists. His untimely death stalled several of his greatest projects, including the improvement of genetically enhanced foods to feed the poor and Deceleroxyn-21, which promises to extend the life span of every man and woman on earth. For the last two years, I've been overseeing Tower International's holdings in Europe. I've also been grooming the man who will lead Tower International into the future—my husband, Nicholas Tower Jr."

The crowd erupted into a frenzy of applause.

Maria felt herself shrinking from the enormity of the response to Kira's address.

"We are living in difficult times, and it is my honor to introduce a woman who has been working tirelessly to save New York City from the effects of Hurricane Daria—Mayor Connie Krycek."

The applause continued, which surprised Maria given the drubbing Krycek had taken in the press in Daria's wake.

Beaming, Krycek approached the podium and

clasped Kira's hands. "Thank you for that warm introduction, Mrs. Tower. And welcome back to the greatest city in the world."

The roar returned.

"Our city has withstood crippling setbacks: acts of terrorism, painful tragedies, economic peril, natural—or unnatural—disasters. Once again, this magnificent city will rise from the ashes like the phoenix. But only if we work together. I'm delighted that Nicholas Tower Jr. has decided to make New York his home, and I can tell you he intends to play a significant role in our recovery."

The applause grew louder.

"Please join me in welcoming the new chief executive officer of Tower International, Mr. Nicholas Tower Jr."

A deafening roar.

Maria had pulled press conference duty plenty of times while in uniform, but she had never seen one become a rally before.

Tower approached the podium, smiling. He had the self-confidence of a movie star, and Maria wondered how it must have felt to have the experience of a seventy-eight-year-old in the body of a twenty-four-year-old. He wore a sharp black suit with a silk tie.

"Thank you very much," Tower said. "I've never spoken in public before, so you'll forgive me if I stammer. My mother was a Croatian immigrant, and I was born in Germany and educated in France. As a child, I knew my father well, but when I was an adolescent he insulated himself from the world, and I never saw him again. I have only his handwritten letters to remember him by, and my mother died while I was in university. I came of age beneath the Tower International logo.

"When Dad died, Kira Thorn presented me with my father's will, which named me as his sole heir and successor. We intentionally buried that will out of fear of reprisals from the terrorist organization RAGE, but its contents can be made public now. I'm grateful to Kira for teaching me my father's business in Europe and for preparing me for the role I now assume. I'm proud to call her my wife.

"We spent much of the last year preparing my immigration to the US and filing the necessary paperwork to collect the US portion of my fortune. France has already acknowledged me as Nicholas Tower Jr., allowing me to receive that half of my inheritance. Due to my father's paranoia regarding terrorism, I grew up under an alias. Now I claim my father's last name. I've submitted to DNA testing, which proves I am my father's son.

"My father was a man of science, but in his quest for scientific achievements to benefit humanity, he lost track of his own humanity. That detachment filtered down to his company. I possess no such detachment. I plan to put a human face on this company and to interact with the people we wish to serve. To that end, I present Mayor Krycek with a check for one hundred million dollars to be used to help rebuild this neighborhood."

For a moment, the audience seemed stunned into silence. Then Tower withdrew a check from his breast pocket, and Mayor Krycek collected it, shaking his hand with enthusiasm, and the crowd burst into applause.

"I'm also setting up the Tower Foundation, which shall provide food and shelter to those people who have been displaced by Daria. This foundation shall distribute another one hundred million dollars to those in need with no overhead."

This elicited another round of applause. Maria almost expected to see the TV cameramen clapping.

"Finally, I'm told by Mayor Krycek that Roosevelt Island is destroyed and its residents are homeless. I'm donating a hundred million dollars to be used for housing, food, clothing, and training for new jobs. We will not let them be forgotten."

The response from the crowd grew deafening.

Maria looked around at the cheering people, then over her shoulder at Jake's building and the construction area around the fallen buildings across the street. The hair on the back of her neck stood on end, and she sensed she was being watched.

Impossible. Everyone's watching the new king.

It had been easy for Gorman to locate Maria Vasquez in the crowd. He had stood behind her for much of Tower's address. Now he had her scent, and nothing could save her from him.

But he saw Nicholas Tower, too, and understood the man's relationship to Kira. To Gorman, she would always be the Widow. She belonged to him, and he would kill any man who stood between their happiness—even Nicholas Tower.

TWENTY-SEVEN

Standing before the bureau mirror, Jake positioned the gray wig on the skullcap he wore. "What do you think?"

Sheryl studied his reflection. "It looks like a bad toupee."

"It's supposed to." Jake booted up his laptop. "I'll show you."

The Tower logo filled the screen, accompanied by the tagline: Tower International—Building Better Life.

"Did you steal this laptop from work?"

"No, I just like a reminder every day." He went to his documents.

"A reminder of what?"

"That this company is still out there and that Old Nick and Kira had you murdered."

She touched his arm. "I'm not dead. I'm right here. If anything, they brought me back."

"No matter how you look at it, they stole your life."

An image filled the screen: a company photograph of a smiling Andrew Jaeckel.

"It's uncanny," Sheryl said. "You look just like him."

"I chose him because we're the same height, not because he's the head mad scientist there. He was forty pounds heavier than me when this photo was taken. Hopefully he hasn't undergone any physical changes. I'd hate to be the victim of bad intelligence like Tower was."

Sheryl leaned closer to the screen. "Your eyes are the wrong color. His are green."

"Right, good thing you reminded me."

"We make a good pair."

Jake took out a contact case from the tote and handed it to Sheryl. "Do you mind opening this?"

Sheryl opened it. "What would you do if I wasn't here?"

Jake touched one of the colored contacts, then raised his finger and pressed it against his eyeball. For a second, he was blind. Then, blinking, he inspected his handiwork in the mirror. His real eye had turned green, but his glass eye remained blue.

"Very exotic," Sheryl said. "Can you wear a contact over a glass eye?"

"I don't need to. I have something better." Jake turned to the tote and removed a black box that resembled an oversize jewelry case. Opening it, he revealed a glass eye with a green iris.

"That's lovely." Sheryl giggled.

"What's so funny?"

"Look in the mirror."

In the mirror, Jake appeared to be proposing.

"It's almost five. Time to get ready. DNAtomy employees clock out at six."

"How am I supposed to prepare?"

"First, I have to teach you how to shoot a gun."

Andrew Jaeckel followed his colleagues through the front doors of DNAtomy, his mind already on the next day's work.

Tower's sudden return and public assumption of control of Tower International and DNAtomy had come as an unwelcome shock to him. Jaeckel had supervised the creation of every Biogen, including those of Tower and Kira, and he had grown accustomed to a certain amount of autonomy while his supervisors had run the company through Daryl Klemmer. Jaeckel found the timing of Klemmer's death suspicious and his superiors' insistence that he rush production of new models burdensome. But what choice did he have but to comply? He had made a deal with the devil when he shook the hand of the original Tower years earlier.

Crossing into the parking lot, he stepped into the path of an oncoming Jetta, which came to a sudden stop just feet away from him. He didn't turn to see who had almost hit him or to apologize for being careless.

He continued to his Lexus and got in. He had purchased a new luxury vehicle every year for as long as he had lived in Terry. His wife had died six years earlier, but he had been married to his work since long before then. He had no real relationships with any of his three children. His daughter and two sons had graduated from college and turned out well enough, though he doubted any of them would leave a significant mark on the world. It didn't surprise him that none of them had chosen to follow in his footsteps.

As he went through the security gate, his thoughts returned to the work that needed to be completed. Jaeckel knew it was just a matter of time before Tower and Kira visited the facility and made unreasonable demands upon him. Not for the first time, he dreamed of retiring. He certainly had more money than he could spend in his remaining lifetime. But retirement was not an option; he knew too much for the Towers to allow him to live beyond their control. Terry was a secluded, easily managed location, and he didn't doubt for an instant they would assassinate him as soon as he attempted to leave. He would go on working until the day he died or until he became useless, which would mean the same thing. Fortunately, he loved his work.

He drove along the main road, which circled the valley, affording him a view of the complex, as orange light from the evening sun highlighted the pine trees. He appreciated the scenery, which came as a welcome relief from the snow-covered alternative. During those long winter months, he sometimes thought he would go insane.

He turned down the side road that wound around

the woods to his house, passing neighbors few and far between. An old stone shed occupied one corner of the land where his dirt driveway started, and he pressed the gas pedal to climb the hill. Woods flanked either side of the driveway, and he drove in the middle to avoid the branches.

Halfway up the hill, another vehicle came into view, and Jaeckel slowed his car to a stop and shifted into Park. A woman crouched at the rear wheel on the driver's side of a Plymouth, inspecting its tire.

Jaeckel frowned. The last time strangers had come to his home uninvited had been during the DOJ's investigation into Tower International and DNAtomy. Journalists had swarmed Terry, and the company had furnished him with around-the-clock security. Then the investigation ended, the media interest subsided, and Jaeckel's life returned to normal. He hoped this woman was not a journalist and he could get rid of her fast.

Climbing out of the car, he approached the woman, who wore a skirt. "Excuse me. What are you doing here?"

Standing, the woman gestured at the wheel. "I had a flat, so I turned into the nearest driveway. I didn't think I'd have to drive up a mountain."

The woman didn't turn around, and the wheel's tire appeared full.

"It looks fine to me," he said in a skeptical tone. "Who are you?"

The woman faced him. She wore a plastic children's

mask of a fox that left her mouth and chin uncovered. "I'm the fox in the henhouse."

Jaeckel stiffened. Footsteps on the dirt behind him alerted him to danger, and then pain exploded in the back of his head. He collapsed on all fours and gasped. The pain below his brain ebbed.

"Get up," a man said behind him.

Jaeckel grabbed the rear bumper of the Plymouth for support. Groaning with effort, he got to his feet. The woman aimed a small handgun at him, and he knew he was in serious trouble. "What do you want?" he croaked.

"Turn around," the man said.

Frightened to turn his back to the man with the gun, he complied.

The man wore a matching plastic mask and a bald cap. He held a gun as well and kept one hand in his pocket. "Listen carefully. Do not scream. Do not run. Do not make any attempt to escape or call attention to us. The three of us are going to get into your car, and you're going to drive us into your garage. Do not ask any questions until we get inside. Move."

Sweating, Jaeckel moved past the gunman to his Lexus. His head continued to throb, and he pressed two fingers against the pain point. They came away free of blood.

The woman circled the front of the car to the passenger side, and the man stood beside Jaeckel waiting to get into the backseat.

Jaeckel opened his door and slid behind the wheel. Before he could consider speeding away, the woman got in beside him. She kept her gun leveled at him, and the man got in behind him. The man stayed out of view of prying eyes but kept his gun aimed at Jaeckel. Without prompting, the woman leaned across the seat. She pressed her gun against Jaeckel's crotch, then laid its head on his thigh, facing his abdomen.

His captors had staged the abduction in a stretch of the driveway unobserved by security cameras, and now they had made themselves invisible to the cameras outside his house. They knew what they were doing.

"Drive at the same speed you do every day at this time," the man said.

Swallowing, Jaeckel shifted the car into gear and passed the Plymouth. Ten seconds later, they emerged from the woods and drove on the paved portion of the driveway that cut through an immaculate lawn to the wide brick house built while Jaeckel's wife was still alive. The house faced away from the valley, so the deck, patio, and swimming pool overlooked the complex.

Jaeckel stopped before one of the twin garage doors. "I have to open the glove compartment to open the garage door."

"Then do it," the man said. "But if you trigger any alarms or do anything that brings help, you will die in a very painful and protracted manner."

"I understand." Jaeckel reached over the woman, opened the glove compartment, and pressed the button on the remote control for the garage door, which whispered open. He eased the car inside and closed the door, shutting out the sunlight.

The woman sat up, removing the pressure from Jaeckel's crotch, and the man got out and opened his door.

"Let's go," the man said.

Jaeckel exited the car, and the man shoved him away from the door and kneed it shut. The woman joined them at the door to the house.

"When we go inside," the man said, "punch in the same security code you do every day, not an alternate one to alert whoever monitors your home. We're prepared to die for our cause, and we're more than prepared to take you with us. If we're forced to kill you, it will be a glorious day for RAGE."

Jaeckel had suspected the male captor belonged to the Righteous Against Genetic Engineering. The domestic terrorist organization had been silent for almost two years. He supposed Nicholas Tower Jr.'s appearance had reignited their fuse.

"I won't give you any reason to make me a martyr," Jaeckel said in a quivering voice. He unlocked the door. Inside, the keypad issued an electronic whine. The woman entered first and he followed. When the man joined them, he closed the door and entered his code, killing the whine as the light on the keypad turned from red to green. He faced the door two steps above, leading into the kitchen.

"Down in the basement," the man said.

TWENTY-EIGHT

Jaeckel flipped the light switch, and Sheryl descended the stairs first. The scientist followed and Jake brought up the rear.

"Lights," Jake said at the bottom.

Jaeckel flipped another switch, and fluorescent lights flickered to life all the way down the immense basement. The ranch house was enormous, and the full basement had clean concrete block walls, a high ceiling, and an unblemished floor. Light seeped through glass block windows; otherwise, the basement could have served as a bomb shelter. Bicycles, toys, and garbage bags bulging with clothing lay scattered about, and bare tables topped with framed soil ran the length.

"What are these?" Sheryl said.

"My wife used to grow plants down here."

"What kinds of plants?"

Jake sensed the edge in her voice might not have been a performance.

"Special plants. Hybrids."

"You mean genetic mutations?"

"Yes."

Jake knew Jaeckel's wife had worked for Genutrition, but he had not thought to tell Sheryl. "Walk," he said, hoping to keep her focused on the task at hand.

Jaeckel started crossing the basement, and Sheryl fell into step beside him. Jake followed in case Jaeckel made for her gun. They reached the middle of the basement.

"Strip," Jake said.

Jaeckel appeared confused at first, then frightened. "Why?"

Raising the Thunder Ranch, Jake nodded to Sheryl. She shifted the Ruger into her left hand, then punched Jaeckel in the jaw.

"We have the guns. We ask the questions," Jake said. "I'll throw the next punch."

Looking shocked, Jaeckel removed his jacket and tossed it on the floor, then loosened his tie, which he also discarded. He unbuttoned his shirt, revealing a wifebeater beneath it.

"Leave your underwear on."

When Jaeckel stood before them in dark socks and boxers, Jake kicked the man's shoes and clothing away. "Back up," he said.

Glancing behind him, Jaeckel backed up to a metal support column.

Sheryl took out a zip tie and secured his wrists behind him.

"Feel free to sit," Jake said.

"I prefer to stand."

"Suit yourself, but you're going to be here for a long time. You might as well get comfortable."

Frowning, Jaeckel slid down the length of the pole and sat on the floor.

"Maybe we'll get you some blankets later." Jake walked over to a desk and pulled its rolling chair away. "Was this your wife's computer?"

"Yes."

"Get on it," Jake said to Sheryl.

She moved to the computer and booted it up, then turned on the monitor. "Password?"

"Successful 02," Jaeckel said.

"That figures," she said with scorn as she keyed in the password. "I'm in."

Jake scooped up Jaeckel's slacks and went through their pockets, retrieving a clip-on security card and a wallet. He handed the security card to Sheryl, who walked over to the printer and powered it on.

"Pay no attention to what she's doing," Jake said. "Pay attention to *me*."

Jaeckel swallowed.

"We know who you are, and we know what you've been doing for Tower these last fourteen years."

Jaeckel appeared skeptical.

"We know about the Biogens."

The scientist's eyes widened.

"We know Nicholas Tower isn't Old Nick's heir but his clone and Kira Thorn—sorry, scratch that—Kira *Tower* is a Biogen, too."

"How could you possibly know that?"

"How many of those things have you made in human form?"

"I can't tell you anything. If I do, they'll kill me."

"Look around. Do you see them? No. You see us. You see our guns. And you know that we'll kill you if you don't start unburdening your soul."

"They don't have to be standing before you to kill you. They can order an assassination from far away and make it look like an accident."

"Like they did with Daryl Klemmer?"

"Yes."

Jaeckel didn't know it but he had already cracked. "How many?"

"More than I can count."

"Sometime in the next twenty-four hours, Tower will be finished. He'll be dead or this entire operation will be exposed. Either way, you'll have a chance to negotiate for immunity with the Department of Justice in exchange for your testimony, but you have to talk to us first."

Jaeckel bowed his head but he did not speak.

"Do you need more convincing? I once tortured a tough old geezer who had served in the military. I used pruning shears to cut off one of his fingers, which opened him right up. I'll kill you if you don't tell us what we want to know, but I'll take my time getting there. You will scream long and hard, and there are no neighbors close enough to hear you. In the end, you'll talk, and you'll wonder why you hadn't done so sooner and spared yourself a lot of agony."

Sheryl printed a document.

"I can't tell you how many Biogens I've designed," Jaeckel said.

"Let me rephrase that. How many different humanoid prototypes are there?"

"Six."

"Who besides Tower and Kira?"

"I only know the identities of those two, because I knew the actual people."

"What was the protocol for activating the two who are in the Tower right now?"

"Old Nick's Biogen was already grown. We had it in stasis. Kira ordered me to activate the genetic program she had sent me before he died. That took as long as it takes to download a program on a computer. By the time the world learned Nick had died, his duplicate had already landed in Hungary. Kira was in control of the company just long enough to appoint Daryl Klemmer the new CEO. When Kira disappeared, Klemmer ordered Kira's duplicate, also in stasis, to be activated. To do that, we downloaded an update from a blood sample she gave the day she disappeared."

"You're doing fine." Jake took a piece of paper out of his breast pocket. He unfolded it several times, revealing the floor plans of DNAtomy. "We know you manufacture the Biogens at DNAtomy. We just don't know where." He set the plans on the floor before Jaeckel. "Tell us."

"There's a subbasement," Jaeckel said in a defeated voice.

I knew it. Tower would have to go to extremes to keep his monstrosities a secret from regulators. "How do we access it?"

"You can take an elevator or the stairs to the regular basement. At the back of the building, there's an office with an unmarked door."

"Does your key card access that office?"

"Of course. People with access—just the scientists and lab techs on my team—enter their password on that computer, which opens a secret panel in the far wall. That leads to both an elevator and a stairway. Both of those lead to the real DNAtomy, which is only accessible by a face-recognition system."

"What about retinal or hand scanners?"

Jaeckel shook his head.

322

"Good, you get to keep your eyeballs and hands."

"You can't seriously mean you intend to go in there?"

"Do the guards still change shifts at midnight?"

"Yes. How do you know—?"

"We've been staking out the place on and off for almost two years."

Dawning realization turned to panic in Jaeckel's eyes. "You're going to destroy my work!"

"Your work amounts to illegal munitions used to kill people."

"There are other applications. Therapeutic cloning, for one."

"You can pretend you're doing this for the betterment of mankind, but we all know better. Tower gave you the keys to the candy store and the bankroll to stock it however you wanted. If you had any misgivings about the ethical ramifications, you turned a blind eye to them long ago."

"That isn't true."

"You didn't have the balls to ever say no to what was requested of you, though, did you? Did you design any of those monstrosities yourself?"

"We have an entire team, but the others lack my . . . imagination."

"Are there guards inside the complex?"

"Six, who split their time between patrolling the grounds and roaming the first and second floors. No one's permitted in the laboratory level."

"Are they armed?"

"Of course."

"White River Security?"

"How do you know these things?"

"Obtaining this information has been our raison d'être. Cameras?"

"This is the twenty-first century."

"Where do they transmit to?"

"Nowhere. That would be too dangerous. The feed goes to a digital recorder maintained in the laboratory."

"What about metal detectors?"

"There's no need. We're a laboratory, not a military complex. No unauthorized personnel even reach the building."

Sheryl walked over to them.

Jake inspected her handiwork. Using the photo he had copied from the DNAtomy website at the Internet café, she had created a security card for Charlene Morrisey. The scientist was two years older than Sheryl and wore horn-rimmed glasses and her dark hair in a bun. The resemblance was not striking but close enough.

"I found this in the desk drawer," she said, holding up a Genutrition security card in a plastic holder.

"Good job," Jake said.

Returning to the desk, she removed the card from its holder.

"Let's get back to your abominations," Jake said. "What's the floor plan in the laboratory?"

"It's hexagonal, just like the structure aboveground. The main floors are rectangular, with side chambers and self-contained environments. The first section is the research center. Beyond that is the containment center for the non-humanoid Biogens, and beyond that is the stasis center for the humans."

Jake knew Jaeckel had a big ego and he wouldn't shut up once he got talking. "Describe the human Biogens who don't look like Kira or Tower."

"There were three males and one female."

"Describe the males."

"All three of them were more or less your height. One had reddish-blond hair. We were instructed to scar his face and remove his left eye."

Jake maintained an even tone. "How many copies of him did you make?"

"We generally make three perfect copies of each model. Two of those we programmed according to Tower's specifications and turned over to Kira."

Good, Jake thought. *That leaves only one more duplicate of me.* "And the imperfect copies?"

"We destroy them, of course."

"Next."

"The second man was also a Caucasian. Muscular, hard jaw, shaved head."

"The human bomb who exploded on flight 3350."

"Yes. That's the only one we released, so there are two more."

"And the third man?"

"He has sandy-brown hair and bland features. Kira took only one copy of him, so two more remain."

"Other than the walking bomb, did the other two have any special features built into them?"

"No. They were ordered into production too fast. We can produce an adult biogenetic clone in thirty-six hours, but the enhancements can take months."

"What about the female?" Sheryl said, moving closer.

Damn it, Jake thought. But he wanted to know the answer, too.

"She was a special enhanced model," Jaeckel said. "We've had the original's DNA for some time."

"Special how?" Sheryl said.

"We incorporated the DNA of a scorpion into her, among other things. If she ever attempts to fly, airline security is in for one hell of a nasty surprise."

Sheryl's body wilted and she turned back to the desk. Jake felt her pain.

"Are there any emergency exits?" Jake said.

"No. Since the facility's existence is a secret, we don't have to worry about being up to code."

"But if you grow the non-humanoid Biogens on-site,

they have to be transported. No one walks them out the front door."

"There's a smaller building off to the side of the complex. It looks like a garage."

"We've seen it."

"It has a false floor. A cargo elevator in the rear of the lab rises into it; the floor rises to the ceiling, and the elevator allows the animals to be loaded onto a truck."

Sheryl moved toward Jaeckel with surprising speed and tore off her mask. "You're a monster!"

Jaeckel's features contorted into fearful recognition.

Sheryl fired four shots into his chest at point-blank range. The rounds tore into his flesh, and blood spurted from the entry wounds, soaking his wifebeater and boxers.

TWENTY-NINE

Jake gaped at Jaeckel as the man slumped to one side, the zip tie around his wrist preventing his upper body from reaching the floor. Jake holstered his gun and took off his mask.

Jaeckel's eyes bulged at the sight of his doppelganger, and then he stopped caring.

"That wasn't exactly the plan," Jake said in a quiet voice.

Sheryl lowered her smoking gun. "For what he did to me . . . for what he turned me *into* . . ."

"He deserved to be punished. No question about it."

Tears rolled down her cheeks. "It's not like my soul can go to hell, right? I'm already in heaven."

A horrible sucking sound escaped from Jaeckel's lungs.

"But I didn't get a chance to ask him about the controls for the Biogens," Jake said. "Each one has a custom-designed Achilles' heel. Now we're walking into DNAtomy blind."

"You're concerned you don't know what my Kryptonite is."

She was right. "On the other hand, neither do you.

Worse, neither one of us knows what will trigger your transformation."

Sheryl looked at the scientist's body. "Should we bury him?"

"He isn't dead yet. I think I've buried enough bodies lately. Besides, I don't trust the rent-a-cops out there. I prefer to make one drive straight to the complex."

She leaned against the edge of the desk and set the Ruger on it. "So what's the plan now?"

"We leave at nine."

"I thought you wanted to go after the guards change shifts at midnight."

Jake shook his head. "I wanted him to think that in case he somehow got loose after we left. Now we don't have to worry about that. I know the midnight crew is less likely to have seen Jaeckel before, but it's more believable that he would go back to work at nine."

"You want us to wait down here? Why don't we go upstairs?"

"I have a weird feeling about it. I don't see cameras down here, but they could be all over the house."

Jaeckel let loose a strangled gasp. An instant later, his flickering soul rose from his body and faded. Jake knew Sheryl didn't see the show.

"Then let's at least get away from him." Sheryl picked up the gun, but it shook in her hand.

"Easy." Even as Jake took the gun from her hand,

her knees buckled and she grabbed his arm.

"I can't stop shaking," she said.

He put his arm around her waist and helped her walk across the basement. "It's the adrenaline."

"You're not shaking."

"I didn't shoot him." *And I've done it before.* He set her on a leather sofa, then pulled on a pair of latex gloves and walked back toward Jaeckel.

"Where are you going?"

"To get his clothes." Facing her, he patted his shoulder bag. "And to dig out those rounds so they can't be traced back to me."

At the scene of the crime, Jake set the bag on the desk, removed a coverall, and pulled it on. He put his plastic mask over the silicone appliance, then tied the hood and covered his shoes. Then he took a hunting knife out of the bag and kneeled beside the corpse.

When he had finished digging out the rounds, a messy procedure that left his protective clothing spattered with red stains, he wiped the blade on one sleeve, then peeled off the garb. He wrapped the knife in the slick coverall, bunched it up, and stuffed it into a garbage bag.

Jake grabbed a sheet of paper from the printer and located a marker in the desk. He scrawled *RAGE* on the paper and left it on the desk. Then he peeled off his gloves, stuck them inside the garbage bag, and tied it.

He gathered Jaeckel's clothes and rejoined Sheryl.

"I have something to tell you," he said as he sat next to her.

She gave him a questioning look.

"They can design Biogens with a predetermined life span. You could live forty more years or—"

"Forty hours?"

"Exactly. If they created you just to screw with my head or to take me out, my guess would be the latter."

She swallowed. "Sucks to be me."

"There's a good chance neither one of us will walk out of this alive, but even if you do, it might be a short-lived victory. I won't hold you to our agreement. If you want to cut out right now, you can have the Plymouth and what cash I have left. Hit the road and don't look back."

She wiped the tears from her eyes. "Thank you but I want to see this through. I *have* to see it through. I need to see the monsters who did this to me."

He put his arms around her shoulders, and she leaned her head against his chest and wept.

"I'm the monster," she said.

At 9:00 p.m., Maria removed her holstered Glock from her belt and set it in her top desk drawer. She was about to lock the drawer when she remembered Jake's instructions

to leave her phone at work. She debated doing as he wished but decided to keep it. Then she shut down her computer and crossed the squad room to the desk of Detective Sergeant Benny Lawson, who served as the shift commander after Mauceri left for the day.

"I'm checking out," she said.

Lawson looked up from her monitor. "I thought L.T. said you were staying late. You came in late and took an hour of personal time you don't even have."

"I'm beat, okay? I've had a long day, even if it wasn't all spent here."

"Is the paperwork on Severn done?"

"All we can do. It's not like we have a person of interest or anything."

Lawson frowned. "Okay, take off. See you tomorrow morning."

"Good night." She walked over to Totty's desk. "I'll see you tomorrow."

"Thanks for your help today," Totty said.

Maria left the squad room. On the sidewalk outside, she stood in a pool of light coming from the building and raised her gaze to the clear sky, then walked to the parking lot. Instead of entering it, she continued walking.

Dressed as Ryan Coulter in faded jeans and a black concert T-shirt, Marc Gorman stood across the street from

Detective Bureau Manhattan, watching Maria Vasquez exit the building. He expected her to enter the parking lot, but she kept walking.

Interesting, he thought. According to the intel Kira had given him, Vasquez drove to work every day. He waited until Maria had gotten half a block ahead of him, then followed her.

Kira wanted him to kill Vasquez, and he intended to make a messy job of it to impress her.

Wearing Jaeckel's work clothes, Jake drove the man's Lexus up to the security booth at DNAtomy and Genutrition with Sheryl seated beside him. She wore her hair in a bun and a pair of nonprescription horn-rimmed glasses. Jaeckel's ID was clipped to the breast pocket of Jake's blazer, and Sheryl's forged ID was attached to her handbag.

They slowed at the gate, and a laser scanned the company ID glued to the windshield.

The security guard glanced at them and raised the barrier, and they drove through.

"I hope the rest is as easy," Jake said.

He drove into the parking lot and counted the reserved spaces facing one side of the hexagonal building. The headlights illuminated Jaeckel's name on a metal sign as he pulled into the spot.

"How did you know right where it was?" Sheryl said.

"I spent three full days watching this place through a high-powered telescope. How does my face look?"

"Old."

"I never thought I'd live to see this age."

They got out. Mosquitoes swarmed in the parking lot lights. Jake slipped his hook into his jacket pocket and carried Jaeckel's briefcase with his hand, and Sheryl carried her handbag. The sky seemed blacker in the country and crickets chirped.

"Good luck," Jake said.

"You, too."

Maria looked up at the Tower. The windows on the first and top floors glowed in the night, with the fifty-eight floors in between them dark.

Damn it, Jake. She needed to know what was happening.

She crossed the street and made her way east, moving around the walled-off debris zone.

Gorman found himself on the same side of the street as Vasquez, so he fell back to be discreet. The woman didn't turn around. She passed an encampment of homeless people standing around metal barrels with flames dancing inside them.

335

At Second Avenue, a police car cruised by, heading downtown.

Where the hell is she going?

Using Jaeckel's key card, Jake opened the glass doors in the front of DNAtomy, and Sheryl followed him into the spacious lobby.

Behind a counter, a security guard looked up.

Jake smiled broader than normal to ensure the silicone appliance conveyed the intended warmth.

"Back for more, doc?" the guard said.

Jake cleared his throat. "The bosses are coming this week. We just need to do a little work to get a head start on tomorrow."

Sheryl gave the guard a perfunctory smile and turned her bag to him so her ID showed. The guard nodded and they proceeded to the inner entrance. Cameras in smoked-glass domes looked down at them. Jake handed Jaeckel's briefcase to Sheryl and swiped his key card through a slot. The door unlocked and he opened it, and Sheryl brushed past him as she entered the workplace.

Fluorescents flickered to life ahead of them as they walked, triggered by motion detectors. A sea of cubicles stretched before them. They entered a wide corridor and passed a cafeteria. Per Jake's instructions, they didn't speak. Anyone could be listening.

Next they passed dozens of closed offices and conference rooms. Accustomed to the absurd level of security at the Tower, Jake found sneaking into DNAtomy a walk in the park. At the end of the corridor, they reached an elevator. Jake swiped his key card and the door opened. They boarded the elevator and took it to the only place it went: the basement.

Maria waited at the corner of First Avenue and East Twenty-third Street until a bus pulled over. The door opened with a hydraulic hiss, and she boarded it and swiped her MetroCard. She moved to the center and sat at a window seat. She wondered how Shana was doing on her first day in her new home. The bus headed uptown.

Gorman's heart beat faster when he saw Vasquez board the bus. He waited until it pulled away to run to the street. Looking in the opposite direction, he waved at an approaching taxi. It stopped at the curb, and he leapt into the backseat.

"Follow that bus," he said to the driver. "But don't get ahead of it."

The elevator door opened, and Jake and Sheryl emerged

into an industrial area with thick pipes and a boiler the size of a bus. Fluorescents continued to flicker ahead of them as they walked, their footsteps echoing. They passed machinery Jake could not identify, a metal shop with cage doors, and numerous offices and closets.

When they had walked the same distance as they had on the first floor, they reached an unmarked door with a key card scanner mounted on the wall beside it. Jake swiped his card through the slot, and the door clicked. He opened the door, and the room beyond it flickered with light.

Jake led the way, and Sheryl sat before the computer Jaeckel had told them about. She tapped the computer's touch pad, and the monitor blossomed with light, revealing a log-in prompt. She keyed in Jaeckel's name, then entered his password.

A section of the opposite wall hummed open, and they faced a concrete anteroom that reminded him of the one separating Kira's and Tower's offices in the Tower. After they entered the room, the panel slid shut behind them. They stepped before another elevator, and Jake swiped his key card. The elevator opened and they boarded it. There were no buttons to push and the elevator descended.

Maria got off the bus at East Eighty-fourth Street, where

glowing city lights made her feel safer. She saw the same signs of destruction she had witnessed everywhere else in Manhattan, but at least the sidewalks were crowded with people going somewhere instead of living on them. Salsa music blasted out of a passing car.

She bought a pack of Marlboro Lights and a lighter at a newsstand. She had quit smoking several times, but this had been a particularly stressful day. She slid the pack into her pocket without opening it and walked east.

Gorman felt a strange sense of déjà vu as he crossed Eighty-fourth Street to avoid being seen by Vasquez. He had been in this neighborhood before. In his mind, it had just been a few days earlier, though he knew it had been almost two years ago. Sure enough, Vasquez stopped outside the building he had staked out. In another lifetime, Helman and his wife had lived in an apartment there. Vasquez resumed walking east and he followed her, his curiosity growing.

Jake and Sheryl exited the elevator and found themselves facing a round vault door like the one that led to Tower's office. A light blinked above a dark glass panel the size of a book set in the wall.

Jake glanced at the duplicate of his wife. If the face

recognition system did not accept his disguise, their ruse would be discovered at once. He stepped before the black glass mounted on the wall and waited for the scanner to analyze his silicone features. The light over the panel stopped blinking, and he held his breath.

The vault door opened with a loud hum.

THIRTY

Tower snarled and laughed as he plowed into Kira, who writhed beneath him, their bodies dripping with sweat. Their lovemaking sessions consisted of acrobatic wrestling matches in which each opponent tried to outlast the other, and their biogentically enhanced bodies had attained the stamina to last for hours before release.

His original body had been unable to perform at all, and he had been a victim of his own brilliance: the powerful pheromones Kira had been designed to exude had sometimes driven him mad with frustration. His new vassal exhibited no such handicap. Kira's scent prevented him from ever tiring of her, and her programming prevented her of tiring of him. They typically spent one quarter of their day satisfying their mutual lust, a most rigorous form of exercise.

Not bad for a seventy-eight-year-old, he thought once more.

Kira buried her long fingers in his hair and yanked

his head from side to side until he toppled onto the circular water bed and she climbed atop him, her body glistening as her opening swallowed his member and her muscles closed around it. He thrust his hips into the air, attempting to hurl her off him, but she held tight and drew her fingernails down his chest and over his taut stomach muscles. She snarled back at him, her dark eyes gleaming with excitement.

Beneath him, eel-like Biogens swam in the bed's water. A layer of micro-steel lined the bed, preventing them from chewing through it, but they rammed at the lining anyway, striking his buttocks, back, and shoulders, desperate to devour human flesh with their piranha-like teeth, their efforts increasing his excitement.

"Come on, old man," she said, hissing.

Tower squeezed her throat with one hand, and she did the same to him. Who would choke out first? A dangerous game: if, in the passion of the moment, Kira believed herself in danger, she might transform into her assault mode. She arched her neck and flung her head forward, her wet hair whipping his eyes. How he loved his wicked Medusa!

The emergency phone rang on the floor, where it had fallen during their match.

Tower turned his head in its direction.

But Kira seized his face in her hands and turned his eyes back to her. "Not yet," she said in a hoarse growl.

Releasing her throat, he threw his arms around her and squeezed with all his strength. Their bodies trembled at the same time, over and over, their warm fluids mixing, and their triumphant cries became one, their climactic pleasure a shared series of pleasure explosions. Panting, Tower dropped his arms at his sides.

Kira rolled off him and the bed and scooped up the phone. "Yes," she said, all business.

Tower wiped stinging sweat from his eyes.

"It's Hanaka," she said.

"Put him on speaker."

She pressed a button on the phone. "Speak to us."

"The guard at the front desk at DNAtomy called a few minutes ago," Hanaka said. "He said Dr. Jaeckel came into the office late. He's in the lab now."

Tower sat up. "So? Is that unusual?"

"No, he's done it before."

"He's probably stressed we're coming in later this week," Kira said to Tower with a knowing smile. "You know how he hates micromanagement."

"He didn't come in alone," Hanaka said. "He brought Dr. Morrisey with him."

"Who?" Tower said.

"Charlene Morrisey," Kira said. "She's a trusted member of the team."

"He's never brought her before," Hanaka said. "He's the only one permitted access after hours."

Tower and Kira narrowed their eyes at each other.

"Bring the surveillance cameras up on the secure feed," Tower said. He had led Jaeckel to believe the cameras were for in-house purposes only.

"It's waiting for you now," Hanaka said.

Kira moved to the console at the opposite end of the enormous bedroom, and Tower rose from the bed. Still nude, she entered her log-in information into the system. By the time Tower reached her, twelve images of the secret laboratory at DNAtomy filled the security monitors covering the wall.

"There," Tower said, focusing on one screen.

Kira stroked her keyboard, and the image of a man and woman entering the laboratory filled the center screen.

Jake led Sheryl into the research center of DNAtomy, and the lights flickered on. Air-conditioning hummed, computers whispered, and small lights glowed. A dozen long tables served as desks. Glass-faced rooms lined the side walls. After twenty-two months, he had finally penetrated the nerve center of Tower International.

"Walk casually, like you know where we're going," he whispered.

They crossed the length of the center. In one of the side rooms, he observed computer servers in a climate-controlled environment. In the next room, one hundred floor-to-ceiling glass tubes contained blood and other genetic materials.

Reaching into his pocket, Jake dropped a plastic packet the size of an envelope and as thick as a hamburger on the floor. He had wrapped it in bubble wrap secured with electrical tape.

"How could they keep all of this a secret?" Sheryl said, matching his whisper.

"This is just the tip of the iceberg."

"Something isn't right," Tower said, watching his scientists cross the research center.

Kira brought up profiles of Jaeckel and Morrisey on two screens.

"Call Jaeckel and see what he's up to."

"I did," Hanaka said. "He's not answering. But I called Morrissey, too, and she's at home right now. That's an imposter."

Kira zoomed a different camera in on the scientists, then blew up the image of Morrissey. "That isn't her. It's our Sheryl Helman." On another screen, she enlarged the image of Jaeckel.

"Then that's Helman somehow," he said with equal measures of awe and self-congratulation. "He's there to wipe out our Biogens. Call Faulkner at White River Security and tell him to scramble a team now."

On East End Avenue, Maria entered Carl Schurz park. Scores of homeless people occupied the benches, and several huddled on the ground.

"Spare some change?" a man said.

"How about some food?" a woman said.

"We need water," another man said.

She kept walking, then climbed the curved stone steps to the walkway overlooking the East River.

Jake and Sheryl entered the next chamber, identical in size and configuration to the research center. The overhead lights flickered on while the lights in the space behind them turned dark. No tables or desks occupied the main floor area, but glass-faced rooms lined both long walls. Jake and Sheryl moved forward, glancing sideways at the rooms, which remained dark.

"Don't look inside," Jake said. "Remember, we're in here every day. Nothing can surprise us.

A large animal crashed against the glass wall of a room, triggering the light in its cage, and Sheryl's body jerked as she cried out. A gorilla with alligator skin instead of fur pounded on the glass, which Jake concluded was some form of Plexiglas. Sheryl clawed at Jake's arm. The swamp gorilla roared at them, its yellow, reptilian eyes dilating and its lips curling back to reveal two rows of fangs. The beast had four long arms, and while its roar could not escape its prison, its blows against the Plexiglas produced dull thuds.

"Jesus," Sheryl said, no longer whispering. "Can I please take out my gun?"

"Not until we reach the next room," Jake said.

Lights blossomed in the Plexiglas cages ahead as the swamp gorilla's attention to them stirred the other inhabitants. Sheryl grabbed his hand but he shook it off.

"Play your role," he said.

Four-foot-long centipedes crawled over their Plexiglas wall, leaving a sticky trail of slime in their wake. Their undersides revealed human lips that parted to reveal bear teeth.

A bald woman with five tentacles, each one longer than her torso, lay back on her elbows, revealing an orifice in the center of the bottom of her squid-like body which sprayed an inky black substance at her Plexiglas wall.

"Charming," Sheryl said. "I suddenly feel inadequate."

A humanoid boy with the arms of a praying mantis and claws of a lobster blinked bulbous black eyes at them.

"I'm going to be sick," Sheryl said.

A lion with eight limbs paced its confines, twin tails whipping at the Plexiglas. An enormous bat with the head of a little girl screeched and extended its leathery wings. An anaconda with the head of a Doberman slithered across its floor. Ratlike creatures with scrawny waists and hunched spines snapped alligator jaws at them. A man with leech suckers covering his entire body scaled his Plexiglas wall. A panther covered with porcupine quills paced as the lion hybrid had. Other beasts proved harder to identify: bipeds and quadrupeds with multiple eyes and mouths. An empty cage caused Jake to think of the monster that had attacked him at South Mountain Reservation.

"I can't be one of these *things*," Sheryl said.

"No. Your breed is in the next room."

Gorman exited the curved stone stairway and saw Vasquez standing two hundred yards away at the railing of the walkway overlooking the East River. Other adults—potential witnesses—walked hand in hand in the moonlight, ignoring the homeless people huddled in groups on the ground. Taking a dog-eared paperback out of his back pocket, he sat on a stone bench illuminated by a lamp and waited.

Without turning in his direction, Vasquez pivoted and walked toward Gracie Manor, where the mayor resided.

Rising, Gorman returned the paperback to his pocket and followed.

Jake and Sheryl entered the final chamber, triggering the overhead lights. Dozens of metal-and-glass cylinders eight feet long and three feet in diameter protruded from the walls, each one connected to a breathing machine, like an iron lung. Plastic tubes fed nutrients into the occupants of the cylinders, and others removed body waste. Jake had seen one of these in the Soul Chamber at the Tower; it had contained a biogenic model of Nicholas Tower Jr.

"This is it," he said. "The end of the road."

They peered through the curved glass window on the nearest cylinder at Young Nick's features. Monitors had been attached to the naked man's chest using suction cups.

"This was the original model," Jake said. "Tower created them for organ replacement and therapeutic cloning."

The next cylinder contained a biogenic clone as well.

And the one after that.

And the next.

Jake counted three Towers in all. Then he and Sheryl stared at two perfect nude replicas of Kira.

"I can see why you found her hard to resist," Sheryl said.

"All the scientific trickery in the world couldn't make what's inside her attractive." He regretted the words as soon as he uttered them.

"This is the man who killed me," Sheryl said in a quivering voice as they gazed at a replica of Marc Gorman, the Cipher.

"Yes, and I killed him." It was strange for Jake to see Gorman without the faces of his victims tattooed on his chest.

A replica of Gorman occupied the next cylinder as well.

The cylinder after that was empty.

"Oh no," Jake said. "They set one loose."

Maria.

Maria descended another flight of stone steps and entered the park proper, ornamental lamps illuminating the path. She saw no other people as she passed the statue of Peter Pan and made her way to the aqueduct where Sheryl had been murdered. It took only a few minutes for her to locate. The lights of Gracie Manor glowed through the trees to her right.

She stood at the mouth of the aqueduct, gazing at the ground within its tunnel. She and Edgar had stood in this same spot twenty-two months earlier, staring at Sheryl's corpse. It had been raining that night, and Sheryl's throat had been slashed twice, as had the other victims of the Cipher. Maria recalled the dead woman's gaze; she had never shaken it. Now empty sleeping bags and filthy cardboard boxes covered the ground.

Turning, she scanned the terrain she had just crossed. Then she took out a cigarette and lit it, trying to ease the edge she felt with a nicotine rush.

Gorman circled the park, keeping Vasquez in sight. She stood smoking a cigarette by the aqueduct—almost the exact same spot where he had collected Sheryl Helman's soul. The park was known as a place where homosexuals went for anonymous sex. Was Vasquez a pervert? Maybe Helman didn't know what he had in her.

He lost sight of her as he ducked behind the aqueduct, but she came back into view soon enough as he approached the opposite entrance to the tunnel. She stood with her back to him, the tip of the cigarette in her left hand glowing red in the darkness. Sliding his dagger from its sheath, he entered the tunnel, moving with caution and deliberation, stepping around cardboard on the ground, gliding along the curved tunnel wall so she could not see him out of the corner of her eye. Thoughts of Kira performing sexual acts with the billionaire Tower filled his mind, and he relished the opportunity to make this cop pay for it.

This is going to be good, he thought.

He waited for her to raise the cigarette to her mouth, so her hand would be occupied, and then he raised the dagger over his head and closed in on her, near enough to smell her perfume. Since he didn't have to take her photo, he anticipated an easy kill.

Jake disconnected the life support cables from the first cylinder. "We have to hurry!"

The breathing apparatus for the cylinder stopped

functioning, and the heart monitor flatlined. Jake ran to the next one.

Sheryl moved to the cylinders protruding from the opposite wall. "This one is you."

"Do it!" He jerked the next set of life support lines out of the wall.

Sheryl mimicked his actions, then ran to the next cylinder. "This one's empty."

Jake skipped the empty cylinder and unhooked the cables from the first Kira unit. The whining sounds of three heart monitors flatlining overlapped each other.

"And this one."

"Keep going!"

Jake unhooked the support for the second Kira.

"It's me."

Jake ran to the first Gorman. "Do you need me to do it?"

"No." Sheryl unhooked her duplicate's life support, then moved to the next one.

Taking a drag on her cigarette, Maria spun around just as a silhouette blocked her view of the opposite end of the tunnel. She held her Glock in her hand, and she stepped back, clasped it in both hands, and opened fire, the muzzle flashes illuminating her assailant. Seeing the dagger in his upraised hand, she continued firing, peppering his chest with entry wounds that coughed blood.

The man's eyes widened in shock as he dropped the dagger, but Maria continued firing until he collapsed in a bloody heap.

.⁜.⸪

"They're killing them all," Tower said, spittle flying from his lips.

"White River Security will never get there in time," Kira said.

"I have a better idea. We can't save our counterparts, but we can save the rest of the menagerie and make sure Helman doesn't get away."

.⁜.⸪

Tossing her cigarette away and exhaling smoke, Maria walked over to the corpse on the ground. Taking out her phone, she shined it on the dead man's features. Even with his slicked-back hair and eyeliner, she recognized Gorman. She knew what Jake would do in this situation: he would run or calmly leave the scene.

Raising the phone, she pressed a number on the auto dial.

"Police dispatch, where's your emergency?"

"This is Detective Maria Vasquez with Special Homicide. I just killed a perp in Carl Schurz Park near Gracie Manor in the One-Nine precinct."

GREGORY LAMBERSON

With the heart monitors whining behind them, Jake and Sheryl fled from the rear chamber and skidded to a stop. Before them, the Plexiglas faces of the cages containing the Biogens rose into the ceiling in unison, freeing the monsters.

THIRTY-ONE

Jake and Sheryl stood frozen as creatures leapt, crawled, slithered, and oozed out of their respective cells. A cacophony followed them: roars, cries, snarls, and sounds impossible to describe. A shrill trilling caused the hair on the back of Jake's neck to stand on end. Sheryl drew the Ruger from her handbag and aimed it in both hands.

"Get back inside," Jake said.

They backed into the rear space too late: a prehistoric monster covered with gray scales sniffed the air and howled in their direction. But before it could move forward, the quill-covered panther leapt upon its back, raking razor-sharp claws over its scales. Then the lion creature tore into the squid woman, who screamed and wrapped her tentacles around the beast's flanks, then sprayed its defensive ink in the monster's face, which smoked. The lion tried to shake her free, but her tentacles held it tight. The rat creatures dove upon the mantis boy, who flailed at them with his appendages. Their metallic teeth gnawed on his arms, whittling them until they fell off in geysers of clear blood. The anaconda with the Doberman head curled around the man with the suckers all over his body, and the leech hybrid drew blood from the serpent. Jaws snapped, teeth chewed, and claws raked. All of the creatures attacked each other in a frenzy, spilling buckets of slime, blood, and jelly.

Sheryl shot a confused look at Jake, who shrugged. Tower had ordered the creation of flesh-and-blood weapons that were incapable of serving together.

"We have to get out of here," she said.

"We can't leave until I detonate the explosives. Doing so would defeat our whole purpose. The computers and DNA strands have to go."

"What are we supposed to do, wait for them to kill each other? That could take all night."

A shriek rose above the fighting, and the enormous bat with the girl's head soared over the melee, beating its leathery wings.

Jake drew his Thunder Ranch and fired three shots at the monster's midsection, drawing the attention of the other monsters. The bat recoiled in midair, the bones that served as a frame for its wing snapping like the spokes of an umbrella in a windstorm, and crashed to the floor. Gazing at Jake, it crawled toward him, a hissing sound escaping from its lips.

Jake fired three more shots into the creature, killing

it. Then he handed his revolver to Sheryl. "Reload."

Sheryl handed him the Ruger, and he shoved it into his holster. Then he removed a handheld trigger from his pocket and squeezed it. In the research center, the plastic explosives he had dropped detonated, exploding Plexiglas and hurling debris. A fireball rose to the high ceiling like a comet, dispersing orange flames. The monsters panicked and thundered in their direction.

"Great idea," Sheryl said.

"Mission accomplished," Jake said.

He squeezed the trigger twice more, and a second set of explosives detonated, flinging the monsters in different directions. The panther creature caught fire and ran in a circle. Several lumps of flesh lay smoldering on the floor. The rat creatures surged forward, their teeth reflecting light. They hopped like rabbits.

Drawing the Ruger, Jake kneeled and opened fire. The critters were hard to pin down due to their speed, but he managed to pick off all four of them. They flopped around on the floor like beached fish until they stilled. Beside Jake, Sheryl snapped the Thunder Ranch's cylinder shut.

A cringe-inducing roar filled the space, and the swamp gorilla charged out of the smoke swirling around him.

"Mother-father!" Jake aimed the Ruger and fired three times at the beast, which kept charging, running on all sixes.

"Oh, my God," Sheryl said.

Jake fired three more times, and he saw the rounds chew into the surface of the swamp gorilla's gator hide, but still the beast did not slow. Then the gun's slide locked in his hand: empty. He had wasted too many shots on the rat creatures.

Baring its tusks and fangs, the swamp gorilla slammed into Jake with such force he crashed into one of the cylinders, toppling it and ejecting a Tower corpse. The swamp gorilla raised two arms above his head and brought them down. Jake rolled out of the way, and the monster's fists pounded the cylinder, producing echoes and dents. Jake scrambled over the cylinder and rolled under the next one. His chest ached, and he feared he had broken ribs.

The swamp gorilla landed on top of the second cylinder and roared at Jake, a sound so loud and ferocious it gave Jake chills. He attempted to slide under the next cylinder, but the monster jumped on the floor behind him and shoved the cylinder onto the floor ahead of Jake. It rolled into the next cylinder with a clanging sound, knocking the Kira Biogen onto the floor. Jake cast a fearful look over his shoulder just as the beast brought its fists down again, smashing his back and right shoulder and flattening him on the floor. He didn't have the strength to pick himself up. He hoped Sheryl could figure out the escape route and prayed Maria was okay.

Three shots rang out behind him, and the swamp gorilla bellowed in pain. Jake forced himself onto his back as the monster turned around. Sheryl stood before it, brandishing the Thunder Ranch in both hands. She fired the weapon three more times at point-blank range. The swamp gorilla dropped onto its knuckles, uttered a pained growl, then toppled forward, its breathing growing labored.

Sheryl screamed: the anaconda with the Doberman head ensnared her legs, its glistening belly covered with red circles from the leech boy's suckers.

Jake got to his feet, his chest tight with pain.

Sheryl pitched forward, the anaconda working its way up her legs, its lips pulled back in a toothy snarl. "Help me!" She tried crawling toward Jake, but the anaconda pulled her back down.

Jake staggered forward. The anaconda had wrapped itself around her legs and waist, and she beat at its scaly hide with the empty Thunder Ranch. Jake ran to the threshold leading to the containment center. Water erupted from sprinklers in the ceiling, dousing the carcasses of burning animals, but no alarm sounded. Creatures continued to battle each other within the hazy smoke. As he picked up his Ruger, something ensnared his ankle and jerked him off his feet. Landing facedown on the floor, he heard a strangled moan behind him and rolled onto his back.

The squid woman clung to the wall to the right of the threshold, four of her tentacles splayed out and her gills contracting. The fifth tentacle held him tight. Blood flowed from deep claw marks across her breasts. She sprang off the wall, and Jake scrambled backward using his free leg. She landed where he had just been and issued the trilling sound he had heard earlier. She tried to rock back to fire her defensive ink, but he raised his leg and stomped on the fleshy webbing between two tentacles, planting her upright. Her trilling grew angry as he bolted into a sitting position and pounded the crown of her bald head with the butt of the Ruger, cracking her skull. She grabbed her head with the hands attached to her humanoid limbs as a pale green milky fluid poured out of the wound.

Jake moved away and got to his feet, and she came after him, her tentacles pulling her along the floor. He ran to a glass case recessed in the wall, smashed the glass with one elbow, and jerked a fire ax free of its clamps.

The squid girl closed in on him, her face no longer resembling anything human, her grimace revealing jagged shark teeth.

Jake tossed the axe in the air and caught its handle, then wound his arm in a complete circle and buried the ax deep in her skull.

The squid girl trembled, then fell back and stopped moving.

In the next room, Sheryl screamed.

Jake grabbed the ax and tried to wrench it free, but the dead squid girl's skull would not relinquish it. He ran to the threshold but slipped in squid slime and crashed onto his ass. Seeing the anaconda hybrid had extended its grip on Sheryl to her breasts, he got up and raced over to them.

"I can't breathe," Sheryl said.

The anaconda creature bared its canine teeth as it growled. Jake chopped at the head with his gun, causing the monster to yelp. It lunged at him, and he pistol-whipped the top of its skull, dazing it. The head recoiled on the serpentine body, and Jake had difficulty inflicting the damage he desired. The creature went on the offensive, snapping its jaws at him, and he jerked his arm back. God only knew what kind of venom those teeth contained. It clamped its jaws over the barrel of the Ruger and flung it away. Jake drove his hook into the creature's right eye, rupturing it, and the monster unleashed an agonized howl. It rolled Sheryl away from Jake, protecting its head. Jake straddled it, raised his arm, and buried his hook in its scaly body, producing a jet of yellow blood.

The anaconda hybrid roared. Sinking his fingers into the creature's scaly hide, Jake drew his hook down, slicing the snakeskin open. He backed up, slicing another length, and the snake flesh separated, spilling glistening innards onto the floor. The head turned in Jake's direction but could not reach him. Grunting, Jake pulled his hook down a third length, and yellow fluid poured out of the opening along with snake guts.

The creature relaxed its grip on Sheryl, who squirmed free of its hold with a disgusted cry. Stepping on the end of the monster's tail, Jake lengthened the slit, then reached inside the serpentine body, braced his hook on the monster's spine, and closed his hand over warm, sticky vertebrae. Pushing with his hand and pulling with his hook, he snapped the spine. The creature hissed, then uncoiled its body, writhing on the floor in its own fluids.

Jake gasped for breath, his heart pounding. He handed the Ruger to Sheryl. "Load both guns."

Sheryl took the Ruger, then screamed again just as Jake felt something wet and tingling on the back of one leg. Whipping his body around, he saw a trio of the three-foot-long centipedes crawling through the threshold. They moved with frightening speed, and the sight of them filled him with revulsion. So did the realization that the fourth one had just crawled over his buttocks.

"It's on your back," Sheryl shrieked.

"Well, get it off!"

"I can't!"

A dozen sharp teeth pierced Jake's back, and he recalled the mouths along the creatures' undersides. His flesh tore, and he realized the monster was *chewing* on him. Another chomp like that could paralyze him. Throwing himself into the air, he landed flat on his back with a crunch and a pop that soaked his back in goo. He raised his knees to his chest, wrapped his arms around them, and rocked back and forth, producing similar sounds. When he got up, he saw the smeared remains of half the creature on the floor.

Sheryl screamed again: two of the creatures moved between and around her feet, and she danced around them. Jake stomped on one, and the other crawled up her leg. The one he had stomped continued to move its legs, so he stomped it again and rubbed it across the floor. Sheryl's screams grew louder, and blood flowed from her thigh beneath the monster upon her. Jake had no choice: spreading his fingers wide, he buried them into the membrane covering the centipede's body. The monster's legs danced in a panicked spasm, but its teeth did not release Sheryl.

Sheryl clawed at Jake's shoulders. "Get it off me!"

Jake forced his hook between Sheryl's thigh and the centipede, separating them, and pulled the monster free. Sheryl backed away, blood flowing from the bite wound. Jake turned the centipede over and gazed in disgust at its gnashing teeth, slick with Sheryl's blood. Crouching on one knee, he raised the centipede over his head and smashed it on the floor several times until he had reduced it to pale mush.

Sheryl crawled on top of a cylinder and pointed past Jake. Tears streamed down her cheeks. "There!"

Jake looked at a wall near the threshold where the final centipede clung, motionless except for a nervous twitching in its legs. Jake picked up Sheryl's handbag, walked to the cylinder, and held it out to her. Blood oozed out of the burning bite in his back. "Load the damn gun."

Taking the bag, she fished for another clip for the Ruger.

He grabbed the Thunder Ranch, and when he handed it to her she gave him the loaded Ruger. When he crossed the floor, the centipede took off. He raised the Ruger, aimed, then fired three times before the centipede dropped to the floor. He fired twice more, yellow fluid exploding from the creature before it stopped moving. He hated centipedes.

When he turned back to Sheryl, she was speed loading the Thunder Ranch with trembling hands. The bloodstain around the hole in her skirt spread.

A deafening roar echoed in the chamber outside, and an immense silhouette formed within the sprinkler water and lumbered forward. The prehistoric rhino creature came at them, its scaly hide crisscrossed with gashes, bite marks, and pieces of glass.

Jake and Sheryl sprinted to the rear of the chamber. The wall had been divided into four panels, with two palm buttons on one. He tapped one button with the butt of the Ruger, but nothing happened.

"It's getting closer," Sheryl said.

Searching the room, Jake located another face recognition camera and ran over to it.

"Hurry!"

Refusing to waste even one second looking at the advancing monster, Jake stood before the camera and prayed it recognized him even with biogenic blood spattered on his features. Behind him, a panel rose with a hum. As he rushed back to Sheryl, he saw the dino rhino had thundered into the chamber. He and Sheryl scrambled into the cargo elevator even before the panel had finished rising. Sheryl aimed the Thunder Ranch with both hands.

"Don't bother," Jake said as he palmed another button. "These bullets won't penetrate its hide. That thing is a living tank."

The green behemoth broke into a gallop that shook the floor and walls. Jake and Sheryl huddled together in the elevator as the steel panel blocked the creature from their view and locked into place. The elevator surged upward just as the monster slammed into the panel. Metal groaned below them, and the monster roared, the sound muted.

"I feel bad for whoever has to wrangle that son of a bitch," Jake said. "We're not out of the woods yet."

Thunder echoed in the shaft below them, and Sheryl turned to him.

"I'm pretty sure it can't climb or jump with all that mass."

The elevator stopped and they stood. A new panel rose, and they faced a small control room encased in Plexiglas and another vault door. Jake moved to the face recognition camera, and the vault door opened. They entered a simple loading bay. He pressed another button, and the vault door closed behind them. Then the entire vault descended into the floor, hiding the elevator, and the loading bay door rose with a grinding sound. Bright light shot in from outside.

Jake and Sheryl traded knowing looks. There was nothing left for them to say.

Three cars marked *Security* had been parked lengthwise thirty feet away, with spotlights shining on Jake and Sheryl. Through the glare, Jake made out half a dozen uniformed men aiming shotguns and Glocks at them. A chopper whirred in the distance.

"Drop your weapons, and come out with your hands up," a man said, his voice amplified by a speaker.

Jake tossed the Ruger on the pavement where it clattered, and Sheryl threw the Thunder Ranch beside it. Raising their arms, they walked into the light.

Brawny security men with military crew cuts surrounded them and jerked their arms behind them.

"Are we under arrest?" Jake said.

"You're in trouble is what you are," one of the security officers said.

The chopper grew closer and louder, pinning them with a searchlight.

"There's a monster down there," Jake said.

"I don't know what you're talking about," the officer said.

The chopper, as black as night, landed just beyond the police cars. The side door opened, and four men in dark paramilitary gear jumped out.

White River Security.

THIRTY-TWO

Maria stood within the perimeter of crime scene tape stretched around the aqueduct. Eight uniformed POs surrounded the area, and Mauceri and Totty approached her from the aqueduct, where the Crime Scene Unit shot photographs and video. A few onlookers, mostly homeless people, stood behind the crime scene tape. She wondered how many of them lived in the tunnel.

"You did quite a number on that guy," Mauceri said.

She knew better than to make a flippant remark.

"Here come the cheese eaters," Totty said.

Hammerman and Klein, two inspectors from Internal Affairs Bureau, ducked beneath the crime scene tape and joined them. Hammerman was tall with dark hair and silver sideburns, dressed in a black suit, while the squat Klein wore slacks and a blazer with a Mickey Mouse tie.

"What's the situation, Detectives?" Klein said.

"I'm a lieutenant, Inspector," Mauceri said. "A bad

guy tried to knife my detective, and she took him down," Mauceri said.

"Nice and simple, huh?" Klein said.

"It sure looks like a clean shoot to me," Totty said.

"That's our determination to make," Hammerman said. "Has anyone taken your gun, Detective Vasquez?"

"Not yet," Maria said.

Hammerman pulled on latex gloves. "I'll take that now, then." He removed a clear plastic bag from his pocket and held it open before her.

Maria took out her Glock, ejected the clip, and deposited both items in the bag. She did not like turning it over, and she supposed her feelings showed.

"Don't worry. You'll get it back pending the investigation," Hammerman said, sealing the bag. "Are you up for being interviewed tonight?"

"Why not? I've got nothing to hide." She looked at Mauceri.

"Let me guess," Mauceri said. "You want to come in late tomorrow."

"It's not like you can send me out on the street. I'll be chained to my desk for thirty days. Right, Hammerman?"

"You know the drill. We're going to look around. Why don't you meet us at IAB in an hour and a half?"

"Can I get a lift back to the squad room?" Maria said to Mauceri.

"Sure," Mauceri said. "I wasn't going back that way anyway."

Two hours later, Maria waited in an interview room at Internal Affairs Bureau, located at 315 Hudson Street. She wondered if this was the same room where Jake had resigned from the force.

The door opened and Hammerman and Klein entered.

"Sorry for the wait," Hammerman said.

They did not enter alone: Geoghegan followed them.

"What's he doing here?" Maria said.

Klein closed the door. "Some freaky details have arisen in this case. This will be a joint IAB–Major Crimes interview."

"Do you want a lawyer?" Geoghegan said.

"I don't need one," Maria said.

Hammerman and Geoghegan sat opposite her, and Klein stood off to the side.

"Let's get started. This interview is being recorded." Hammerman identified the date, case number, and participants. "Tell us what happened tonight, Detective."

"It's all in the statement I gave at the scene," Maria said.

"Humor us and this will go faster."

"I left work at 2100 hours. I was feeling restless. Earlier in the morning I had to say good-bye to a little girl I fostered, Shana Robbins. I didn't feel like going home to Brooklyn, so I took a walk. I ended up on the Upper East Side."

"Carl Schurz Park is sixty plus blocks from the Detective

Bureau," Geoghegan said. "How'd you get there?"

"I took a bus."

"Wasn't your car parked in the lot?" Klein said.

"Yes. Like I said, I took a walk. I didn't really have a destination in mind."

"But you ended up taking a bus to the park," Hammerman said.

"No, I ended up taking a bus to the Upper East Side and walked to the park."

"What did you do there?"

"I stood at the railing for a while, watching the tugboats on the water. Then I walked toward Gracie Manor. I started thinking about an old case of mine. The Cipher killed Sheryl Helman in the tunnel of the aqueduct in the park."

"You're seeing Jake Helman, right? Sheryl Helman's widower?"

"Right." She knew Geoghegan had filled them in.

"Are you living with him?" Klein said.

"Temporarily. Daria left him homeless."

"What happened next?" Hammerman said.

"I decided to visit the aqueduct, and I smoked a cigarette there. I heard footsteps behind me. When I turned around, I saw a man lunging at me out of the darkness. I stepped back and saw he had a knife—a big one, not a pocketknife. Sensing my life was in danger, I drew my gun and fired."

"Did you identify yourself as a police officer?"

"I don't remember. Maybe not. Everything happened so fast. But he didn't stop when he saw my weapon. If I hadn't fired, he would have killed me."

"Maybe he didn't see the gun," Hammerman said. "It was dark."

"He saw it. I held it in both hands and stood in the light. If I saw his knife, he saw my gun."

"How many shots did you fire?" Klein said.

"I don't remember, but I counted six entry wounds after he went down."

"Isn't that excessive?" Klein said.

"I fired until he stopped coming at me."

"Couldn't you have shot him in the leg?" Hammerman said.

"That would have required me to look away from his eyes and his knife. There wasn't time."

"What did you do after you shot him?" Klein said.

"I checked for a pulse. There wasn't one. Then I called Dispatch on my phone."

"How long would you say you stood at the aqueduct before the perp attacked you?" Hammerman said.

"Not even long enough to finish my cigarette."

"So you went for a walk and ended up taking a bus to the same park where your boyfriend's wife was murdered. You stood in the exact spot where a famous serial killer killed her with a dagger, and another man tried to kill *you* with a dagger."

Maria held Geoghegan's gaze. "I wouldn't say it was the same spot. Sheryl Helman was killed inside the tunnel."

"Are you ready for some shit?" Geoghegan said. "The perp you killed has the same fingerprints as Marc Gorman. It looks like you killed a dead man."

Maria tried to look and sound surprised. "That isn't possible."

"You don't say. I've seen the crime scene photos. That stiff even looks like Gorman."

"He was alive when I shot him."

"Didn't you notice the resemblance between him and Gorman?"

"No. This guy had eyeliner on, and his hair was all gelled up. I don't usually make mental comparisons between perps and people who have been dead for two years."

"Even when you took his pulse, you didn't get a feeling about him?"

"It was dark and I've never killed a man before." She had killed plenty on Pavot Island.

"You went to that aqueduct thinking about Sheryl Helman and Marc Gorman, and seconds later a man who looked exactly like Gorman, who even had his fingerprints, tried to kill you in the same manner that Gorman killed Jake Helman's wife. How the hell do you explain that?"

Maria sat forward. "I don't. I can't. And I don't have

to. I have to answer your questions about what went down in that park. I killed a perp who tried to kill a cop. I don't have to know or understand who or what that perp was."

"Why do you say 'what the perp was'?" Hammerman said.

"I saw Gorman's corpse after he was killed, so I know he was dead. Dead people don't tend to visit the scenes of their crimes. You're telling me the man I killed tonight has Gorman's fingerprints. I have to take your word for that. Why would you lie? No two people have identical fingerprints, not even identical twins. I can only guess how this is possible: we live in an age of scientific wonders."

"Say what's on your mind."

"Am I the only person in this room who has the balls to say what we're all thinking? Maybe the guy I killed *was* Gorman or a clone of Gorman. Or maybe his fingertips were genetically altered."

Klein guffawed and Geoghegan smiled.

"Let's just say for the sake of argument that your theory is correct," Hammerman said.

"It's a shot in the dark, not a theory," Maria said. "You've presented me with an impossible scenario. I'm just grasping at straws to provide a possible rational explanation."

"Why would a clone of Gorman want to kill you?"

"Maybe he didn't. Maybe I was just the wrong person in the wrong place at the wrong time."

"Or maybe you were the right person in the right place at the right time," Geoghegan said. "Maybe he wanted revenge against whoever killed him."

Maria gave him a dismissive look. "I was on duty when Gorman was killed. Edgar Hopkins and I worked around the clock to catch him."

"You also cleared Helman of executing him."

"I didn't clear Jake. Kira Thorn did. Oh, shit, look at that: Kira Thorn works for Tower International, the leader in genetic engineering, and she just returned to the US after an extended stay in Europe. Damn."

Hammerman and Klein glanced at each other.

Geoghegan's face tightened. "Where's Helman now?"

Maria sat back. "I have no idea, but you've really got to let go of this obsession you have with him. It makes the whole department look bad."

Geoghegan sat fuming.

"So you think this department should investigate Tower International for allegedly creating the clone of a dead man who tried to kill you?" Hammerman said.

Maria shrugged. "It's a thought."

THIRTY-THREE

The chopper flew over Manhattan with Jake and Sheryl strapped into seats in the fuselage. From this height, Jake saw where the electricity cut off: buildings gleaming in the night gave way to black zones peppered with occasional lights powered by generators. His face, head, and muscles ached, but one of the four White River Security contractors guarding them had bandaged his back and Sheryl's thigh.

The chopper veered to one side, and the Tower came into view, its top floor illuminated. The Flatiron Building remained dark along with most of the rest of the neighborhood; work lights illuminated the work zone on Madison Avenue and Twenty-third Street even though debris removal stopped at sundown. Jake imagined police officers or security guards protected the zone from scavengers. The lights highlighted his office building.

This is my neighborhood, Jake thought. He wasn't sure what that meant to him.

The chopper circled toward the Tower, and the heli-pad on the building's roof came into view.

Back to the beginning.

He looked at Sheryl. She had performed well in the DNAtomy lab, and in a strange way he felt proud of her. The chopper descended to the landing pad below, rocking its passengers as it touched down. The rotary blades continued to spin.

One of the contractors opened the side panel, and Jake saw Hanaka standing expressionless outside. Two of the contractors hopped out with machine guns in their hands.

The other two unbuckled Jake and Sheryl and prodded them to the exit. Jake jumped onto the roof, the deafening rotary blades whipping his hair in the warm night air. Sheryl jumped out beside him. Hanaka gave them a measured stare, then turned and led the entourage into a small structure atop the roof: a control room facing the chopper. No one occupied the station, and Hanaka brought them to an elevator and aimed his security ID at a scanner. The elevator opened, and the seven people crowded into it.

Glancing at the camera mounted on the ceiling, Jake knew Tower and Kira watched them. With some effort, he could wrestle his stump out of the prosthetic holding the hook, which would allow him to free his hand, but what good would that do? Four men held guns on him and Sheryl in the confined space, and Hanaka didn't need a gun to kill at least one of them. It didn't matter: he didn't want to escape.

They got off on the top floor of the building. Jake recognized the corridor, which wrapped around Tower's atrium on the opposite of the building from where the living units and the Demonstration Room had been. They stopped at a door, Hanaka unlocked it with his ID, and they entered an anteroom identical to the one leading from Kira's office into Tower's. They faced a gleaming vault door. Hanaka threw a lever, and the halves of the vault door separated, receding into the walls and revealing the atrium inside: a man-made park complete with a stream, a waterfall, and trees.

A lot had changed. Once upon a time, the atrium's existence had been a secret. Now Tower permitted his lackeys a peek inside his world.

Hanaka led the party into the park, and they crossed a footbridge over the stream. Tower and Kira stood outside the structure housing his Soul Chamber in the center of the park. Tower wore a tuxedo and Kira a gown, as if they had just returned from a gala event.

God knows what they've been up to, Jake thought.

Sheryl glanced around with an expression of wonder. Jake supposed the atrium resembled Oz or Willy Wonka's chocolate factory to a newcomer.

Scanning the trees, he noticed another difference

from his last time here: the wombs containing genetically enhanced Biogens no longer hung from the branches, a concession to transparency.

They stopped before their scowling hosts. He and Sheryl had managed to piss them off.

Good.

"Take that ridiculous mask off him," Tower said.

Two of the contractors seized Jake's arms, and Hanaka pulled off his wig and then the bald cap. Jake felt glad to be rid of them. After discarding the items, Hanaka felt along the edges of the appliance, tracing it from Jake's jaw to his hairline. He tugged at the appliance, but it did not come off.

"It's glued on," Hanaka said.

"That's his problem," Tower said. "Tear it off."

Hanaka worked his fingers between the silicone and Jake's forehead, and the adhesive tore at Jake's skin.

"Hold his head," Hanaka said.

One of the contractors standing behind Jake grabbed the sides of his head with both hands and pulled it back. Staring at Jake with zero emotion, Hanaka raised his elbows level with his eyes and jerked down on the silicone, ripping it off Jake's face.

Imagining that one thousand needles had just pierced his flesh and the nerves beneath them, Jake screamed. His cuts reopened, and the sweat that had collected beneath the silicone poured into them. Liquid flowed over the contours of his face, but he could not tell how much of it was sweat and how much was blood. Tower and Kira's growing smiles suggested the latter.

Stepping back, Hanaka examined the silicone mask, then held it up to Tower and Kira. The mask had torn in several places during its removal, and blood dripped from it. "Now it looks like him."

"The mask still looks better," Kira said.

Hanaka opened his fingers, allowing the appliance to drop next to the wig and bald cap.

Tower looked Jake up and down with contempt. "Remove that contraption on his arm."

"Both his arms will be free then," Hanaka said.

"Trust me. He's more dangerous with that thing on."

Hanaka nodded to the contractors behind Jake, who recognized the sound of a butterfly knife opening. Pressure on the zip tie binding his wrist to his prosthetic dug the plastic tie into his flesh, and then the zip tie fell away. Jake flexed his fingers and closed them, increasing the circulation in them. The contractors pulled Jaeckel's blazer down his arms and threw it aside. Then they ripped off his tattered shirt, revealing the harness for the prosthetic.

"Such a cumbersome device," Tower said with disapproval.

Jake kept his eye on Tower and Kira as the contractors unfastened the harness straps. When the prosthetic came off his arm, sweat gushed out of it.

"Give that to me," Tower said.

Hanaka handed the prosthetic and harness to him.

Tower glanced at Jake's hand with suspicion in his eyes. He held the prosthetic upside down, allowing more sweat to pour out. "So unsanitary." Reaching inside the prosthetic, he drew out a straightedge razor with tape folded over its blade. "But not as unhealthy as this."

Kira narrowed her eyes at Jake, then smiled at Tower's ingenuity.

Tower handed the razor to Hanaka, who slid it into his pocket. Then Tower stepped before Jake and drove his fist into Jake's nose, breaking it again and triggering a supernova of pain throughout Jake's head that engulfed the stars he saw before his eye.

Jake collapsed to his knees, half supported by the contractors, and his head slumped forward.

"Stop it!" Sheryl crouched beside Jake. "Are you all right?"

Raising his head, Jake glared at Tower. He spat blood in his direction, then snorted more up his septum and spat that, too. "Yes," he said in a strangled voice, still disoriented by pain.

Tower focused on Sheryl. "How touching. You were supposed to seduce him. You obviously failed, or he wouldn't be here, and billions of dollars' worth of work wouldn't be in ruins now."

Sheryl stared back at him. "I don't know what you think I am, but I promise you that isn't me."

For the first time, Tower smiled. "I assure you, I know you better than you know yourself." He turned to Jake. "I guess I can't really blame you for not wanting to sleep with this mess."

Every breath caused a wheezing sound in the cavern that had been Jake's nose, and he opened his mouth for relief.

"Take them inside," Tower said to Hanaka.

"This way," Hanaka said to the contractors.

Hanaka entered the hub, and the contractors prodded Jake and Sheryl forward. Hanaka stopped at the viewing window that faced the Soul Chamber. The glass and curved, vacuum-formed plastic had been replaced, and a door had been installed. Hanaka opened it with the touch of a button. Hanaka nodded at the interior of the Soul Chamber, and the contractors shoved Jake and Sheryl inside.

"Leave now," Tower said as the Soul Chamber door hummed shut.

Crossing the mosaic floor, Jake glanced up at the stained-glass skylight in the high ceiling, another replacement. Lowering his gaze, he watched the contractors exit the hub.

Tower, Kira, and Hanaka stood at the viewing window.

"Do you wish to call on your angel or demon friends for help?"

Jake did not answer.

"You never had any intention of honoring our agreement," Tower said.

"Neither did you." Jake searched the Soul Chamber for anything he could use as a weapon or to aid in their escape. The smooth walls offered nothing.

"I was curious to see how you'd react. That was my mistake. I had no idea you knew so much about DNAtomy. My police force has disposed of Jaeckel's body, by the way: compacted it in your car. He'll be reported missing tomorrow."

Damn it, Jake thought. *Edgar's going to kill me.*

"The lab is unsalvageable, the genetic strains we spent years developing lost. But everything can be replaced when you're the richest man in the world. All it takes is time, and I've got plenty of that."

Jake walked up to the viewing window, his reflection appearing over Tower. "What about Maria?"

"Unfortunately, she killed the Gorman Biogen."

Good girl.

"We'll take care of her soon enough," Kira said. "Maybe even tonight. We can't allow her to live, and once you've undergone your transformation, she'll become as problematic as you've been."

It hurt Jake to squint. "Transformation?"

"As much as I'd love to throttle you with my own hands, I have no intention of killing you. That would be

384

too simple. I want you to suffer." Tower gestured at Kira. "My dear."

Kira manipulated a control out of Jake's sight, and a moment later a hissing sound filled the chamber.

Jake looked up at a vent near the ceiling as black smoke escaped from it.

Black Magic!

"Jake?" Sheryl said.

"It's a narcotic that turns people into zonbies," Jake said.

"I just love when people use the correct pronunciation." Tower faced Sheryl. "It's a slower process than Jake just described. You'll become an addict first, craving nothing more than your next fix, which we'll happily provide. You'll wither away, becoming an emaciated animal—a human scarecrow. Eventually, you'll suffer a fatal overdose. Jake will return, his soul trapped inside his lifeless shell. How appropriate to turn you in here, eh, Jake?"

Jake swallowed.

"I don't know what will happen to you," Tower said to Sheryl. "We've never tested the effects of Black Magic on a Biogen. Since you have no soul, it stands to reason you won't reanimate. But it will be fun to see you wallowing in your own filth anyway. You'll even enjoy it in the beginning."

Sheryl backed away from the window as the sweet-smelling black smoke spread.

"Jake will resurrect before you die, because he's already an addict. Aren't you, Jake?"

"Yes."

"Tell me: how did you get Jaeckel to turn on me? I'm told his body showed no signs of torture, just the gunshot wounds that killed him."

Jake looked from Kira to Tower. "I told him Sheryl and I were members of RAGE. That opened him up better than Sodium Pentothal. We had to shoot him just to shut him up."

Kira just stared at him, as if trying to read his mind.

Tower stared at Jake. Then a smile spread across his face, and he burst into laughter. "Oh, that is rich. You used my own imaginary domestic terrorist organization against me. I played the terror card too often for my own good." He clapped. "Bravo."

"Jake," Sheryl said, "get down on your knees."

Jake snorted. "For this soulless bastard? That's not happening."

Tower's smile faltered. "Once you've inhaled enough of that Magic, you'll do whatever I tell you to do—even kill Vasquez, if I decide to let her live that long." His smile returned. "Yes, I like that idea."

"I wasn't lying when I told Jaeckel we were RAGE." Reaching up, Jake plucked his glass eye from his socket. "I *am* rage."

Jake ran to the center of the chamber and assumed a perfect pitcher's stance. He wound his arm, raised his leg, then pitched his glass eye at the viewing window.

Tower, Kira, and Hanaka all seemed to realize what was happening at the same time, and Hanaka dove into Tower, knocking him out of the way. The plastic explosives packed inside the eye exploded as soon as it struck the window, blowing out the window and the vacuum-formed wall around it in a blinding flash and deafening roar.

Jake tackled Sheryl and pinned her to the floor, protecting her from any blowback. He thought he heard a scream but couldn't be sure.

When the debris stopped raining, he jumped to his feet. The explosion had dispersed the Black Magic lingering near the skylight and had also destroyed the pumping system that spread it.

He helped Sheryl to her feet, then tore out of the Soul Chamber. Hanaka's bloody corpse lay on the floor. One of his arms had been blown off, and smoke rose from his trousers. Jake searched the dead man but found no weapons.

Sheryl emerged from the Soul Chamber behind him.

"This is it," he said.

Sheryl cupped the sides of his head in her hands, then kissed him. The sensation of her tongue pushing against his surprised him, but he allowed her the kiss. He knew she loved him, and he could not deny his feelings for her. Then he broke away from her and ran after Tower and Kira.

He didn't have to run far: they stood outside the

hub, waiting for him, and he slowed to a stop. He stared at Tower, then Kira, and they stared at him.

"You did everything today wearing a glass eye full of explosives?" Tower said.

"I told you I'd bring this building down around you," Jake said.

Tower pointed at him. "Take him now."

"With pleasure, Daddy." Kira clenched her teeth. Her entire body trembled. Then a milky substance ruptured her sides, and four extra arms burst free of her body. She tore the gown to shreds, freeing her breasts and shrieking.

Jake had witnessed this transformation before, but this time he didn't have a knife for defense. She charged at him, and he searched for something to use as a weapon. Kira knocked him to the ground. Using two hands, she pinned his arms to the earth; using two others, she held his head in place; and she used the final two to choke him, all the while grinding her pelvis against his. He knew what lurked between her legs, and it wasn't pretty.

"Finish him once and for all," Tower said.

Kira's eyes dilated, and a serpentine tongue flicked out of her mouth. Jake snapped his jaws at the long tongue and sank his teeth into it. Kira's eyes bulged, and he bit the forked end of the tongue off and spit it out. Arching her back, she screamed.

A second scream drowned hers, one of rage, and

a new creature stormed out of the hub, one with four arms and four legs, crawling like an insect: Sheryl. Jake did a double take and glanced at Tower, who beamed. Sheryl bore down on Jake at a high speed, and Jake knew he could never contend with two monsters at the same time. Sheryl opened her eyes and mouth wide, her hair flying behind her, and unleashed an inhuman growl. But she crashed into Kira, knocking her off him, and the two female creatures rolled on the ground, their arms and legs entangled as they shrieked at each other.

Rolling into a crouch, Jake gaped at the monster brawl. The women kicked and punched each other with multiple limbs at the same time, drawing nails over flesh. Kira raked Sheryl's face with her claws, and Sheryl pulled Kira's head back and bit her cheek. Their arms and legs never stopped moving.

Rising, Jake picked up his prosthetic hook, then slipped its harness over his bare shoulders. The bite wound in his back started bleeding again. Moving around the frenzied creatures, Jake faced Tower, and the two men glared at each other. Jake sensed fear in the Biogen and thought he might run, but he should have known better: every Biogen he had seen had kept going until it had been killed.

Tower's upper lip twitched, then he unleashed a scream. Jake screamed, too. And they charged at each other.

Tower sprang into the air, aiming a flying kick at

Jake, who ducked and punched straight into the air, connecting with Tower's groin. Tower jerked in midair and crashed onto the earth. He spun into an upright position, but Jake had already gotten to his feet and kicked him in the face, dislocating his jaw. Tower dove at Jake, a half-hearted roar escaping from his loose jaw. Jake threw an uppercut into the jaw, damaging it further.

Tower retaliated by punching Jake in his crushed nose. Jake staggered backwards, exhaling and spitting blood. Tower circled Jake like a boxer, throwing jabs Jake fended off with his hook. Then Tower jumped high and delivered a roundhouse kick that smashed Jake's swollen eye, and Jake fell onto his back.

"Get up," Tower said in a strangled voice.

Groaning, Jake got to his feet. He wanted to say, *I'll never give up, either,* but he was too exhausted to speak. His chest rose and fell, and he heard animal snarls behind him. Tower lunged forward, throwing a jab with his left that Jake blocked, then connected with Jake's chin. Then he punched Jake on the left side of the face, and Jake heard a soggy impact.

He's killing me, Jake thought.

Jake caught the next jab Tower threw with his hook and it twisted until Tower's wrist snapped. Tower screamed, and Jake punched him in the throat, crushing the man's Adam's apple. Tower gasped, his eyes bulging, and then he backpedaled, but Jake's hook jerked him back and he fell to his knees.

Jake raised the man's limp arm. "Look at me."

Clutching his throat with his free hand, Tower raised his gaze to Jake.

"Who's on his knees now?"

Scarlet-faced, Tower keeled over, and Jake released his wrist. A death rattle escaped from Tower's lips, and he stopped blinking.

Jake turned to Sheryl and Kira, whose movements had slowed. Kira sank her teeth into Sheryl's throat and tore off a piece of flesh, and Sheryl screamed. Jake lumbered toward them: he had to help her. Exhausted, he fell facedown in the dirt. With a banshee cry, Kira rolled on top of Sheryl, choking her with two hands while the other four pummeled her. Jake raised his head. Sheryl's four arms flailed at Kira with decreasing strength, and Kira's snarl quivered. Sheryl opened her mouth wide, and a dark, phallic shape shot out and struck Kira's breast.

Kira's body stiffened. Sheryl retracted her stinger, then shot it out again, this time into Kira's other breast. Again and again. Kira's eyes rolled in their sockets, and drool poured out of her mouth. She toppled over.

Jake crawled to Sheryl, who stared upward at him.

"We did it," he said, gasping. "We both did it. You and me."

Sheryl blinked tears out of her eyes. "Hold my hand."

Jake curled his bloodied fingers over hers.

"Don't let anyone find me," she said. "I don't want anyone to know . . . I was like this."

Jake's eye filled with tears.

"I never stopped loving you," she said.

Jake's chest heaved and he choked up. "You *do* have a soul and it's good."

Sheryl stopped blinking, then stopped breathing, and her hand turned limp.

Groaning, Jake managed to stand and wipe his tears on his arm. Dense smoke billowed out of the hub, and he staggered into the structure. Hanaka's body had become a bonfire, and Jake gagged on the stench of burning flesh. Crouching, he reached out with his hook and snagged the corpse through the roof of its open mouth, then dragged it out of the hub and onto the grass, a few feet away from the corpses of Sheryl, Kira, and Tower. He took his time pulling on Jaeckel's bloodied shirt and blazer, watching the flames spread across the grass. Picking up the silicone mask, he pressed it against his face, inducing shock waves of pain. Flames licked the trunks of the trees, and the leaves caught fire. Black smoke swirled through the atrium. The mask held. He prayed to God no fire sprinklers would come on.

THIRTY-FOUR

Jake remembered the way to Tower's office. The monitors showed the security bay and the downstairs lobby; the rest of the floors were dark. He opened the drawers of the massive desk until he found what he was looking for: a gleaming, pearl-handled Colt revolver. He popped the cylinder open: full load. Snapping it shut, he threw the lever that opened the vault door and entered the ante-room. Passing through Kira's office, he glanced at the Flatiron Building below, then entered the empty security bay.

The guard on duty spun in his chair at the security station. His eyes popped at the sight of Jake aiming the Colt at him.

"The atrium's on fire," Jake said. "Everyone in there is dead. Long live RAGE!"

The guard swallowed, an indecisive look on his face.

"Who else is working on this floor?"

"No one," the man said.

"Cleaning staff?"

He shook his head. "Just the other guards in the downstairs lobbies."

"And in the security level in the basement."

"They closed that down more than a year ago."

"Take your gun and set it on the desk."

The man unfastened his holstered Glock and set it down where Jake could see it. "I'm a family man."

"I doubt that." Tower liked to hire expendables. "Get up. We're getting the hell out of here while the getting's good."

The guard rose and circled the station. "Shouldn't we call the fire department?"

"That would defeat my purpose in coming here. *Long live RAGE.*"

Jake followed him to the glass door, where the man palmed the lock release. The door clicked and he pushed it open. They walked to the elevator bay, where the guard palmed another button. One of the golden elevator doors opened, and they boarded the car. Standing behind the guard, Jake slid the Colt inside a blazer pocket as the elevator descended.

"When we get down there, I'll do the talking. The only thing that matters is that we all get out of here alive, understand?"

The guard nodded. "I want to get out of here alive."

"I want you to take out your phone and slip it into my left pocket without turning around."

The guard reached into his pocket, took out a phone, and reached behind himself.

Turning sideways, Jake removed his hook from his pocket. "Six inches back. A little to your left. There you go."

The guard eased his phone into the left pocket of Jaeckel's blazer. At least Jake would be able to call Maria now. The elevator stopped, and Jake nudged the guard out into the security lobby, where two guards sat at their station, facing the side doors. Both of the men watched the guard exit the elevator with his hands raised.

As they rose, Jake aimed the Colt in their direction. "Guns and phones on the counter."

"Do as he says," the guard from upstairs said.

The guards set their Glocks on the station counter, then their phones, and raised their hands.

"Drop your hands." He didn't want anyone who happened to pass by thinking he was robbing them. "The fiftieth floor's on fire. This whole building's coming down. We're all walking out of here, and when we get outside I want you to run toward Broadway. I don't care if you keep running or stop to look for a cop, but you'd better run at least that far if you don't want to get shot in the back. We're leaving now. Move."

The three guards walked ahead of Jake, who resisted the urge to glance at the security cameras.

"There's more guards in the other lobby," the guard from upstairs said.

"I know. You two unlock the front doors."

The downstairs guards used keys to unlock the glass doors.

"Pull the alarm over there," Jake said to the guard from upstairs. By now the entire fiftieth floor should have been an inferno.

The guard pulled the alarm, and a klaxon filled the lobby.

"Now get the hell out of here. Run!"

The three guards ran out the doors and sprinted toward Fifth Avenue and Broadway beyond it.

Sliding the Colt into his pocket, Jake ran outside, too. Fresh air filled his lungs. The side street appeared to be empty.

"Jake?" Maria stood at the corner of the building across the street.

Jake sighed at the sight of her. He removed his hook from his pocket and held it at hip level. Even from here, he saw her body relax.

"My car's parked at the station," she said.

He beckoned her forward and she crossed the street.

"What the hell have you got on your face?"

He took her hand, which felt good. "We're going to my office."

"Why?"

He dragged her to the corner, then turned left. "Because I need to see this place burn to the ground."

396

Maria looked above them. "What are you talking about?"

"You'll see soon enough."

"They sent a clone of Gorman after me."

"I know. You did well."

"Where's . . . Sheryl?"

"Dead. Just like Tower and Kira and my replacement. This is almost over for good."

Jake took out the guard's phone and dropped it down a storm drain. When they reached the curb, they crossed Twenty-third Street. Due to the work zone, there was no traffic. They hurried toward Jake's building.

"Are you going to tell me what happened?" Maria said.

"I took care of business. The less you know the better."

When they reached Jake's building, he opened the door to the foyer. "Do you have your key?"

"Of course." Maria unlocked the inside door.

They didn't have to worry about the alarm because there was no power.

"Do you have your phone?" Jake said.

"Of course."

"You never listen to me."

"Good thing I don't."

She took out her phone and set it on bright mode, casting blue light around them.

Jake took off his mask, which made a peeling sound as it separated from his skin. He didn't mind the pain this time and stuffed the mask into one pocket and took a deep breath.

Maria held the phone up to his face. "Jesus, what the hell happened to you?"

He continued walking toward the stairs. "Like I said, I took care of business."

She followed him, lighting the way. "It looks more like it took care of you. You need to go to an ER right now."

"Later."

They climbed the stairs, their footsteps echoing.

"The department knows what Gorman was," Maria said.

"They'd be fools not to," Jake said.

On the fourth floor, she unlocked the door to his office and they entered. It reeked of mildew.

He collapsed into Carrie's chair. "Grab some disinfectant out of the bathroom, will you?"

"You sound like Rudolph with that nose." Maria went into the bathroom, taking the light with her.

Sitting in total darkness, Jake glanced out the replacement window. The upper floor of the Tower flickered, and he heard the first sirens.

They'll be too late, he thought.

Maria returned with disinfectant spray, a healing gel, and Band-Aids and set them on Carrie's desk. Raising the phone, she studied Jake's features in its pale blue glow. "I don't even know where to start. Close your eye, I guess."

He did, and she sprayed his face with cold, sting-ing disinfectant, causing him to scrunch up his face and hiss. She sprayed his entire face again, then a third time.

"You've got no nose."

"I noticed."

She applied antibacterial gel to his cuts and scrapes and around the outside of his nose.

"That's really ghastly. This is the worst I've ever seen you look."

"You're just trying to make me feel better. Let's go up on the roof."

"What for?"

"We can make out like kids."

Emerging onto the roof, they moved to the protective wall at the edge. Sirens filled the streets below, and a fire-ball consumed the top of the Tower, lighting the clouds in the sky.

"Oh, my God," Maria said. "Did you do that?"

"I'll never tell," Jake said. "But I wish we could roast marshmallows over it."

Their hands found each other, and they interlocked their fingers.

"I love you," Jake said.

Maria looked at him. "I love you, too."

They watched the Tower burn.

"Helman!"

They turned at the sound of the gruff voice.

A figure with broad shoulders stepped forward, his features highlighted by the fire across the street. The man held a semiautomatic pistol with a silencer attached to it.

Geoghegan.

"What did you do, Helman?"

"Did you follow me, Lieutenant?" Maria said.

"If you came to arrest me, you don't need gloves and a silencer," Jake said.

"What did you *do*?" Geoghegan said.

"What did *you* do, Teddy?"

Geoghegan's gaze darted to the burning Tower, then back to Jake. "Is he dead?"

"Who's that? Say his name."

"Tower. Did you kill him?"

"He told me he'd been keeping tabs on me, and you keep hauling my ass downtown. How long have you been on his payroll?"

Geoghegan snorted. "Who the hell are you to judge me? You're no one."

"I'm Jake Helman. Who the hell are you? You're just some fat cop on the take. Every time you've had me in the hot seat you've waved your sanctimonious bullshit in my face. What a hypocrite you are."

"Look who's talking: a junkie ex-cop who's always neck deep in shady activities. So what if I took some money to keep an eye on you? You're always getting yourself into trouble, sticking your nose where it doesn't belong. What's it gotten you? You don't even *have* a nose anymore. You look worse than a scarecrow, you goddamned freak."

Maria raised her hands. "Okay, look, I hate to interrupt this macho bullshit you two have going on here, but let's turn it down a notch. Tower's probably dead, Lieutenant. We don't know what arrangement you had with him, and we don't care. It's moot. This doesn't have to happen."

"Yes, it does," Geoghegan croaked.

"Why?"

"Because Tower promised Teddy a big payday to kill me if anything happened to him," Jake said.

"That broad of his contacted me after you wrecked your car outside One PP," Geoghegan said. "All she wanted was basic intelligence about anything you got involved with. She got all hot and bothered after Madigan and those rich old farts got killed at that Brooklyn shipping yard. Whatever went down there really stirred her up. Then she upped the ante when you went out of town."

"How much are you getting to cap me?"

"A cool million, tax free. It's already been deposited in a Swiss bank account, and the account number will be delivered to me by courier when news of your execution follows news of Tower's death."

"A million dollars isn't what it used to be."

"Tell that to my grandkids when they want to know why they have to go to some shitty community college. Tell me you wouldn't have made a deal for a million bucks."

"I turned down an offer for ten million from him. That's what makes me better than you."

"That's what makes you a sucker." Geoghegan squeezed the trigger of his pistol three times, the silencer spewing muzzle flashes and making spitting sounds.

Jake took all three rounds in the chest and tumbled backwards over the protective wall, his arms waving in the air.

"Jake!" Maria seized the lapels of his blazer with both hands and pulled him back onto the roof before he could plummet to the sidewalk below.

Jake's body turned numb, and out of the corner of his eye he saw the gun in Geoghegan's hand. He draped his arms over Maria and took three more rounds in the back.

"Stop it!" Maria shrieked.

Jake's body went limp, and he felt himself sagging in Maria's arms.

"Don't die. Please don't die," Maria said, tears in her eyes.

Geoghegan moved closer, aiming his gun at Maria's forehead as she wept over Jake.

"Kill him," Jake said, but only an unintelligible garble escaped his bleeding lips.

The sky ignited, flaring solar bright. For two seconds,

the intensity of the light blinded Jake. Then the light receded into a sphere seven feet in diameter, descending from the sky, as dazzling as the sun, and the night around it turned dark once more.

Geoghegan turned to the sphere as it floated above him. The look of wonder in his eyes turned to fear, and he incinerated even as he screamed, shriveling into ashes that spread through the air in slow motion, like snowflakes.

With the last strength he possessed, Jake reached up and turned Maria's head to him. "Close your eyes," he said, choking on his own blood. This time his words made sense. "Don't look. For once in your life, do what I say."

With tears still streaming from them, Maria closed her eyes. "I don't want to lose you. Please don't go."

He pressed her head against his shoulder, forcing her not to look.

The sphere moved toward him, and as it drew closer, he discerned a humanoid body within it, androgynous and beautiful, with golden skin and fiery eyes, long silver hair floating around it as if submerged in water. The beautiful creature's arms were extended at its sides as if crucified, its fingertips touching the sphere itself. Both the creature and the sphere appeared to have been constructed of pure energy. It moved closer to Jake, its radiation causing him to squint, but he refused to close his eye.

I'm Jake Helman, he thought. *I won't look away. I won't back down. I'll stand toe to toe with anything that comes my way, and I won't be afraid.*

The creature moved closer to Jake, radiating warmth. He realized *creature* was an inaccurate term for the entity before him; it was a seraph, a celestial being that had existed longer than mankind. He knew in a heartbeat that this was a true angel, not a spirit of man that had ascended to a higher plane like the Realm of Light. As the seraph's glowing eyes focused on him and filled his vision, he experienced a peace he had never known before.

Take me with you, he thought. *I'm ready. I've suffered enough.*

No, one thousand voices sang to him. *We need you here.*

The seraph grew brighter, whiter, and Jake felt nauseated and dizzy. The white light enveloped him, absorbed him, and he felt warm purity coursing through his veins, transforming him. Then he lost consciousness.

Jake felt warm air on his face and in his lungs.

He heard Maria speaking to him, but he could not understand her words.

She came into focus above him, looking at him, tears in her eyes but a relieved smile on her lips. His stomach constricted and he wanted to vomit, but he controlled the feeling, beat it down.

Maria's words crystallized. "Jake . . . Jake . . . I love you, Jake."

Jake raised his hand to his forehead and blinked in astonishment. He gazed at his left hand and opened and closed the fingers on it. His depth of field perception had changed: the world felt three-dimensional again. He used his restored fingers to touch his left eye.

I'm whole again, he thought, swallowing. "Help me up."

Maria stood and pulled him into a sitting position. "What happened?"

"I don't know," she said. "The light got so bright and intense. I tried to hang on, to stay with you every second I could, but I passed out. When I came to, you were like this." Cupping his face in her hands, she kissed him.

Jake responded in kind, enjoying her warmth as much as her taste. Then he separated from her and touched his face. His nose was intact; the swelling above his right eye was gone; his cuts had vanished.

"Your scars are gone," Maria said.

He rubbed his cheeks. She was right. Then he tore open his shirt, popping its buttons. There were no entry wounds in his chest. Reaching behind him, he felt along his back; the bite wound had disappeared as well. Standing, he gazed at the roof where he had lain. Six rounds lay there.

Sheryl stood beside him. "It's a miracle, just like what happened on flight 3350." She rustled his hair and he felt no pain. "Your hair's turned white, though."

He chuckled. "I can live with that."

Across the street and one block over, the Tower had

become an inferno, and fire trucks, police vehicles, and ambulances surrounded the area. Had any of the emergency response people experienced the white light as well?

"Check your phone," Jake said.

Maria took out her phone and frowned. "It's dead."

Jake looked behind him. Abel stood two dozen feet away. So did Sheryl and twenty-four other agents of the Realm of Light. Laurel Doniger stood among them, and Ripper and Marla Madigan. He saw young Victor Rodriguez and old Andre Santiago. So many familiar faces. It felt good knowing they had ascended.

Agents, not angels, Jake told himself.

Their faces filled with awe—and fear.

"Do you see them?" Jake said.

Maria looked in the same direction. "See who?"

The beings before him vibrated, their expressions turning to panic, and they disappeared.

"Never mind." He cupped his hands over her face. *Both* of his hands. "Let's go home."